Lying flat in the dust outside, Dunlee waited. A figure took shape out of the darkness and crept to the door. Another man reached a window on the west, hardly ten yards from Dunlee. The man at the door eased in, rifle poking ahead

shots
brutal protest
against the night's stillness.
A match flared inside the
cabin.

"*He ain't here,*" Dunlee heard the man rasp. "*Git down! He's laying for us.*"

The man at the window hissed an oath,
ducked low, and dug hard for the
brush. Somehow, perhaps by
instinct, his frantic eyes
searched out Dunlee's shape.
He jerked up his pistol
to kill. . . .

TREACHERY at CIMARRON

JIM ROSS

LIVING BOOKS
Tyndale House Publishers, Inc.
Wheaton, Illinois

First printing, Living Books edition, November 1984

Library of Congress Catalog Card Number 84-51058
ISBN 0-8423-7330-6, paper
Copyright © 1984 by Jim Ross
All rights reserved
Printed in the United States of America

TREACHERY AT CIMARRON

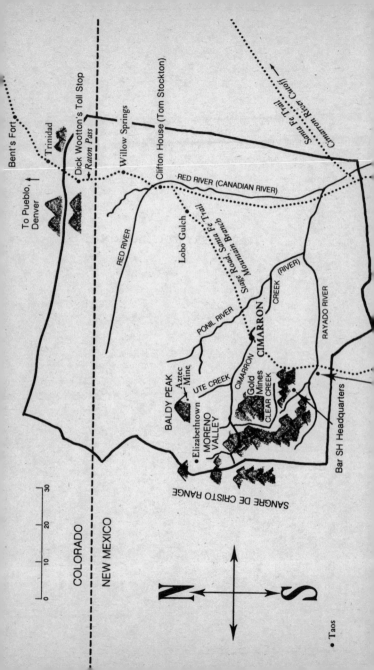

CIMARRON AREA—Early 1870s

———— Boundary, Maxwell Grant.

••••••• Santa Fe Trail. Two main routes ran from SW Kansas into New Mexico, one via Bent's Fort and one across the Arkansas and Cimarron Rivers. The Cimarron River runs from NE New Mexico into the NW corner of the Oklahoma Panhandle, north into SW Kansas, then southeast into Oklahoma, where it meets the Arkansas River. It is distinct from the creek that runs through the town of Cimarron.

The Red River, also called the Canadian River, dips far south then runs eastward through the Texas Panhandle and into Oklahoma. Texas has another, distinct Red River.

Lobo Gulch and the Bar SH headquarters are not actual, historical places. They have been added for the purposes of the storyline.

The scale of miles is accurate only within the boundaries of the Maxwell Grant.

Kit Carson's Home; L. B. Maxwell also lived here before moving to Cimarron.

•Wagon Mound

•Fort Union

Las Vegas•

Santa Fe•

1

Marks Dunlee cast a wary eye on his back trail. He was not a man to be caught by surprise, and the men who had haunted his tracks these three weeks had made him doubly cautious. The pack of two-legged killers was sure to come sooner or later.

He craved refreshment and rest under the cottonwood canopy at the water hole. The magnificent black he rode, not so grand after the grueling sixty-mile trek of the night and early morning, needed the stop, too. Both mount and rider were exhausted by the tortuous miles of trying to shake the relentless pursuers. They were gaunt from the toll of pushing hard in the hot summer of 1874.

Dunlee swung his wiry, six-foot-two frame from the saddle and winced at the stiffness within him. He let his mount stretch eagerly for the tiny pool in the rock basin. With the instinct of a hunted animal, he peered back across the flatland to the east, between two flanking ridges. Before he slaked his own thirst, he must be sure.

The price of survival had been vigilance and cunning. Even now his searching gaze lingered on the horizon before he sank to his stomach to drink.

He and the black were alone for the moment. Besides the clink of the bit and squeak of saddle leather, their sensitive ears picked up only the familiar sounds of the oasis. A cheering gurgle came from the spring. A locust sang in the brush beyond a nest of rocks. A dove moaned its dirge from a cottonwood limb, and occasionally a falling leaf kissed the ground.

Infused with a fresh surge of life after drinking only a few swallows, Dunlee stripped the gear from his horse. Raking up leaves and dried prairie grass, he rubbed his mount's lathered coat. Then he hid the animal behind a nest of boulders to graze beneath a cottonwood, and sprawled gratefully on a shelf of rock. He could look back over the desolateness behind, and not be spotted by eyes probing the oasis through field glasses.

Never pursued by more ruthless men, Dunlee had trained his senses to note everything that moved or made a sound. The riders prowling out there had dogged him hundreds of miles from Fort Worth into northern Territory of New Mexico. They meant to kill. His only hope lay in outwitting them. One bit of carelessness and they would leave him for buzzards to pick.

But amidst this deadly drama, one lovely thought drifted back. Though he was now a long way out of Virginia, the image of the girl passed before his mind, lingering to his sheer enjoyment. She seemed so real, decked in that pink dress with the frilly white lace, the broad white belt, the large white buttons from bosom to waist. Her straw-gold hair cascaded halfway to her trim waist. He wanted to reach out and touch her.

"Mandie." He crooned the name aloud. A swirling dust devil, rustling the grama grass and cottonwood leaves, seemed gentled by the name, and played itself out to a hush. Dunlee brightened at the music of the word. A faint smile pressed its way into his sun-darkened cheeks. His utterance floated like a melody in this remote solitude. He could linger for hours, entranced with her loveliness, heedless to passing time.

But the past weeks had sharpened him into a more disciplined man than ever. He could not risk drifting along on a cloud of pretty thoughts. Ugly scenes struck as if from ridges of ambush in his mind. The hunters had tried to kill him two times.

That first try had come suddenly. A few days out of Virginia he and his horse had gotten off the Texas and Pacific from St. Louis to Dallas. Then he had ridden the black to Fort Worth, where he spent two weeks.

One day in Fort Worth he bet some cowboys at a corral that he could bust an outlaw sorrel nobody had stayed on until the count of ten. He climbed aboard and they turned the wild one loose. Dunlee stuck like a burr to the savage, snorting animal right around the corral until the horse had exhausted all its tricks. Then he reined the sorrel back near the crowd of onlookers lining the poles, and settled the bets.

Just then a rider named Lefty Stubbs pushed past the others to the fence. He had galloped up just in time to see the last, weary jumps of the sorrel and Dunlee's triumph. He drew Dunlee off a few steps from the others.

"Somethin' yuh need to know."

"Yeah. What's on your mind?"

"I jest heard some fellers askin' fur yuh back by Brown's store." He jerked his thumb toward the public square. "Hankerin' bad to catch up to yuh. Four of 'em. Man doin' most of the talkin' goes by the handle Pugley. Built stronger than a Nueces bull. Wouldn't want him askin' after me if'n it wasn't friendly. An' he don't sound friendly."

That news was more jolting than the sorrel's first pile-driver jumps. Pugley and his cutthroats, all the way from Virginia! How had they trailed him here?

Well, maybe that letter he'd sent off to Mandie had wound up in the wrong hands. Finding out where he was, they had lit a shuck.

They had come all the way from Virginia, and they wouldn't be here to take him back alive. Not likely. That wouldn't be Pugley's way. First, they'd try to get their hands on the money he'd won from them in the card games. Fair and square it had been, but that would never slow Pugley and his mad dogs.

"They know where I am?" Dunlee was calm.

"Naw, not when I left 'em. I didn't cotton to the looks of 'em. See heah, if yuh need help some of us can. . . ."

"No need," Dunlee said, thanking the cowboy. "They're tryin' to pin a murder on me I didn't have anything to do with. Pugley's out to nail me because I cut him down after he'd hit the bottle too hard. He was takin' out his rage on a Negro servant. After that I stripped him and some others in a card game. He's a sore loser."

"One thing I can do, then," Lefty pursued. "Yuh get yur bedroll at the hotel, an' I'll mosey 'round back with yur hoss. I know 'im, the black down at Tacky's

Livery. Yuh light outta heah an' ride due west. Soon as yuh hit the Brazos, yuh foller it nawthwest. Yuh'll be pointin' toward Fort Belknap, where the Butterfield road passes from Fort Smith toward Horsehead Crossin' an' El Paso. Yuh'll see a line shack on the nawth bank. Nobody's usin' it right now. Stay the night. They won't find yuh theah. I'll spread the word yuh was talkin' about goin' east."

A short time later, Dunlee reached the two-story hotel by a back route and went in, careful not to run into Pugley. He checked the register, but Pugley and his men hadn't checked in here.

He was arguing with himself. He could just ride out and give the men the slip. On the other hand, he was not afraid of Pugley and his toughs. He could stride right up to them, face them down, and have it out. Pugley himself was somewhat handy with a pistol, but his men were not. And Dunlee was a heller with a shooting iron. He could run them out of town.

He had made up his mind not to ride when he got to the top of the stairs. He'd no doubt find them in one of the saloons near Joseph Brown's store, and get it over with.

That was when he saw the leg. A man had just taken a step into his room. Apparently the door lock had not been hard to pick. He flicked the thong loose from the ivory-handled Colt .44 that rode his right thigh. Sliding the gun out of its holster, he eased along the hallway with catlike quickness. Loud, raucous laughter in a room down the hall drowned out the squeaking of the floorboards.

"Let's git outta here. I got 'em." The voice came from within the room. "Pile of money here."

That could mean only one thing. They had pawed around until they found his saddlebags with the money, a small fortune, won in Virginia. He had figured nobody would find them above the ceiling where he'd hid them beyond those boards that did not look loose.

He heard a man shuffle from the door to the bunk near the window. Then Dunlee leaned around the doorpost, jabbing his gun before him.

"You can drop 'em right there," he barked. Two of Pugley's men were standing by the open window, peering at the money in the saddlebags. One of them had slung the bags over his left shoulder. The other intruder hissed and clawed for his revolver. He spun and swung the gun up, but shot in the reckless haste of a man caught by surprise. That proved fatal. His bullet chipped wood from the edge of the door and rapped into the wall across the hall. Dunlee's slug slammed him in the chest, staggering him wide-eyed one step to the left, where he buckled heavily to the worn carpet.

Falling sideways, the wounded man shielded his partner, who fired around him and bored a hole in the rose design on the wall only inches from the doorpost. Then he whirled and dived through the open window to reach an adjoining roof three feet below.

Dunlee's second bullet tore a hole high in the robber's left arm, and in his frantic dive he could not shift the saddlebags to his right arm. The leather strap looped on the sharp end of the window sill, jerking the bags loose from him before he tumbled to the roof below.

Dunlee, sure that the man on the floor was out of the action, leaped to the window. The escaping robber had dropped over the edge of the low roof. Rather than shoot him in the back, Dunlee checked his shot. He lunged through the window and raced to the roof's edge. The man, scrambling past an empty wagon, looked back and snapped off a shot. His own Colt barked, and the man was knocked by another impact in the left shoulder. He flung himself low, bawled a torrent of profanity, and scurried out of sight behind some stacked drums. Over the sound of steps pounding a hasty retreat, Dunlee heard his screaming threat.

"We'll git you, Dunlee. We'll be comin'!"

"I'll be ready for you," Dunlee muttered.

Dunlee climbed back into his room and looked at the dead man. He recognized another of Pugley's cohorts. He felt sick in the pit of his stomach. Yet the man had asked for that kind of end.

The proprietor and Lefty peered in at the door. Lefty had arrived with the horse, heard the shots, and guessed the rest. He had raced up the stairs ahead of the proprietor.

"Two thieves ransacked my room," Dunlee explained. "I surprised 'em making off with my bags." He grabbed up the saddlebags.

"Sheriff rode out of town to one of the trail herds," Lefty said. "We can explain this for you. I say you ride, or there'll be more gunplay."

"Pugley and his bunch won't stop without it," Dunlee agreed. Lefty led him to the horse. Dunlee climbed on the black and rode out, keeping close to the Trinity River for the first mile. Then he swung due west across an immense rolling prairie. He planned the route he would take into the Territory of New

Mexico to the Maxwell Land Grant country north-east of Santa Fe. He'd hug the north line of the Brazos River and later the White River west from where it joined the Brazos. Then slant northwest across buffalo prairie to the Red River, and on to the Canadian. There he could pick up the government wagon road from Fort Smith, Arkansas, toward northern New Mexico.

Late the second afternoon after leaving Fort Worth his steady pushing brought him to the line shack by the Brazos. He ate a simple supper of biscuits and jerky that Lefty had rustled up for him. As darkness laid its heavy shroud over the vastness, he decided he would get a good night's rest. He stretched out his bedroll on a broken-down bunk, and went to sleep.

He was suddenly snapped awake. The black had snorted warning. Something prowled out in the murky darkness. He snatched up his Winchester '73, eased out the door on hands and knees, and bellied down in a patch of brush south of the shack. Scarcely had he settled when his ears caught the soft footfall of a man slinking in the brush to the east. Hugging the dust, he waited. A figure took shape out of the darkness, cir-cling in from the river, and crept to the door. Another man reached a window on the west hardly ten yards from Dunlee. Then the man at the door eased in, rifle poked ahead.

A few seconds slipped past, then three rapid-fire rifle shots cracked a brutal protest against the night's stillness. A match flared inside the door. Deep guttur-al cursing followed the rifle blast.

"He ain't here," Dunlee heard the man rasp. "Git down! He's layin' for us."

The man at the window hissed an oath, ducked low, and dug hard for the brush. Somehow his frantic eyes searched out Dunlee's shape, perhaps by instinct. He jerked up his pistol to kill. Dunlee had taken deliberate aim and now he shot him in the chest. The man shrieked his agony into the night as he pitched through low brush into the dirt and lay still. His gun crashed through brush near Dunlee.

The man caught in the shack was near the window, trying to find Dunlee from the bark of his rifle.

Dunlee's eyes probed the darkness for a third man. Sure enough; a large figure loomed up from rocks toward the river. Dunlee pressed off a single rifle shot, and heard a nasty snarl before the man dropped out of sight.

As he shot, Dunlee bolted toward the wall of the shack, hugging the brush to avoid making himself a target for the man at the window. The man fired at the place from which he had seen the tongue of orange flame. But his bullet harmlessly whacked through brush and kicked up sand. Dunlee shot at the window and heard the man sputter. The sound made him think of Pugley's voice.

The door burst open and banged against the wall outside. The man hurtled through the doorway and dropped into the brush. The form was burly, like Pugley's. Dunlee heard him swishing hastily through the brush toward the river, apparently to get to the horses.

Seconds later he heard hoofbeats heading eastward through the brush flanking the Brazos. The two surviving attackers were tearing pell-mell out of there.

Dunlee went to the black. The horse had saved

his life by waking him, so he thanked him with soothing words and gentle hands. The thud of retreat faded
on the Texas plains. A frog croaked above the gentle
drone of the river, and a coyote yapped in the distance.

A desperate groan drew Dunlee from his horse
to the man who had tumbled into the brush. He crept
cautiously lest he fall victim to a trick. The man had
flopped on his back, one arm outstretched and the
other clutching his side. In the light from the sliver
of moon Dunlee looked at his face, blackened by thick
growth not shaved for days, and twisted in pain. When
Dunlee lifted the attacker's head, the man spoke.

"Water," he rasped. "Jest a drink . . . 'fore I'm
done." Dunlee fetched his canteen from the shack and
the ambusher gulped eagerly. Then, nearly stran-
gling, he spat out water and blood. Striking a match,
Dunlee studied his face. The match burned almost to
his fingers and he jabbed the stub into the dust.

"Carmack," he muttered. A vivid remembrance
flashed back. Men hovered near a gambling table in
Virginia one night. Here was one of them, a member
of Pugley's treacherous killer pack. But not as vicious
as Pugley himself.

"Yeah," Carmack claimed the name. "They'll see
you pay. They'll always be comin' . . . till they git
you. You've done two of us in . . . today."

"You started this," Dunlee reminded him. "Slymer
died back in town robbin' me, then tryin' to gun me
down. Now you came askin' to join him."

"Humpf!" Carmack winced and fought his agony
in the light of another match. "You got our money.
Besides, Pugley figgers to collect the reward. You're
up for murder."

18

"The money I won fair and square," Dunlee again reminded him. "And I didn't have anything to do with a murder. How did you know right where to find me here?" He doubted Lefty would set him up for this, yet it was possible.

"Trowling ... told Pugley about the shack. He ... he was ... sore you won ... his money ... ridin' a sorrel. He ... overheard some man ... Stubbs ... tell you ... where to go. Said ... he expected ... his own money back for tellin' ... or he'd come after us ... with a gang."

That made sense. Trowling had been a scowling loser when he forked over money at the corral. A couple others, no doubt sidekicks, had also lashed Dunlee with dark glances.

"Now," the man rasped, "Pugley and Trowling ... both ... will be comin'. They say ... Trowling ... tracks ... like an Indian. I'd like ... to see it ... when ... they catch you." He coughed and tried to laugh at the same time.

"They come an' more of 'em will die," Dunlee said grimly. "A man does what he has to do."

"You ... for sure ... will die." Carmack spoke with great finality. Then came his death rattle. He slumped into stillness.

Dunlee left the body in the shack, set the bunk up against the window, then shut the door. That way wolves wouldn't be able to get to the corpse. Pugley's pack would regroup, slink back, and bury him. He hoisted the saddle to the black, cinched up, and headed northwest. An hour later he reined the horse into a nest of big rocks. He spent what remained of the night there, feeling safe from the killers should they

19

double back to the shack for another crack tonight. That was unlikely, for now they knew—Dunlee was a hard man to catch napping.

Long before the crack of dawn he heated coffee over a small fire; the smoke was thinned and spread out by overhanging branches of tall brush. He hunkered close to the flames, chewing on jerky and hard biscuits. He pondered his situation.

Trowling was a bad loser and a vengeful man. It seemed fitting for Pugley to fall in with him. Birds of a feather. . . . Trowling might just fulfill Carmack's death wish. Tie in with Pugley, throw in his own sidekicks, and come gunning to grab the money back.

There had been talk in Forth Worth of Trowling riding the outlaw trail—rustling, holding up stages and banks, and being an all-around heller. No lawman had gotten anything on him that he could make stick, and in a vast land where good lawmen were few and far between, men of Trowling's breed could get away with a lot.

Besides, few could stand up to Rube Trowling's speed or treachery in a showdown. If Pugley lured Trowling into the chase, he'd be a devil to shake off a trail. So Dunlee figured he'd better ride any rocky ground to advantage and lead off on false trails to throw his pursuers in the wrong directions. He'd need to cast an eagle eye on his back trail at all times. None of the pursuers would hesitate to steal fresh horses, and they might push on day and night to close the gap. Vigilance was crucial—they might even slip around him and lurk in ambush.

Ambush? Trowling would be a past master at that. To kill from the front or strike out of hiding would pose no problem to the man's mind.

As Dunlee picked his way through the rugged country, he thought of the destination he had in mind when he fled Virginia. *Cimarron . . . southwest of Raton Pass.* He whispered the words. They sounded good. They drew him on deep into the Territory of New Mexico, to the northeast of Santa Fe.

Shoat Hartman, the towering and rugged king of the Bar SH outfit, would be glad to see him back. Wasn't Dunlee like a son to him, indeed the son he'd never had? Hadn't Hartman pled with him to stay on? Sure, and held his peace when Dunlee swore he would look up his little Mandie on that Virginia estate. Hartman would be eager after these months to hear first-hand about his little. . . . Well, that's how he still thought of her, remembering a seven-year-old "angel" who used to throw little arms around his huge bear neck before her mother took her away twelve years back.

Now there was a story Hartman never told anybody except his closest friends. And he had few close enough. A man of massive strength and iron will, he had absorbed the deep hurt and the bitter loneliness a few miles southwest from Cimarron in the rugged country of his canyon. There he'd whispered his losses into the ears of a big horse, or spoken them to the winds of his canyon rims, which moaned back the only answer he got.

Then Dunlee happened onto Hartman suddenly one day when the rancher *really* needed a friend. Dunlee thought back to that incident. But all the while his eyes swept warily in a searching circle. And he listened to the rhythm of the black's hooves, the creak of leather, and the swish of buffalo chaps now and then against the brush.

On that day Hartman had crested a knoll and reined his horse in a shaded glen. Suddenly he stopped. Thirty paces away two men were busy altering a Hartman steer's brand with a running iron. He hauled down on them with a Henry rifle and was going to read them from the book before he stretched their necks with a rawhide riata. The cow thieves reckoned that doomsday had come.

Then Hartman stepped on a rattler and leaped sideways just in time to evade its lethal strike. But he was not in time to dodge the running iron that one of the rustlers hurled. It banged him in the rib cage and he half fell, then jerked off a shot that whined out its song in the brush just before a slug from a Colt .44 shattered the Henry out of his gun hand. His rifle slammed against a rock and clattered to the ground.

The rustlers moved in fast. They ordered the rancher on his face. They drove down stakes, and laced his outstretched hands and feet to them. One savagely ripped the shirt off Hartman's back, and the other brought the running iron, heated to a glow.

"You've got an iron will, Hartman," one man sneered. "Now let's see how you like our kind of iron!"

They both snickered. The brand changer with the iron lowered it close enough for Hartman to grit his teeth at the heat. But that was only to tease him.

"Ah, ain't that a shame," the man with the iron said. "I didn't get it hot enough. Do you mind waitin', Hartman? It'll jest take a...."

He swung around to stride back to the fire. His eyes saw the long shadow.

Dunlee was simply standing, Colt in hand and a twig in his teeth, chewing casually.

"Go ahead. Heat it again," Dunlee drawled. "By the time you peel *your* shirts off it'll be nice and ready."

The faces of the two contorted into a grimace of pain that amused Dunlee. Hartman, twisting his neck to look, found it amusing, too.

"You wouldn't do that," the man wielding the iron said, his words knife-edged with dread.

"You reckon no human being would do a thing like that?" the newcomer replied. "Move!" The man gripping the iron took the dreaded steps to the fire.

"Shore, shore," he mumbled. "Jest be careful with the shootin' iron." He bent toward the fire, then suddenly dived with great quickness beyond the bound steer. At the same time he whipped his gun clear of leather in a blur of speed. But Dunlee's bullet was faster, and as the rustler hit the ground on his belly, his shoulders up, a small crimson hole appeared on the side of his shirt near the heart. His rustling days finished, he buried his face in the hair of the steer's back and died before he could draw another breath.

His partner, nerves keyed to hair-trigger action, needed only that split second that Dunlee's one shot afforded. He was fast, very fast. His gun leaped into his hand as if by magic. He fired, but Dunlee had lunged sideways, and the bullet whacked through the brush behind him. Dunlee's own slug tore through his left shoulder. He was knocked halfway about, but threw himself down a grassy bank into a tangle of brush. Then he scrambled through brush, hidden from Dunlee, to his horse that stood with a riata still stretched taut to the steer. Getting the animal between himself and Dunlee, he took the dally of the rope off the saddlehorn. Flinging the riata aside, he led the horse away as he covered his back trail. Then he mounted, drove rowels savagely into the horse, and slapped through the brush for a getaway.

Dunlee quickly drew a Bowie knife and cut Hartman free.

"You saved my bacon," the rancher said, rubbing his wrists and smarting from the pain of the rawhide. "They'd a scorched a brand on me to watch me suffer, then strung me up." He nodded to a lofty cottonwood limb not far away.

An unusual friendship sprang up between the two. Hartman liked to call Dunlee "Son." One day he shared the heartbreak he had kept bottled up within for twelve years.

He had married an eastern girl, Sheila, whom he met in St. Louis and brought to the Cimarron range. But she did not take to the ranch life with its hazard of attacks by Utes, Navajos, Apaches, or wandering Comanches out of Oklahoma. She felt the range men were uncouth, and she detested the hard work, grime, sacrifices, simple living, and the ache of loneliness.

At that time a Virginia estate owner, Henri von Ehrencroft, was in New Mexico with his daughter Teresa. They were visiting relatives in Santa Fe after the death of Mrs. von Ehrencroft, Teresa's mother. Now they were on their way home, following the Santa Fe Trail through Cimarron.

It was during von Ehrencroft's brief stay that he met Sheila, who was admiring a dress she could not buy. She asked him and Teresa to join her, Mandie, and Hartman at lunch in a restaurant. During the meal Hartman had to leave because of an accident at a nearby stable—a horse had crushed one of his cowboys in a stall.

Sheila became infatuated with the visitor, a man of smooth, cultured ways, nice compliments, and a bulging wallet. She invited him and his daughter to be guests at the ranch, and during their week-long visit, von Ehrencroft simply swept her off her feet. She fell for him hard, and he for her. Hartman, too trusting, had been slow to read the signs. But when he saw the truth, he loaded the von Ehrencrofts in the buckboard and drove them to Cimarron to put them on a stage. He would be rid of them.

Sheila followed him into town, bringing little Mandie, and announced to Hartman that she was leaving him. She'd be rid of this life in the raw. Hartman figured by now that he'd be better off rid of her so-called refined tastes, love of ease, and nagging. But he was stung by von Ehrencroft's tactics and the threat of losing Mandie.

When von Ehrencroft belittled him the words led to a fight. Hartman battered him into the dust, and towered over his crumpled form. By the code of the land, he had let the man off light. Sheila had the battered Virginian doctored and put on a stage. She insisted on taking Mandie, but Hartman refused to let her go. Then three men, whom Hartman was later to learn had been hired by von Ehrencroft, challenged Hartman to a gun fight over a grudge they had harbored. Hartman and his outfit had killed a brother of one of the men, when they caught up with some rustlers who drew on them.

Hartman pushed Mandie safely to the side and turned to face the men. One of Hartman's cowhands arrived just then, and the two of them slugged it out with the three. Sheila snatched Mandie away to the stage, and it pulled out. Hartman and his man won the fight but Hartman was laid up for a couple days. Then he was afraid to leave his ranch to go after Mandie because rustlers were working his range.

A severe winter hit and he lost a lot of cattle. He'd almost gotten back on his feet again when another harsh winter blasted his hopes. By then his passion to retrieve Mandie had cooled. Besides, Sheila had written to tell him what a nice life Mandie now knew, with a good school and lots of playmates. Hartman did not have the heart to pry the youngster away from advantages she could not possibly have in the Cimarron country.

Twelve years went by. Hartman drew about him a rugged, salty outfit that knew how to stop Utes, Apaches, Comanches, and rustlers. He was a feared man—a terror to outlaws—but kept mostly to himself, a few trusted friends, and the men who rode for the brand.

It was then that Dunlee rode into the Cimarron range from a stint as a cavalry scout in Texas. The rancher he had saved from the two rustlers was, behind his rough exterior, a man with a heart—a heart for his riders, for Dunlee, and for Mandie. Hartman longed to see his daughter, and yearned that she should love her pa. He cherished the dream that she might someday return to the pass, and love whom her mother had spurned.

Dunlee hankered to go to Kentucky to visit some of his own family. He promised he would also go to Virginia and find Mandie, so Hartman finally gave his hand to it. His request still stood out in Dunlee's mind.

"Hurry home, Marks. It won't be the same 'til I see you comin' back." He laid a big paw on Dunlee's head affectionately. Then, turning away quickly, he busied himself tanning a horse hide.

Dunlee swung aboard a claybank, and headed out. Halfway to the rim that flanked the ranch pass on the north, he looked back and saw the tall man raise his hat to wave. Hartman was a lonely figure, a man he loved like a father.

Now, as his mind flashed back to that scene some months before, Dunlee was glad to be riding home. Within a couple days he would feel the emotion of coming down into that canyon to the ranch house.

What would he say to Hartman about Mandie? Again he found himself retracing the rapid-fire events leading up to his decision to run for his life.

2

An old German, Johannes Mueller, had taken on Dunlee at his factory, Mueller Implements. The company produced plantation equipment for the area around Big Lick, Virginia, on the Roanoke River. Dunlee threw himself into the work with driving energy and a quick grasp of things. Because of his good work, business began to pick up at an unprecedented clip. Mueller, seeing the truth of it, promoted him into the office as his special assistant.

That sorely rankled Roe Pugley. Pugley was a dark, brooding, blocklike muscleman of middle age with an ample beer-belly slouched over his belt. The surly Pugley had been with the company for fifteen years, but two things held him back from advancing from the yards into management. One was his tendency to be argumentative and to rub people the wrong way. The other was his inordinate love affairs, partly with the bottle, partly with gambling, and most intensely with bawdy women.

Yet he bitterly resented the young man who blasted his way above him and issued him orders. Dunlee quickly sensed that Pugley was out to nail him, and spoke to Mueller about the problem. But Mueller, kindly sort that he was, had been very close to Pugley's deceased father and felt that by helping Pugley he was doing right by his father's honored memory. He spoke gently with Pugley about the situation, and naively assumed that he had put the squelch on the matter.

Teresa von Ehrencroft glided into Dunlee's thoughts. A stunningly beautiful, large-eyed girl of twenty, her presence at the parlor, porch, or estate grounds seemed a fragrant caress to the atmosphere around her. She fluttered pulses, and dispatched most men into tongue-tied shock or awkward fumbling. In fact, she had become more dazzling than her stepmother Sheila, herself a charmingly striking southern belle of class and carriage.

Dunlee shook his head as he recalled watching Teresa dance with finesse about the ballroom. Every movement was perfection. She was the rage among the young, unmarried men of position, and the envy of other belles. Only her stepsister Mandie, a year younger, drew some of the eyes away from her. For this Teresa was insanely jealous. Teresa, he reflected, had excelled in the polished art of manipulating others, of tipping her world whichever way her impulse desired. She knew how to get what she was after. Delicately balanced in her pretty head was the ability to wrap people about her finger. Men stumbled over one another in a rush to please her.

Dunlee, a ruggedly handsome man with a powerful body and an indomitable spirit, had become a favorite with some of the eligible ladies of the area. He had hauled Teresa's runaway carriage to a stop one day, and that won him her gratitude. Then she consented to accompany him to a play at the community center. In a few weeks he was escorting her on carriage rides amidst the Blue Ridge grandeur. For the time being, he had lost the driving urgency to head back to Hartman's canyon.

Mandie was friendly also, and Dunlee exulted at signs that she would like to be in Teresa's shoes. She was just about as pretty as Teresa, but not as forward, and Teresa was clever to keep his attention.

But Dunlee had a rival, a formidable one. This was none other than the dashing, rich Trevor Endicott of Ridgetop Manor a few miles southeast of the von Ehrencroft estate. He owned one of the choice, old tobacco estates of Virginia, passed on to him by his father and his grandfather before.

Endicott soon decided to put Dunlee out of the running. And Dunlee expected the attempt to come at any time. He'd picked up surprising bits of information while traveling about the area to sell equipment. Dunlee began to hear that Endicott was making cocky boasts. Given his estate, money, and influence, it was just a matter of time until he showed up the western man as a hick from the sticks.

Dunlee, shrewd in his judgment of horses, had found a superb animal, the black he now rode. The horse was the finest he ever had laid eyes on for looks and speed. And Dunlee liked good horses. He'd bought the black from a man who needed desperately to pay his wife's hospital bills. Dunlee cut deeply into his savings, but believed he could challenge some local horsemen to races and win the money back fast.

He rode him out one evening under the cover of

darkness just to find out what the animal could do on one of the smoother roads. He let him open up for a mile, stopwatch in hand, and was amazed at the explosion of muscle and speed under him. He drew up in a clump of trees to give the horse a breather. Striking a match against his boot, he gazed eagerly at the timepiece. The black had cut loose even beyond his expectations.

"A minute thirty-seven," he whistled. Then he dismounted and stroked the sleek neck that glistened in the moonlight. A man may invest in business and bring in a fortune, or discover gold out in Californy and be rich overnight, or go to a gambling table and rake in a big pot. But what about a man with the fastest horse in Virginia? It was an interesting thought.

"Black, you're wonderful," he said aloud. "You did that without any horse to push you. What could you do if you had to get down and really do some running?" He was still shaking his head, exulting at his prospects, when he heard a shout from over a knoll.

"I'll teach you to show up late!" Then as distinct as the flat report of a rifle came a sharp crack like that of a bullwhip laid to flesh.

Dunlee mounted and nudged the black to a gallop over the knoll and down the slope. In the light of a full moon he could make out a buggy drawn up off the road in a little glen. A burly, powerful man was giving a Negro a brutal flogging.

"Have mercy, Massa, I done come back 'fo you say." The Negro's voice was pleading and desperate as he shook from the pain. Dunlee figured he was witnessing a great injustice.

The man wielding the whip cocked his arm. The leather laced the back again, splitting the shirt and cutting an ugly gash in the flesh. The black man's whole body quivered, his face twisted from the torture, and he screamed.

Dunlee swung down, as yet unseen, and caught the whipper's right wrist with his left hand when it was thrown back for another whack. The massive, muscular man with the whip was jerked about by the powerful arm of the newcomer. The two men came face to face, and the reek of whiskey almost hurled Dunlee back.

"What you buttin' in for?" the man demanded meanly. It was then that Dunlee realized what he had not known in the darkness. The assailant was Roe Pugley.

"Ah, it's you, Dunlee," Pugley sneered. "I mighta known. I oughta horsewhip you for this."

"You've done enough whipping," Dunlee said curtly, maintaining his grip on the wrist. Pugley tried to wrench free, and threw a lot of muscle into it. He wanted to use the whip. But Dunlee's grip clasped him tightly. Pugley then planted his feet, cursed, and chopped hard with his left fist. As he started the swing, Dunlee shoved the man's right arm around to meet the blow.

The swing was cut off and Pugley was thrown off balance. Then Dunlee's right hand shot up, tore the whip from the clenched hand, and tossed it slithering like a snake through the grass.

Pugley bellowed, a bull aroused to his rage. He lowered his head and charged. He was mad to kill. Dunlee neatly stepped to the side with catlike quickness, caught the thick neck as it plunged by, and rammed it down. The drunken man fell heavily to the grass—nose first. He picked himself up, shaking his dazed head. Dunlee could see the darkness of blood oozing from his nose and mouth.

Obsessed with a craze to destroy, Pugley wiped his face on his sleeve, then smashed at Dunlee with a murderous, brutal right. It glanced off Dunlee's arm; if it had landed squarely it could have staggered an ox. Now Pugley was boring in, slugging with both hands.

Dunlee stepped under a wicked swing that would have struck with the impact of a sledgehammer. Grabbing the man's legs, he flopped him on his back.

"You'd better stop right here," Dunlee warned. "I don't want to hurt you."

"Hurt *me?*" That really infuriated Pugley. He leered in disbelief. "No . . . no! I'm gonna break you in two once an' for all."

He lurched up, smearing the blood on his sleeve again, and landed a jolting blow to the jaw. Dunlee staggered, warded off another, and shook his head clear. Then he threw all his power into a left uppercut that snapped Pugley's head back and sent him reeling. Then a right to the jaw smashed the raging man sideways. His legs buckled and he went down heavily. This time the fight had gone out of him, and he lay moaning in the grass.

The Negro, leaning against a wheel of the buggy, was shaking his head with amazement.

"I nevah knew no one could do dat to Massa Pugley. You helped me, suh . . . Mistah Dunlee. He was gwinna skin me within an inch o' my life."

"He whipped you because you were late?"

"Yessuh, but I wasn't late. He jest gets it in his mind I was, an' Massa Pugley he don't change his mind. He played cards at da Green Haven Inn, he an' some others like Massa Endicott. I drives him ovah an' he says be back by nine. I was back a half hour 'fo dat jest to be sho I'm on time. But his luck done run bad an' he lost, so he was done earlier dan he 'spected. So he had to wait a few minutes. Soon's he done get me fur enough from da inn so no one would see, he made me pull ovah, and he done pulled out his whip."

"Who are you?"

"Tom Jackson, suh. I used to be a slave fo' his father, a good man. I stayed aftah us slaves was set free, an' now I live by da lane near Massa Pugley's big house. I works fo' him."

"Will he beat you again for this?"

"Well, if he does, I'se gwinna leave. He'll sulk, but when he done gets sobah he'll be tolerable. I worry fo' you, suh. He'll mean to get you fo' this. Massa Pugley he don't nevah foget."

The next day was Saturday. Early in the afternoon Dunlee got off work, cleaned up, and headed for Teresa's. He wanted to show her his horse and ask her an important question. In a short time he had fallen head over heels.

She came into the parlor decked out in a white dress with dark blue lace. She looked very pretty. He took her out to the black.

"He's a beauty," she said. "You keep on working, Marks, and one day you'll be an important man. You'll have a lot to offer."

He had hoped he was important already—to her.

"Oh, that?" he laughed. "I think I already have a lot to offer. I've worked my way to a really good position and done it fast. There's a bright future. Now I've got the finest running horse in Virginia."

"Oh, but there are some fine horses, Marks. Yours really hasn't been tested. I'd hate to see your hopes dashed. You must get into these things gradually. Trevor, for instance, has a whole stable full of incredibly fast horses."

He winced. "He'll prove himself. You'll see. I've been around horses all my life, seen some great ones. I've never had one under me respond like this one. He's a bolt of lightning."

She laughed cheerily. He couldn't tell if it was a laugh of happiness for him or of sympathy because she thought he'd be in for a fall. She *had* seen Endicott's horses win.

They walked into the garden and she sat down upon a white bench, backed and flanked by huge pink roses.

"Terry," Dunlee said, fumbling with the difficulty of words. He cleared his throat. Why was it so hard? "I've got this position with Mueller. I'll do well. You've made my life a very happy one. I want to make you happy—I mean always, Terry. I'm askin' you straight out—will you marry me?"

He had found himself on his knee before her. He couldn't remember getting into that position. He was gazing into her face, anxious to catch a good reaction. Nothing else mattered.

Her big eyes grew wide, and her lips flew open in a whistle of surprise.

"Why Marks Dunlee!" She hesitated, and studied his eager face in amazement. Then she looked down.

"I'd do you proud," he said. "You'd see."

"But, Marks," she replied, and her tone was strange, condescending. She laughed uneasily. He suspected it was not his day. "You know," she purred, "I'm fond of you, and I expect you to do well. But I . . . well, I would really never be satisfied with the life you could give me. I—"

"Never be satisfied?" He searched her eyes. They were filled with a look of pity for him. Then she turned away and gazed at a servant toiling in a field beyond the garden. "What is it you'd really *need* that I couldn't satisfy you with?"

"Oh, Marks." Her tone was tinged with . . . what was it, feeling irked at being trapped . . . or contempt? "Please, don't let this hurt you. But you have nothing except a good job and a promise. I must have money. I must be rich. That's the life I've chosen—the really good life. If I have that, everything else will be lovely. But I *must* have that. Can't you see, Marks?"

"Yes," he said weakly, swallowing hard and still watching the graceful curve of her cheek turned away from him. She could not meet his eyes. "It's getting clear now. If that's what you want. I thought life was made up of things of far greater value than . . . than being rich. I thought it included character, sacrifice for people you love, loving even when things aren't easy, facing challenges and rising to them, peace in your heart—."

"Oh, yes, of course, I'll have all of those. But why not have them *and* a lot of money?" She spoke now as if she were really in command of things. "Why, Marks, you *know* I could have any man I fancy. That's just the way it is. I've got to make the choice that's best for me."

He bit his bottom lip and measured her squarely in the eyes. "Any man, huh? So who is it going to be?"

"Why, I haven't decided, Marks. But I should think it will be someone like ... Trevor Endicott. He's a man with style. He has just about everything."

Yes, a plantation, a fine line of horses, beautiful hills with vines, expensive clothes, many servants, a position of prestige in the area, plaudits that wouldn't quit.

"I see." He spoke in a low voice. It was difficult to utter a word. "And if I had a lot of money as Endicott does, would that make things different?"

"Why, I ... why, I should think so, Marks. You'd have so much you could offer then. You'd be a man of power. Isn't it all clear?"

"Yes," he said scarcely above a whisper. "Only then it wouldn't be me you loved, but the money." By now he had put on his hat. He stood up, turned, and walked away. "Good day, Terry."

"Marks, don't go now. I don't wish this to be an unpleasant evening."

"Oh, you needn't worry," he said coolly. "I think I'll find it pleasant when I realize what I've been saved from. And when I mull over the lesson I've learned, the feeling will be ... great! Beauty is only skin deep— sometimes."

She gasped, flung her nose into the air, and pulled herself up very stiffly. He strode quickly out of the garden to his horse. When he rode away, she heard him whistling cheerfully. Along the lane to the front gate she watched him meet Trevor Endicott, who was coming in mounted on the seat of a shining black buggy. Dunlee waved, smiled, and shouted. That really peeved her.

"Great day, great day!" Dunlee's words floated back.

Endicott scratched his head, threw a questioning glance back at Dunlee who had ridden on, then turned toward the house. Had Teresa made Dunlee that enthusiastic? Was this Dunlee's flair in announcing a triumph? He shrugged it off. Dunlee . . . win out over him? He killed the fear in a smile of disdain.

That week Dunlee met Tom Jackson again. The servant came to the equipment yards to see Pugley, his boss. Pugley was gone at the moment.

"I'se hopes Massa Pugley wins tonight," Tom said. "Dey's havin' a big card game at da inn. It's always real big when Massa Endicott will be deah."

"Oh? Is Endicott as good as I've heard?"

"Yessuh! He wins a lot. But he only plays when da big, important men are gwinna be deah. Da money gotta be big. Deah'll have mo' money dan I'se evah seen in my whole life."

"Can anybody play in those games?"

"I'se thinks so. Dey jest needs lots of money. Mistah Marks, you ain't thinkin'. . . ."

"You just keep quiet about it," Dunlee cautioned. "Maybe . . . maybe. . . ."

At four o'clock Dunlee, dressed in a padded black suit and a heavily bearded disguise, rapped at the door of the inn's back room. It opened only a crack and a thin-faced, pallid man peered inquiringly out.

"I understand I might encounter some men who like a gambling game." The visitor's voice took on an air of importance and business. "I travel a lot of late and haven't had this chance before. May I come in?"

The man hesitated, unsure. "Well. . . ."

"Thank you," Dunlee said, and pushed the door forcefully open, moving the man back by sheer muscle. Dunlee saw a card game already in progress. Four men glanced up curiously, and two others hovered near to watch the game. Four lamps on the wall cast bright light on the table top. Endicott was one of the men at the table. Pugley was among the onlookers.

Dunlee smiled confidently. He had dressed in a black derby hat, put on a wig and a beard, and darkened his eyebrows. His voice was different. They did not recognize him.

"Gentlemen," he said cordially, "I learned quite by surprise I could find a game here. I came hoping to meet men who are serious about the game. Serious . . . and skilled. I hope I have not wasted my evening."

That had its effect on the men.

Endicott pushed back from the table and arose to his feet. He was a swarthy man of six feet three, a bit heavier than Dunlee. His green eyes possessed a hunting look that reminded Dunlee of a wolf. His square jaws were well-shaved, and a dark mustache curved on both sides of his mouth like Texas longhorns. He wore a dark gray suit, a white shirt, and a striking crimson bow tie.

"Daniel Edward," Dunlee offered, and that was true. Marks was only a nickname that had stuck, short for "Marksman." He had stood out above others as a crack marksman in a cavalry of Texas. His first and middle names were Daniel Edward. But nobody here knew that.

Endicott eyed the newcomer as a timber wolf might gaze on a young calf. He decided he savored the well-heeled look, the cut of refinement, the brash confidence of the man—and the challenge.

"We only throw this open for big stakes," the estate owner said.

"Yes, yes, by all means, a bit of a challenge, to be sure! I do have $500. That, my friend, is not chicken feed."

Two of the men at the table slyly winked at each other. They had no idea that Dunlee noted this effect clearly out of the corner of a vigilant eye.

"Wait around," Endicott invited. "When there's an opening, come on in. Jamsy, pour Mr. Edward a drink."

Endicott sat back down. The pallid little man who had come to the door went over to a bar, poured a drink into a glass, and delivered it to Dunlee.

Endicott smiled as he continued the game in progress. He felt his evening would be rescued from boredom. He was winning big already, early as it was, against easy opponents who had recently come into money. And along comes a stranger with $500. Astute observation told him that the visitor's hands were not those of a man who spent his days at gambling tables but at hard work outdoors. But he also had the signs of a man of money. . . .

Not long after, one of the four dropped out. Dunlee took his chair, and was glad it was the one in the corner. He could easily keep an eye on all the men.

He lost the first game, intentionally making some bad moves. Then he won the second and third. After an hour the other two men dropped out and Pugley came in. He lasted only a short time, losing heavily, and went out growling like a sore grizzly.

Now it was Endicott and Dunlee.

Some of the stories he'd heard about Endicott came back to Dunlee. He was glad he was here. The man across from him had stripped money from a lot of people, had been brutal to some of his servants. Dunlee saw a fitting justice in cutting the man down to size.

His mind leaped back three years to a snowed-in cabin in a Texas winter. Across from him had sat one of the sharpest card players who ever played the game, willing to teach Dunlee. Dunlee had saved his life, had carried him in from a blizzard. After they had played for days, he told Dunlee he had never seen a man develop so fast. "You'll take many of the good ones," he'd said.

Endicott suggested Dunlee put in his whole $500. Dunlee won. Then Endicott lighted a cigar and blew smoke across the table. He was being pushed in a way a man seldom pushed him. He was tight but eager to go on. He could yet make a killing, and this newcomer had really aroused him for the kill.

"Are you willing to bet it all again?" He hurled the challenge at Daniel Edward. The stranger tapped his fingers on the table for a moment, deep in thought, then accepted.

"I can use the money for some investments," he said. "And I figure it's a lucky night for me. It's all or nothing."

In the next hour he cleaned Endicott out and raked in $5,000. But he had watched the man like a hawk to catch any card produced from a sleeve, under the table, or the bottom of a serving tray that Jamsy brought frequently.

Endicott called a recess after the latest game to stretch and catch a breath of fresh air. He said he wanted to go get more money at his estate and would hurry back within the hour. He and Pugley went out.

Dunlee wondered if they were setting up some plot to stop him even, should he try to leave a winner. He had studied the room carefully. Two windows in the back, both open due to the heat, he noted. But they would *expect* him to leave the front way.

The master of Ridgetop Manor must have driven his horse unmercifully. He was back well before the hour with a wad of money. Pugley, he explained, had a stomach cramp and was lying on a divan in a side room of the inn. Dunlee wondered . . . was he on a divan or staked out in the darkness?

Dunlee went on to give Endicott a lesson in cards. He took every bill in the wad. Endicott was deeply agitated. He had expected to make short work of this visitor, but everything had gone awry. As he had continued to lose, he had continued to drink. Now he'd had too much, both of losing and of drinking.

"Well, then, that's all for tonight," Dunlee said as he pulled in the winnings, $10,000 worth. His opponent, a bit bleary-eyed, threw his coat open and produced an envelope.

"No!" he shouted. His face was approaching the redness of his tie. He was drunk, but his tone was emphatic. He was accustomed to saying what would be and making sure that was the way it was. "I've lost too much. I'll have my chance to win it back. Here's my title deed to Ridgetop Manor. I'm putting it up. I'll win or be damned."

A tremor of shock ran through the spectators. Dunlee's eyes swept the faces of the men, then came back to the envelope. He opened it and removed a document, then spread it out in front of him so that he could detect any movement out of the corner of his eye. He read it deliberately, then inserted it back into the envelope.

"This," he said, "would be a huge loss for you. I would advise you to stop while you've still got the Manor."

Endicott leaned far over the table, and slammed his fist so hard into the wood that the money beside Dunlee jumped at the impact. His face was dark and intense, his teeth bared like those of a snarling wolf. "I'll have my money back—and keep the Manor. Are you afraid your luck's run out?"

Dunlee smiled thinly. "Your decision."

A while later, Dunlee coolly laid down four aces he felt would win the game. But Endicott put down a winning hand. A cackle of enjoyment, or triumph, ran through the huddled crowd.

"No," Dunlee said very confidently, "*that* card won't work. Reason is," and he was speaking slowly, matter of factly, "you had it up your sleeve." He reached over the table faster than a wink, fixed his opponent's right arm in a vise-like grip, and shook another card free from the sleeve. It spilled on the table, and gasps came from several of the men.

"Why, you . . . you!" Endicott shouted, his face livid with rage and embarrassment. He was totally losing his composure. Now it was clear that he'd probably cheated even in his wins against the others.

Dunlee, his fingers appearing to straighten his

coat, drew his gun and laid it on the table. His left hand quickly gathered the money into his coat pockets.

"My game is fair. I beat you fair and square. The Manor is mine. Now, if anybody's hand as much as moves toward a gun or the door, he'll take the first bullet."

Endicott looked all about.

"Don't anyone make a wrong move. Do what he says."

"Good," said Dunlee. "Here's paper. Endicott will write out a brief note that I won the money—$10,000—plus the Manor. Then each of you will sign that you witnessed it as fair and square."

The work was grudgingly done by the six men.

"You've beaten me," Endicott fumbled huskily. "I never had such a run of bad luck. But nobody says I fail to make a deal good. Come, be my guest tonight at Ridgetop. Tomorrow I'll show you what you won."

"Right gracious," Dunlee replied. "But no thanks. I already have plans for the evening. I'll ride over tomorrow morning."

Out of the corner of his eye Dunlee caught Endicott's wink to one of the men. The man ducked his head in a nod of understanding. Dunlee frowned.

"Now," he said, nodding to the door, "after you all, please."

They filed out, and he closed the door, then moved quickly to snuff out the lamps, watching the windows all the time. Once the room was plunged into darkness, he went to a window, climbed through quickly, and crouched in the bushes along the wall to look and listen. Then he ran with a sudden burst of speed into the deeper darkness of the trees a few strides out. He reached the black, well-hidden in the trees a couple of hundred paces from the inn.

He rode parallel to the inn along a blunt ridge, and came to the fringe of the trees near the road in front of the inn.

"He slipped out the back," someone exclaimed in a surprised tone. Then he heard a muffled order and a clatter of hard heels drumming quickly across the boards of the porch. This ceased abruptly as the men vaulted the end railing and hit the grass. He saw, in the pale glow of a lantern hanging out front, dark figures darting across the grass toward the rear of the inn. Clearly a couple of them held guns.

Just as he suspected. They wanted badly to stop him. A plot to jump him—perhaps bury him in some hole in the woods—had failed.

He lifted a howling laugh of derision loudly into the early evening air. The black's hooves clattered sharply on the hard-packed road away from the inn. He swung into a lane cutting north toward town. A mile farther, he veered west on a lane that would lead to the road out to the von Ehrencroft estate.

Back at the inn, Pugley waved Tom Jackson to wait at his buggy and trotted over to Endicott as the big loser reached his horse.

"You know who that was?" Endicott asked.

"Naw, just a stranger. Why should I?"

"Dunlee!"

"Dunlee?" Pugley grated on the word. "No!"

"When he stuffed some money into his inside pocket, I glimpsed the initials—M. D. That made sense, because I'd been looking at his left hand. The knuckles had some bruises. They came from his fight with you. It all became clear right there at the last— the eyes, the chin, the height. It's him all right."

"Yeah." Pugley was convinced and hotly aroused.

"It adds up," Endicott went on. "He asked Teresa to marry him, and she told him he needed money the way I have it. Money . . . of course! How would you like to get your money back, Roe?"

3

Dunlee halted his horse at the gate to the von Ehren-croft farm and peeled off his beard and wig. Then he rode in, asked a servant if he could see Teresa, and waited in the parlor.

She came, dressed in a pink evening dress with frilly white lace down the front to the waist.

"Marks," she said with some surprise, "I thought you didn't visit me anymore."

"Hello, Terry. I kept recalling our last conversation. You said you had to have money. Endicott could make you happy."

"Of course. That hasn't changed. He does have much to offer, and he fancies me. It isn't just promise with Trevor. It's money in hand, and the Manor." She seemed to be savoring her words, her head tilted in her snooty, defensive way.

He smiled. She had stated things more aptly than he could have asked.

"Money in hand, and the Manor." He let the words drift through the room.

"Yes, Marks." He detected condescension in her tone. "Not everybody can have that kind of life. I would be a fool if I turned my back on it. Surely you can understand that. And you know I wish you well—whatever you do. Things haven't changed."

"Oh, but they have, Terry. Very quickly, in fact. You see, Endicott no longer has the money, or the title deed to the Manor."

"Oh, come now!" She stepped back, a little surprised and impatient. "Why that's utter nonsense. Trevor would never part with his Manor. And even if he did he would have his money. The Manor would bring a very handsome price."

"No nonsense, Terry. Late this afternoon the money and the Manor became mine."

He unfurled the note with the signatures before her eyes on a coffee table.

"Why, that's Trevor's handwriting." She slid her nail up to the top of the note and read line by line very carefully. At the end she saw Endicott's signature, familiar to her from notes he had written. Below it were names of men she knew or had heard mentioned. A couple of the signatures she recognized from the writing on letters that had come to the house.

She looked baffled. More than that, she was confounded and deflated. All the breath seemed to have gone out of her.

Dunlee slipped the title deed from its envelope and laid it out where the note had been. After a moment the impact of it all hit her more squarely.

"This . . . this simply can't be." She wilted weakly down into a soft chair. Some of the rose tint had fled from her cheeks, routed by a deathlike pallor.

Dunlee returned the title and note to his coat pocket and laid several stacks of bills on the table. She leaned over and noted the denominations in one stack and gasped, awe-stricken.

"What . . . how? You . . . Marks, you wouldn't steal. The note . . . it . . . I don't get it. All this money. . . ."

"It's simple," he smiled, relishing every moment. "Seems Endicott, Pugley, and their ilk like to gamble. That's one of the big reasons why Endicott has done so well. I cut in on their little game today, and I was better than they figured. Endicott is proud. It hit him like a ton of bricks, right where he lives. He drank too much, as he was being beaten. He lost his head in a blind rage to stop me. He made a mad ride home and brought more money. On a whim, I guess, he even stuck the title deed in his coat.

"Of course, he figured even if he lost he'd still win. That crowd never figured to let me out of there alive, so they had nothing to lose . . . nothing they couldn't get back if things went wrong. They'll be in town by now searching for me to rob me, kill me, and cover it all up."

He returned the money to his pockets.

She sat shaking her pretty head. Groping for words, she found herself at a loss.

"Money, the Manor. . . . Things change, Terry. When you come right down to it, it takes more than these to make a life."

"Yes . . . yes, Marks." Her voice was faint. A tear formed like a dewdrop at the edge of an eye, poised for a moment, then slid down her delicate, quivering cheek. "Oh, Marks, you must think I am very foolish. And I am. You . . . you have proven yourself. In my heart, I kept telling myself I knew you would. You have the way of a winner. I have wondered a hundred times since you left, wondered how I could have said what I did. Your words came back to me. It isn't the money at all. It's the person and whether you love that person or not."

She daubed at her eye with a handkerchief from which he caught the tantalizing whiff of perfume.

"As I've fought this out, the thing that keeps speaking is, 'Banish your silly pride, Terry, and tell Marks what your heart really says. Admit it's him you truly love, it's him with whom you would always be happy, it's him you wish to make happy.' " She arose, ran her fingers through his dark hair, and pressed her cheek against his chest. "Marks . . . oh, Marks, I do love you."

"Do you?"

"Yes!"

"I don't reckon so," he said slowly. "You love yourself—only!"

"Why, of course I love you. And you love me, too, Marks. I'm the only one who can make you happy—ever."

"No, Terry." He pushed her shoulders out to arm's length. "You are not the one who can make me happy. I don't think you have it in you to make any man happy. You're too obsessed with making Teresa happy."

"But you are wrong, Marks. You'll see. You couldn't live without me. Not really live." She fondled her long hair and tossed it coquettishly over against her cheek, spinning one of the strands around a nimble finger.

"One thing I know," he replied firmly. "A man

can learn fast when he opens his eyes. And the words you said to me in the garden did me a great service. I reached within myself then, and I reached up to the Lord, and I got some understanding. I wouldn't risk you now, Terry. Not even if you were the last person left."

She stared at him in unbelief. Her eyes grew very wide. Her mouth dropped open, a flush of red came back to her cheeks, her fingers seemed to freeze stiff in her hair. She found no breath for a long, awkward moment. Then she hissed through her teeth, and it was a hiss of scalding fury, or burning scorn. It had in it the breath of hell.

"Then I will see you put in hell!" she sizzled. "No man . . . I mean *no* man casts me aside!"

"You said it," he spoke coolly. "That's another mistake." She drew herself up stiffly and spun about, a deep rage scorching her face. Her fists were clenched and shaking.

Just then Mandie walked into the parlor. She saw Dunlee and smiled innocently. She had no idea what had transpired between the two. He liked the smile. She had always smiled at him. And come to think of it, her smile always seemed genuine. Now it was a refreshing, gladdening thing—like a cooling zephyr on a blazing day.

Thoughts rush through a man's head. Mandie had never tried to cut in on Teresa. Only a year younger, she dressed more plainly and did not strive so hard for glamor. But she was pretty. As he watched her glide across the room to extend her hand in welcome, he marveled at how much like Teresa she looked.

Confound it, he thought. *Why was I so moon-*

struck over Terry, and so blind to Mandie? She's the real jewel.

"Hello, Marks. Oh, did I come at the wrong time?" She glanced at Teresa and noted her rigid, fuming posture. It was clear she was in a huff, that she was slicing Dunlee into thin strips with daggers from her eyes.

"No, I'd say you came at the right time." Dunlee smiled, bowing and rolling his black hat in his fingers after he had taken her hand for an instant. "I don't think you could come in at a wrong time."

"Why, Marks, what a nice thing to say. May I bring you two some tea?"

"Well, I . . . I'd love that, Mandie. But I was just ready to leave. Terry doesn't want me to stay."

"You can say that again!" Teresa blistered him.

"Oh, that's rude, Terry." Mandie turned to Dunlee. "Please don't be dismayed. *I* would be pleased for you to stay. I . . . I hope you will not think I am being forward. It's just that I want so much to hear more abut Pa and the ranch. We can stroll out in the garden, and when we come back we can enjoy tea."

So they walked out into the garden behind the house and he began to tell her more than he ever had about Hartman, his men, horses, and cattle. Time seemed to fly. Two hours had raced by when they heard shouting and walked over past the corner of the house where they could see out to the lane coming in from the gate. Old Whitehead, a former slave who had stayed on as a servant after Lincoln's Emancipation Proclamation, was tearing along the lane on a big, hard-running bay. He was yelling, "Massa Dunlee, Massa Dunlee!"

They hurried around to the front porch to meet him. Teresa, too, had been drawn by his cries. The Negro left the horse at the low white fence of the yard and scrambled to the porch.

"What is it, Whitehead?" Dunlee asked.

"Oh, Massa Dunlee, dey's comin' fur you. So I came lickity split."

"Who's coming? Why?"

"Massa Endicott an' Massa Pugley. Dey done got da sheriff. Oh, Massa Dunlee, it's awful, awful! Massa Mueller . . . somebody done murdered him. Dey say dey found money done been took an' your knife in da grass by da back fence. Dey say you must have da money."

Mandie glanced at Dunlee's face. It was etched in agony. She gasped and grabbed his sleeve. Teresa cleared her throat. She reminded Dunlee of a witch.

"So you got the money from Trevor, did you? What kind of low-down trick is this?" He looked at her, bit his tongue, but hauled his racing emotions into mastery. He was weary, stunned, heartbroken, angry. Yet he spoke calmly.

"Mandie, why would anybody do this to Mr. Mueller? Such a kind man." He paused. It seemed like all the breath had gone out of him in his grief. Finally he was able to speak again.

"As for me, this is some kind of monstrous frame-up. I won some money from Endicott and some other men in a gambling game at the inn. If that's wrong to you, I beg you not to judge too harshly. I played fair and square. Here, I have all the signatures of the men that I won there, all dated, that I won the money. I—."

"Marks, it's all right," she said gently. "I believe you. You could not have done that kind of thing to Mr. Mueller. Never. We can trust you."

"Oh, can we now?" Teresa sliced at her. "Speak for yourself, Mandie. You haven't even heard all the evidence."

"No," Mandie replied sweetly. "For that matter, none of us have. But I'm sure when it is all settled Marks will be in the clear. Marks thought very highly of Mr. Mueller."

Dunlee studied her face in the pale light. He would never forget, never get over what he saw there. He had never realized what a beautiful person Mandie was.

"Thanks, Mandie." Her trust was a tremendous reassurance. He felt a fresh surge of strength. "Someone has murdered Mueller, stolen my knife, and planted it to shift the blame. I have this note with signatures as to where I was this afternoon 'til late. I rode here from the inn. I wouldn't have had time to go into town."

Then an awful realization hit him, piercing like a Comanche arrow. The men, run by Endicott and Pugley, could deny he had won the money from them. They could lie through their teeth. One of that bunch could have done in Mueller on purpose to strike back at him. Or to get a pile of quick money. Or to get at Dunlee. Or all of these. But he couldn't prove any of this, and the evidence could be twisted against him—if the men claimed he had left the inn much earlier, or if the signatures were disposed of or doctored to look like a forgery.

He felt like kicking himself. Pride had mocked

him. He had fancied he was being so smart cutting Endicott down to size and showing Teresa a thing or two. Now he realized his foolishness. Even in going alone to the inn, and to a back room, unseen.

Only Tom had seen him go in there, while waiting at Pugley's buggy. But Tom's word, honest as it was, would not be believed. Not above that of Endicott and his henchmen.

Pugley? He could claim he'd had to discipline Tom, that Dunlee had interfered, and Tom had a powerful motive to get back at him.

"I hope this whole thing can be straightened out," he told Mandie. "I can tell the truth."

She walked to his horse with him. "Marks, go to the mayor. He's a good man. I stayed with his wife one weekend when she was sick, and he had to be away. He said if ever there was anything I needed, to call on him. So! I'll go write a letter for you to give him."

She dashed into the house.

"You be careful, Massa Dunlee." It was Whitehead, coming out. "Dose men, dey's in a wicked mood. Dey's got blood in dey eyes to pin da blame on you."

Dunlee settled into the saddle, waiting for Mandie.

"Tom, he done drove da buggy home," Whitehead went on. Massa Pugley done told him to get on back. Massa Pugley, he's on a horse with da others."

Mandie brought the note, and stood watching him ride out toward town.

Spotting men riding toward him, Dunlee reined into a grove of trees before they saw him. They thundered past and merged into the darkness. Endicott and Pugley led the pack, pounding pell-mell to the von Ehrencroft place.

A few minutes later, Dunlee drew up to a clump of trees near the shabby cabin Pugley let Tom Jackson use. Tom came out of the darkness from a creek behind the cabin, relieved to see Dunlee safe.

"Ahhhh, good. I been powerful worried. Some of da men stopped by heah. Dey's searchin' everywhere fo' you. Da sheriff is in another group. Even got men hid out 'round your cabin in town to grab you if you come back.

"I was out by da crick where Endicott an' Pugley was sittin' dere horses." He motioned to a bend in the lane between his cabin and Pugley's big house, near a patch of brush and trees. "While da others was lookin' heah fo' you, I sneaked up an' heard what dey was a sayin'."

"What was it, Tom?"

"Ahhhh." He shuddered. "Massa Pugley tells him he's layin' fo' da chance to shoot you in da gut. He wants to do it 'fo da sheriff comes with his group. He said he could tell others he stepped up to say hello an' you tried to kill him. So he had to shoot. An', if dat didn't work, he'd make sho he got hold of your coat, got some papers without anyone knowin' what he was doin'. An', if worse comes to worse, he'd kill you at da jail."

"So Pugley would stoop to that?"

"Ahhhh, Massa Dunlee. Dat man's like da devil hisself. He done killed some other folk, too. Ain't nobody know it but me."

"Well, I don't aim to be murdered in jail. I'll take

care of one more matter, then I'll be gone. But I'll write. Word will come to Buell McCoy. I'll ask him to get the letter to you, secret. You take it to Mandie. Nobody sees it but Buell, you, an' her. Nobody." The jolly blacksmith McCoy had his shop near the Mueller yards. Dunlee knew he could depend on the smithy to keep a tight lip. He glanced at Tom's cabin. "Got any paper I can use to write a long letter?"

"Yessuh, I has brown wrappin' paper from da store."

In the light of Tom's lamp, Dunlee wrote to the mayor. He wanted to have it in writing to save time when he visited the man.

First he concisely and frankly traced the facts he knew: his foolish disguise to help take Endicott down a few notches . . . the fact that Tom Jackson had seen who went into the inn and when they came and went . . . the way the games had progressed . . . the signatures of the men vouching that his winning was fair and square . . . the men's attempt to stop him with guns . . . his ride to the von Ehrencroft's and the time he arrived.

He wrote down a list of people who would confirm his honesty and his splendid relations with Mr. Mueller.

Then he made some suggestions. Cross-examine each of the men who had been at the inn. Check every person in the area of his cabin to see if anyone saw the killer come or go, taking his knife. Talk to those along the back way to Mueller's yards and office, also along the road from the inn to town.

Finally, he gave information to be held in strictest confidence. He spelled out where he would be after the next few days, if none of these suggestions paid off.

Tying a wrapping string around Mandie's note, with his own letter and the list of signatures inside, he said good-bye to Tom and circled by back ways avoiding as many barking dogs as he could.

A few minutes past midnight, he knocked on the mayor's door. But there was no response.

Dudley Neal, who lived in the next house, stuck his head out from his doorway. Dunlee walked over. He recognized the man; they had met at Mueller's occasionally. Here was a good man he could count on.

"Oh, it's you, Dunlee. I'm watchin' the mayor's place while he an' the missus are away. Won't be back from Richmond 'til tomorrow evenin'."

"I'll just push this message through the slot in the door," Dunlee said. "He'll have it when he gets back."

Back near his cabin, Tom slumped on a tree stump. For a long time he sat motionless, lonely under the moon, hoping the best for the man who had rescued him from a bloody flogging.

"Yessuh, Lawd. You knows I'se gwinna do jest what Mistah Dunlee says. Now, Lawd, jest keep dose strong hands on dat man."

How long he kept to his meditations, he did not know. But some time far into the night he heard the drum of hooves passing Pugley's. The riders searching for Dunlee were tearing back to town.

Tom shuddered at the thought of Endicott or Pugley laying hands on Dunlee. Pugley was a vicious animal, a man Tom knew well. Endicott was of the same breed, though his wealth made him "respectable." He could provide the brains and money to find Dunlee.

Tom knew he must be extremely careful. When word came from Dunlee, he must see that no information fell into the wrong hands.

4

Shoat Hartman was a lonely man. The loneliness gnawed at him, and the men who rode for the brand could sense it. Yet only those who had been around for twelve years knew firsthand the reasons. And even they kept a tight seal on their lips. His bitter heartbreak was best buried in the past.

Hartman relaxed on his long ranch-house porch, boots propped on the aspen-pole railing and his body lounging in a recliner stretched over with cowhide thongs. It was dusk on a Saturday night. One of his cowboys was riding the line on the west range where rustlers had been at work. His trusted foreman Luke Savage and six others had gone off to Cimarron. Coot Dresher was staked out on the north rim that flanked the canyon pass which gouged west and east through low hills. He was guarding the area. Farr Bucher would arrive back from town to spell him shortly after sunup, and Coot would get his turn to whoop into town. Hartman had started a round-the-clock guard a month earlier, pushed by several reasons.

He fondled his pipe, blew smoke rings at the porch ceiling, and scanned the horizon with ever-watchful eyes. Men learned to be alert in this land; they were seldom caught off guard. And Hartman had won a reputation as one of the most alert. A new Winchester '73 was laid across his lap. His trigger finger was never far from the trigger.

One reason for the vigil was that twice he had caught fleeting glimpses of mysterious riders at a distance. They prowled where they had no business—on his range. They vanished like ghosts, their tracks leading off into rocky ground toward Elizabethtown, where many outlaws skulked. Those rapid exits told him they were up to no good. They did not hanker to be asked why they haunted the terrain near his headquarters.

No doubt their motive was money. Rumor was that he had it stashed away.

Due to frequent stagecoach robberies in and around Santa Fe, Taos, Elizabethtown, Las Vegas, and Cimarron over the past few years, he had shrewdly figured out ways of hiding his money. "Coal-oil Jimmie" Buckley and some of his holdup bunch had been killed in 1871, but other outlaws could strike from nearby hideouts, especially in the mountainous wilds near "E-Town" only a half day's ride to the northwest. The town was past its big gold boom, and had dwindled from nearly five thousand people to a few hundred. Some of the hangers-on, though hit hard by failure to get rich, were honestly trying to eke out a living. But, as before, others would rob or kill at the slightest promise of fast money. And desperate times set them on a hair-trigger to spill blood.

There was an urgent reason to keep a sentry posted on the rim of the ranch. One of Hartman's riders had been bushwhacked to death a few weeks earlier—shot in the back in a brush-choked gully over on the west range several miles south of E-Town. Another came back from there sporting a bullet crease burned across his cheek. Still a third had been cut down from a stand of piñons only a couple of miles from the pass. His horse had been scared off, and he'd had to stagger back. Later, he died.

To top it off, Hartman himself had ridden to a close brush with death just a couple weeks back. A boulder had come crashing down a slope as he followed a deeply-sliced canyon a few miles from the house. His spooked horse nearly lunged out of his skin, evaded the boulder, and jerked him half out of the saddle. A thick piñon limb then swept him the rest of the way and dumped him, just as a rifle slug screamed past where he had been. Then, as he scrambled to get to deeper cover, a voice yelled from the rim of the canyon.

"Not this time, big man? Be patient. We'll get you."

Two men who had been on his payroll just six months asked for their time and lit a shuck away from the pass. But the rest of the outfit stuck fast. He knew he could count on them.

As Hartman mused, he spotted a buck in the darkening shadows. It had ventured out of the brush near the garden fence. He lifted the rifle and was about ready to pull the trigger. Then he waited, eager to define a sound he had heard that had just caught his ear.

He recognized it as the heavy, dull clop of hoof beats and the clink of metal. As he strode to the railing at the western reach of the porch, rifle poised, he saw a team of mules taking shape from the brush. They were in full harness.

The thing that grabbed his attention most was the man. He was slumped low over the mane of one mule, swaying as if ready to plunge into the dust. Hartman moved cautiously into the yard, his eyes sweeping the brush for any sign that a trick ambush was being set up. He shouted to the mules, and halted them near the porch. The man slid off heavily into Hartman's free arm, and instantly he felt the blood that soaked the visitor's shirt and pants. As he stood looking down at the whiskered face in the moonlight, he recognized a prospector he had grubstaked some weeks before, an older man. Emmett Dawkins!

Hartman had wondered how Dawkins' prospecting would go. He had been so confident about finding gold near other strikes in Moreno Valley. Hartman, too, believed there was plenty more gold for those who could find it. He had seen piles of stones on Ponil Creek that could have been left from washings long ago by Spaniards or Mexicans. And he had heard stories of Spanish placer operations in the vicinity way back around 1650. Already since the late 1860s millions had been taken from such sites as the Aztec and the Montezuma. One miner had plucked from a creekbed a nugget worth $40 that had washed down from a slope.

Hartman let the mules trot on toward the stable with its smell of hay. He carried Dawkins to a bed. Then he came back to the porch, lit a lantern, and waved Coot down from his vigil on the rim.

Rushing back to Dawkins, he quickly peeled off

the soaked shirt and gazed at a gaping hole torn by a rifle slug in the left side, another in the right shoulder. Dawkins had spilled a lot of blood, and obviously had little time left.

A horse's hooves drummed on the trail coming down from the ridge. Coot hurried in.

"I heard the mules come in. What—?"

Dawkins opened glazed, weary eyes in the lantern-lit room. He tried to fight off a daze and to figure out the rough-hewn, sun-darkened face that hovered like a shadow above him.

"Obliged." He choked out the word. Then Hartman reached forth a huge hand possessed of a great gentleness. He wiped blood from the man's mouth. Tenderly he turned the man's face toward the pillow so that he would not strangle. But Dawkins was desperate to talk.

"You . . . you're Hartman. I made it." His voice was weak, but he struggled hard to speak. "A man . . . like a lion. . . . A man you don't . . . tangle with." He was gasping out the words. "But a good man. You done right by me when I needed a stake."

"I deal fair an' square." Hartman began to clean one of the wounds, and Coot held a bottle of whiskey for Dawkins to take a drink. "Who put you in this fix?"

"Two partners . . . shot each other . . . over to Clear Crick. I . . . was off fetchin' firewood. Pockman . . . murdered Burl . . . turned on me. I staggered back of a tree . . . an' got him. They . . . was greedy . . . wanted it all. After . . . we was partners. Greed—" he grated at the word, and quivered with emotion. "Stinkin', filthy greed. Now we're all dead."

Tears trickled down his weather-beaten cheeks to the pillow.

Hartman shook his head knowingly. The rugged country had its good men, but also the bad breed. He had felt something soft in the shirt pocket when he laid the shirt inside. Now he reached over, dragged out a small, heavy leather pouch, and opened it. Gold dust!

Greed, huh? It figured. All for one pouch?

"Get in touch with . . . my sister. In . . . my . . . wallet . . . the address. Only kin I've got . . . in the world. She . . . and you get it all. See she's . . ." He could not finish. Hartman knew he had checked out.

A small diary from Dawkins' shirt had several brief notations. These provided a sketchy picture. Dawkins and two others, Burl Seaton and Enos Pockman, had for several weeks worked some creeks in the hills south and southeast of E-Town. They were nearer the ranch headquarters than E-Town, where so much gold had been found the past few years, especially at Humbug Gulch. They had been elated about finding some gold nuggets as well as gold in their pans. It had been mounting up big. They laid it aside in pouches until they had gotten quite a lot out. Then they decided to bring the gold down, find a buyer, split the fortune three ways, and file on some claims.

Hartman shut the diary, not mentioning its contents to Coot. Dawkins' last, labored words had carried the account up to tonight. A fight had erupted when the men, en route to Cimarron to the northeast, had made camp earlier in the evening. Somehow Dawkins, though slammed by two bullets, had managed to get to the team, unhitch them from some kind of wagon, and get astride one of the mules. Then he had set out for the pass, aware he could trust the help there.

The rancher told Coot that he would take the mules and find the scene of the shooting. He sent Coot back to his watch along the lip of the pass. After pumping water for the mules, he let them drink and fed them a generous helping of oats and hay. Then he saddled a horse and swung astride, taking the mule team along by a lead rope. He'd need the mules when he located the wagon to which they had been hitched. He rode westward out of the canyon.

For three hours he picked his way through rugged terrain to the northwest, using the moonlight to good advantage. Many shale-covered peaks seemed to loom like hulking dark giants above spruce forests, black as printers' ink. Highest of all, several miles off to the north, towered Mount Baldy at over twelve thousand feet with its white snow cap draining into many streams that spilled tortuously down.

A few hours' ride away were the famous yet infamous gold gulches of Moreno Valley—Humbug, Grouse, Nigger, Willow Creek. They mockingly offered riches but soaked up the crimson of lives offered on the altar of the killers' greed. The gulches gouged into the broad, flat Moreno Valley which separates the Cimarron Mountain range from the greater Sangre de Cristo steeps of the Rockies.

Upon reaching Clear Creek, which Dawkins had mentioned, he began checking the places where prospectors might have chosen to make camp. The third spot that occurred to him turned out to be the right one.

There he found a pack of lobos snarling over the two bodies they had already slashed and partly devoured. He chased the wolves away, heaped up brush wood, and built a fire. He dragged the pitifully ripped bodies near the fire.

The warmth felt good against the cold breeze from Mount Baldy's snow cone. But the reason he had built the fire sent a shudder up his spine.

Tromping through long bunchgrass, he searched for a wagon amidst the aspens and brush that whispered in the wind. He found a small one concealed in a thicket. Striking a match, he examined the load in the bed. Back behind some prospecting equipment, meagre food supplies, and utensils he came across several leather pouches. The prospectors had bound them at the tops with leather thongs. He loosened one, poured some of the contents into a cupped hand, and peered at it in the flare of a match.

Gold nuggets and dust!

He whistled, and felt his heart pound faster. Excited, he poured the contents back and tied the thong. He hitched the mules to the wagon and loaded the torn remains from the two victims of greed into the bed. He could see the green glares of eyes where the wolves lurked.

Finding a wooden bucket in the wagon, he dipped water from the creek and doused the fire. When he drove away, he kept glancing back at the wolves. They were slinking behind, eager for more of the taste they had relished.

His aim was to hide the gold where nobody would find it, to make sure it would be safe. Then he would tote the bodies into the house for the night.

Early the next morning, just before sunrise, he rode up and told Coot Dresher some of the details. However, though he trusted Coot, he felt it best to say nothing about the pouches. At sunup, he and Coot loaded the bodies into the wagon and went to Cimarron. Farr Bucher had just arrived from town to assume the day's patrol along the rim in Dresher's place.

In the days that followed, Deputy Sheriff Dike Bellis checked the campsite and was satisfied with Hartman's account. Hartman himself caught the U.S. Mail and Express Coach that ran south from Cimarron to Santa Fe to locate Dawkins' sister. He discovered that she had died of a fever a few weeks earlier. The editor of a territory newspaper, the *New Mexican*, told him her closest friend was a cook at the Exchange Hotel. In a visit to the friend he learned that the deceased woman had no surviving kin except a brother, a prospector named Emmett. He had written to her now and then and had visited a few months ago before gold fever lured him north.

Hartman told her that Dawkins had been shot in a double cross.

Before catching the stage back northeast from Santa Fe, he had a small pouch of the dust assayed, and it tested out very rich. That set him thinking. If so little was worth so much, the contents in all those pouches would add up to a fortune.

Hartman called in Luke Savage, his ramrod. Luke, he knew, was a man to ride the river with. He could trust Luke til' the stars fell. So he sketched the story, swore him to secrecy, and finally said, "Luke, I'm askin' you to take a trip to Virginny. Locate Mandie an' Marks.

Tell 'em I long to see 'em before I go. I'll give you a strip of range all your own, seein' as how you've stuck by me."

"Whatta you mean, Shoat? You've got a heap o' good years left in you."

Hartman's eyes lifted to the Sangre de Cristo peaks in a faraway, wistful gaze. He did not reply for a moment. When he did it was slow, quiet, and labored. It was the speech of a man relieving his heart of a great burden.

"Luke, I had it figgered like that, too. But maybe it ain't so. It bein' you, I can say it right out, but I don't want the boys to know.

"Doc Cunningham warned me a few weeks ago, 'fore I went on the trip, that I may have five years. I have a lump on my chest. Well, Doc didn't want to scare me, but he said it looked like some he's read about an' some he's seen. He wired a doctor friend that knows near as much about such things as any man in the world. His friend promised to send some fuller information. Doc will know more. But some of the people with signs like that were marked for death."

Luke's eyes had been getting bigger and bigger, and his jaw sagged. He scowled, his face a study in pain, and his hands clenched into fists.

"Boss," he finally managed, "that can't be. It . . . it . . . they ain't nothin' like that can destroy you!" He swallowed hard, and got up, pacing back and forth, a man beside himself. He gazed off to the rim flanking the pass to the north, and the snowtopped summits to the west, like wedding cakes with white icing. These had always given him perspective. "I've seen you caught in a crossfire an' walk free of it. Another time I saw you from the butte when that heller longhorn knocked you on your back and charged in for the kill. I never rode so reckless in my life to reach you in time, an' when I got there you had twisted his neck. It was him on the ground, not you. You've come through stampedes, fought off whole bands o' Utes an' Apaches, swam flooded rivers. You're goin' to whip this thing, too."

Hartman put his big hand on his friend's shoulder. The two stood staring into each other's eyes.

"You just don't know how I admire you," Hartman said huskily. "We talk the same language. Like you say, that's how I figgered, too. Doc just listened while I had my say. Then he sat me down an' talked like I never heard a man talk, quiet but deep. I never saw Doc's eyes get all wet like that. He told me an enemy inside stalks with greater cunning, and is more deadly than any bushwhacker, bull, or roarin' river. By the time Doc said his piece I reckoned that if this lump is what he fears, I'd be a fool to fancy I can talk myself out of it. This enemy has struck down kings of empires larger than the Maxwell Land Grant, and warriors commanding armies men figgered were invincible.

"So I thought it through. If it turns out to be so, I want to be ready. Ready before God, 'cause I bowed to his peace terms a long time back. An' ready . . . ," his voice dropped into a soft, wistful tone hardly above a whisper. ". . . ready before the child they took away. I've got a powerful hankerin' to set my eyes on my girl, Luke, on my own flesh an' blood. I just yearn to see what Mandie's growed up to be. She lives in my mind's eye, a fairer flower than anything that blooms in these hills. I want Mandie to come out here, . . . even if just for a good visit. Maybe . . . maybe she'll decide to stay."

He savored that for a moment.

"Marks wrote me she's a fine young woman, prettier even than her ma. An' you remember what a picture Sheila was. Course, it would be news to celebrate if what Doc said doesn't pan out. But I won't risk makin' a mistake. This is too important.

"Luke, I want you to go. Fetch Mandie back here. An' however it goes with me, I'll see to it you have that north range you always thought was special. It'll be yours before this year's out. You go to Virginny, bring Mark and Mandie both back right away, at my expense. I figger if one of us actually goes to Mandie, he can press home the invite more'n a letter can. This means more to me than anything ever happened to me. I'll be waitin', mighty anxious to see 'em. I've got a suitcase you can use. You'll need a couple new suits. An' I'll count on you to persuade Mandie to make the trip."

So it happened two days before Dunlee rode away to elude the men plotting to railroad him on a murder charge. Luke Savage stepped onto a northbound Abbott-Downing Concord coach more than fifteen hundred miles to the southwest. He'd ride the Barlow and Sanderson stage, board the Denver and Rio Grande train at Pueblo headed to Denver, and from there ride the rails east.

5

Luke Savage was in his late forties, almost as old as Hartman. He had thrown himself body and soul into the hard toil, kept his word, been loyal to the brand, and never hit the outlaw trail. Since his youthful years he had yearned for a spread of his own, some horses and cattle, a future he could offer a woman. But 'til now his dream had never worked out.

Once he had bought a small cattle outfit in Texas, but two harsh blizzards wiped him out. He'd been happy riding for Hartman. The baron of the pass was his estimate of a man's man, and not just a boss but a friend. And now he had dropped the chance of a lifetime into Luke's lap.

That, coupled with the fact that he had been spending a lot of his off time courting the widow Ellie Tallam, gave him a new lease on life. The friendship had grown, and it was plain Ellie thought a heap of him. He had never broached marriage, but only because he didn't have much to offer her. Now, several days after one of those pleasant times in her company, he looked at the world through new eyes.

"One thing," he mused as he looked out from a

café in Big Lick, Virginia, "this is a job I don't dare fail. It means everything to Shoat, everything to Ellie an' me."

"Eh, what's that?" A silver-haired oldtimer was bending over a cane, fixing Luke in a curious stare.

"Oh, 'scuse me, partner. Just mumblin' to myself," he said through a broad grin. "Where will I find the von Ehrencroft place?"

An hour later he stepped down from the buggy that brought him from town. He mounted the steps of the huge white house to the front door. Self-conscious about southern manners and finery, he straightened his suit collar and checked the fabric of the dark gray cloth. Any spot of dust must be slapped off.

A white-haired old Negro servant invited him into the plush living room. Almost immediately, a beautiful, golden-haired southern belle in a blue cotton dress glided in like a graceful swan.

"What is it, Whitehead?"

"Oh, Miss Terry, dis heah gentleman done come to see Miss Mandie. He come on a long joney."

"Hello." She smiled inquiringly at Luke. "I am Teresa von Ehrencroft, Mandie's sister."

Luke swept off his gray Stetson, bowed, and was almost struck speechless by her loveliness. Seldom on the wild frontier had he laid eyes on a woman this attractive and refined. A sense of uneasiness stirred within him. The situation called for poise and polish. He felt his inadequacy, rough and simple plainsman that he was. Little had been his formal schooling, fleeting his brushes with genteel society. He hoped he would not be too awkward or show his ignorance.

"A pleasure, Miss. I'm Luke Savage, from out west of Texas, the New Mexico Territory, a place called Cimarron, where you. . . ."

"Oh, yes, Mr. Savage. Of course." Recognition flashed in her big eyes. She rolled those eyes in a way that fascinated and left him spellbound. "I remember. You were a hired man on the ranch of Shoat Hartman. I am the little girl who came there for a few days with my father. You took me riding on a pony."

"Why, yes. You . . . you've growed up, Miss Teresa. You're a beautiful lady. I'm honored to speak with you."

"Thank you. Won't you please sit down? Whitehead, bring us tea, please. Now, Mr. Savage, you are a very long way from home. Marks Dunlee is the only person who *ever* visited us from out there before. To what do we owe this unusual visit?"

He rolled his hat in fingers he was certain were clumsy, and shifted his legs as he sank down into the sofa. He was searching for words he had carefully rehearsed for such a situation. They did not come easily.

"I've come to bring Mr. Hartman's best wishes. He asked me to make the trip. He is not well, or he could've come hisself." He avoided reference to the rustling. That might create apprehension and work against Mandie going back with him. "There are things he wants to see to. I have a letter he asked me to deliver to Miss Mandie, personal. An' I need to find Dunlee."

"Oh, I see. That is so nice of Mr. Hartman. Very nice. Here is our tea, Mr. Savage." She poured a cup and handed it on a saucer to the guest. He was very careful when he took hold of the handle of the cup so that he would not spill the contents. He did not care for hot tea, but drank to be polite.

Teresa went on. "Mandie is not here just now. She's due back in a couple of days from her school. But you could leave the letter. Yes, that would be the thing to do. I will be very careful to see that she receives it immediately."

"Why, thanks. That is kind of you. But it won't be no trouble at all to come back when she's here. I could give her the letter then. I promised to talk with her anyway, and. . . ."

"Of course." She shook her head in her bewitching way, and pushed an errant strand of hair back from her cheek. "Oh, Whitehead, I have been so impolite to our guest, and him so special. Please take his coat and hang it in the closet. He must have dinner with us, and we must show him about the place. Then he must stay in one of our guestrooms. He must remain as our visitor while he waits for Mandie."

"That's kind," Luke said. "But I have a driver waiting. And I need to look up Dunlee."

"No problem," she waved this aside. "We'll simply ask the driver to go on back. Besides, Mr. Dunlee has recently left the area. Nobody seems to know where he is until some word comes."

Luke was downcast at this news. But he tried to hide his disappointment. If he could not locate Dunlee, part of his mission for Hartman would be a failure. He did not want to fail his friend.

"I don't want to put you folks out," he said. "I can get a room in town."

"Why that would be out of the question. You

must stay with us," she insisted. "It would be to our shame to have you come all this distance and be so inhospitable."

Whitehead was reaching to take his coat. And so Luke stood up, took it off, and thought about removing the envelope from an inside pocket. But Whitehead, anxious to be prompt, had already taken the coat. Luke figured that removing the envelope would look strange and too obvious. No need to bother. Whitehead was only going to hang the coat up. No one would dare take an envelope from a guest's coat. Certainly not in a place of refinement like this. Whitehead hung the coat in a closet near the front door and closed the door. *See*, Luke comforted himself, *nothing to worry over*.

"Whitehead, please take our guest out and send the driver back to town," Teresa ordered. "Show Mr. Savage around the grounds close by. I'll slip into some other clothes and join you as soon as I can. I must also tell Mother and Dolcie we'll have a guest for dinner."

A few minutes later Teresa returned to the front room, straight to the closet. Slipping nimble fingers into the visitor's coat pockets, she drew out an envelope addressed to Mandie. She opened it by steam and hurried to her room. From a window she saw Whitehead taking Savage through the garden to look at a field, then circle back to the stables. That would take some time. She drew out the letter and spread it on the table. She whispered aloud as she read:

> *Dear Mandie,*
> *I'm not skilled to say what I want to say, but I love you. I've thought many kind wishes for you,*

and just as I've tried to remember your birthdays, I'm thinking of you now. It's best if I say it straight out. Doc Cunningham made some tests on me and tells me I may have just five years left, perhaps only one. That kind of news can prod a man to do a lot.

It would be a pure delight to see you again. I can't leave here because of some things I need to look after. Will you please come and bring Marks as well? Luke Savage is bringing money to pay for your trip. We'll do our utmost to assure your complete safety and comfort. Come without fail. Come very soon.

Mandie, something happened I never figured would happen to me. I struck it rich. Before I see my last sunset or lay my last gaze on these hills, I have to see you. You will mean more than anything I've ever seen.

Before I go, I want to leave some of the ranch to you, some to Marks, and some to my trusted men like Luke. It is urgent that you come now.

I wait to see you. All my love, Your father, Shoat Hartman.

Teresa snickered mockingly, slipped the letter back into the envelope, and put a layer of glue on the flap. When she neatly pressed it shut she saw no sign it had been opened. She pushed it back into the visitor's coat pocket.

Back in her room, she dressed in an outfit suitable for walking. As she headed toward the front porch she spied a picture of Mandie on the mantel of the fireplace in the living room. Lifting it, she studied the face thoughtfully, and took the picture to her room. Setting it side by side with a picture of herself, she could see how people had thought the two girls looked enough alike to be twins. She was a bit more trim than Mandie, and a person who knew them both well could distinguish them. But it would take only some clever touches of special makeup to transform her into the image of Mandie.

Her mind flashed back through the years. A pitifully beaten man sprawled in a dusty street. . . . Shoat Hartman towered as a victor over him, fists still clenched. A few feet away, her sobbing face buried in the folds of Sheila Hartman's dress, she saw herself. Oh, how she despised Hartman! Many times she had wished she could get revenge on him for that humiliation. But he was so far away.

The man crumpled and broken in the dust was her father. He, the great lord of a southern estate, a man of class and pride, battered down into shame by an uncouth, wild bully of the sticks.

"Well, Teresa," she hissed, "you are going to relish this. Tough Mr. Hartman is going to wish he never laid a hand on a von Ehrencroft!"

Shortly before dinner, Tom Jackson came by. From a window Teresa saw him hand an envelope to Whitehead. The old servant shook his head knowingly and tucked the envelope quickly out of sight in a pocket of his shirt. Teresa smiled as she began plotting a way of getting a look at the letter Whitehead held.

During dinner Teresa "accidentally" spilled gravy on Whitehead's shirt by turning suddenly toward him when he brought another tray from the kitchen.

She staged a convincing act of apology, then told him to go change shirts but to rush right back. He was at his task again immediately after hurrying out to obey her. She noticed that his fresh shirt had a smaller front pocket—too small for the envelope.

Right after dinner she mentioned a book in her room Luke might like to see, and dismissed herself to get it. Stopping at Whitehead's room, she found his soiled shirt hung on a chair. The envelope was in the pocket. She took it to her room.

"So, it's to Mandie," she said, "and it's Marks' handwriting." Then she quickly but carefully opened part of the envelope so as to work the letter out. A hasty reading told her Marks was in Fort Worth, Texas. He planned to "bust some broncs" for a few more weeks. Then he would ride on to see Shoat Hartman. The nice things he said about Mandie left Teresa incensed.

She jotted down the address, a hotel where Marks was staying, and slipped the letter back into the envelope. Again, a bit of glue covered up for her. Picking the book from a shelf, she hurried to Whitehead's room, returned the envelope, then rejoined the others at dinner.

Trevor Endicott drove over in his buggy later that evening. Teresa drew him aside on the front porch and laid before him all she had found.

"He struck it rich, did he? The past six or seven years I have read accounts of gold near his ranch, at Elizabethtown." He liked the sound of his own words, and felt a strange surge of enthusiasm. "Do you figure Hartman's telling it straight? Or could he be using a device to lure Mandie out there as a tonic for his loneliness?"

"Oh, it's true. Hartman may be crude, but he is a man of his word. Mother will vouch for that. If he says he struck it rich, he did. If so, it would repay our efforts and a lot more. Besides that, I've longed for a way to smash Hartman for what he did to Pa. Pa never got over the humiliation of those brutal blows, and never was as handsome. He once thought of sending a man out there to kill Hartman, but the man was injured in a horse race, and Dad died soon after."

"Let me give it some careful study," he proposed. "You do the same, and I'll be over in the morning. There may be a way we could give the man his 'Mandie,' and cut Dunlee out of the picture before he gets back to the Cimarron ranch. As for Savage, we can take care of him, too. But I want to think through on all the steps. We don't want any slipups. However we do it, we could get Hartman's riches. And we could wind up with the ranch to boot. From what your dad once told me, the cattle and horses Hartman runs ought to bring a fancy sum in themselves, considering the prices. As I've heard, we could sell it for a pile of money.

"Pugley will jump at the chance to put Dunlee away for us."

6

Dunlee sprawled on the ledge of the boulder, enjoying the comfort of a cottonwood limb that shielded him from the blazing sun. The peaceful rest for an hour had been refreshing. But now he needed to press on.

Three hours of daylight remained. He could make it to Pop Harbin's stage station at Lobo Gulch by sundown. He slapped the blanket and saddle on the black, drew up the cinch, and let the animal drink again.

One more check to his back trail with the field glasses, he told himself. He thought he had detected a tiny puff of dust in the distance. Still holding the reins, he bent forward to steady the glasses on the saddle seat. That saved his life. A rifle bullet whined just inches above his head before it tore through the leaves of a piñon. Instinctively, he ducked even lower, twisted about with a startled gasp, and avoided the impact as the startled black lunged sideways.

Somewhere off in the brush and rocks nearby a man crouched, eager for a second shot. Dunlee got the black behind a large boulder, shucked his Winchester from the saddle boot, and peered over the rock. A glint of sun flashed on metal half a stone's throw away at the top of a little knoll. The flat crack of the rifle broke the air again, and the slug chipped at the rock a foot to his left.

At the same time, out of the corner of his eye, he saw a sudden, shadowy blur of gray. A second bush-whacker was slinking behind a patch of brush. Obviously he would circle and come in for an easy, wide-open shot from the side.

How many others were out there?

Dunlee snapped off a dried stick from brush over-hanging the boulder and poked his hat up to draw a shot. Sure enough, the man on the knoll squeezed the trigger, narrowly missing the hat.

An instant later, Dunlee's rifle spoke. The am-busher's left forearm was partly shattered and torn loose from the rifle it steadied on the gnarled stump of a juniper. He yelped in pain, flinging himself down out of sight.

Hugging his boulder, Dunlee checked his left. He waited patiently for the other man to show him-self. Within seconds, he did. Pulling his body over grass and leaves on his elbows, he reached a fallen cottonwood limb roughly fifty paces from Dunlee. Then he raised himself for what would be an easy shot from an unguarded direction. Like popping down targets in a shooting gallery. The head, shoulders, and rifle came up. Then they went down. The man's body jerked, then flopped backwards in a roll. His fingers clutched at his throat, half torn away by a slug. He came to rest face down in the grass.

Dunlee stood up warily and glanced toward the

desert expanse. He saw that the tiny puff of dust in the distance had grown. Two, maybe three horses were now visible. They were coming fast, less than a half mile away. From that close the riders could surely hear the shots out across the flatland between the ridges.

No time to waste! He leaped astride the black, which was nervous from the shooting. His rifle was still in his hand, and he rammed it into its scabbard. In its place, he whipped out his Colt .44, and reined around the boulder to the east. Touching spurs to his mount, he raced past the man in gray, caught a glimpse of his crumpled form lying lifeless in the grass. A great feeling of sadness cut through him, sharp like a Bowie blade. But he swished through the brush and cut to the north toward a long strip of benchland he had studied while approaching the spring. Up there it would be easier to throw off the pursuers in one of many twisting gorges or gullies that gutted the land.

Scarcely a dozen jumps from the man in gray he saw three horses standing between a bank of shale and a thick barricade of piñon limbs. A man, rifle in hand, was on guard beyond the horses, looking right at him.

The black was bearing down on the rifleman, moving like a cannonball. The guard's mouth sprang open and lost its cigarette as he made a frantic lunge toward the bank to escape being slammed by one of the three horses or run down by the black. Dunlee sent two bullets whining over the horses' heads and they, too, surged toward the wall, clearing a way for the black. The black's left shoulder rammed one animal in the rear flank, and the powerful impact made him reel sideways into the man on foot. Both horse and man were spilled, the horse screaming and the man's rifle blasting a hole in the dirt before it flipped out of his hand. Dunlee flashed past the man. A few strides later the black leaped down a bank and into the soft sand of a wash. The horse nearly lost his footing from the sheer and sudden drop. But he recovered and veered right, spraying sand as he disappeared from the sight of the fallen rifleman.

A mile or so into the benchland, Dunlee gazed back through the glasses and counted five men near the spring below. One was sitting on a rock, another was wrapping his arm. One of the other men also had a wrapped arm. The men seemed to be having a parley over their next move, probably trying to predict what Dunlee would do next. They would want to cut him off and set up a welcoming party—a vicious ambush. That was their specialty. He watched until he saw two of the men lug the body of their dead sidekick toward some rocks. They'd probably give him an unceremonious burial.

That would take a while. They would stick around the spring for a time, since they had ridden hard through wearying country to catch him.

He was wheeling the black northward into the hills when a thought made him rein sharply to the west.

They were five. He was one. They might split into two parties. He did not know these ridges and gullies. Any box canyons or dead end trails could spell death. Furthermore, Dunlee had run out of food, and did not want to risk a shot at a rabbit lest he attract the pursuers. He dare not afford them help in the hills.

So Dunlee figured he'd better make a beeline for

Lobo Gulch, a stage stop on the trail from Raton Pass to Cimarron. Old man Harbin kept the outlying stage station at Lobo Gulch. From there it would be a three-or-four-hour ride to Cimarron. And if he headed toward Lobo Gulch, well, Trowling would no doubt figure on that happening sooner or later. He would have some of his pack ride hard to get there right away to lie in wait for him.

If Dunlee rode directly to Lobo Gulch, he'd beat the killers there. He could get food and be out of there before they came. Come to think of it, the Barlow and Sanderson stage crossed that strip of country from the pass to Harbin's station, sometimes about sundown. The driver would stop to change teams, let the passengers quickly eat, then drive on in the cool of the evening hours to Cimarron. Dunlee knew that if he could catch sight of the stage, then ride on the road ahead of it a ways, the stage's four-horse team plus the wheels would blot out his tracks.

He pushed his mount hard for an hour, sure that none of the ambushers' horses could match this animal's pace.

He was crossing a land where Utes, Apaches, Navajos, and Comanches had long roamed. Spanish conquerors of Mexico had been here, and Mexicans had driven oxen and sheep across this land. French trappers had plodded this way, as well as freighters, settlers, and government agents over the Santa Fe Trail. The U.S. Cavalry often had tried to rid the area of the Indian troublemakers here. Rustlers had pushed cattle through here and over Raton Pass into Colorado.

From a brush-covered knoll Dunlee spotted a

cottonlike fluff of dust on the gradual slope several miles back; eventually he made out the team and coach. Then he angled over to the road, did his best to brush out his tracks coming in near the trail, and headed southwest along one of the wheel paths. He was a couple of miles ahead of the coach.

A sudden thought disturbed him. Three attempts had already been made on his life. His pursuers would stop at nothing. So he wondered. What if Trowling or Pugley hit on the idea of sticking a man or two aboard the stage? That would be a smart trick to catch him unaware if he should be at Harbin's just ahead of time.

He cautioned himself. It wouldn't do just to go riding right in and be at the stop when the stage pulled up. He would hold off near the station, stay hidden, and take a good look at those who climbed from the coach.

His idea paid off, but in a way he never expected.

The stage rumbled through the gulch from which the station derived its name. A bugle blast lifted on the late afternoon air to signal Harbin. A dusty-faced driver hauled the lathered horses to a halt in the yard near the front door of the adobe building. As the swirl of dust settled, the man riding shotgun clambered down from the seat and swung open the coach door. An elderly woman and young girl stepped down stiffly. Then a man emerged; he had all the marks of a gunman.

Dunlee, who had trained his glasses on the door, now followed the gunman as he walked around the stage to enter the station. He could be one of Pugley and Trowling's outfit. Not one of Pugley's own men from Virginia, but possibly one of Trowling's crowd. The gunman looked about cautiously, then followed the elderly woman and girl inside.

All in a flash Dunlee saw the face clearly. He knew that man. Choc Chenault! The man who had fled from the shooting at the rustler's fire after nearly branding Shoat Hartman! Dunlee felt his anger flare at the sheer evil of Chenault and his partner while they had Hartman down. They were playing with him before they dangled him from a limb, dragged him to death, or shot him. Chenault had recovered from his arm wound, and was still haunting the land.

Could he be working Hartman's range again?

Then Dunlee shifted the glasses back to the coach. What he saw made him forget the gunman. A tall man in a dark hat and suit was walking around the rear of the coach. He looked a lot like ... but, way out here it couldn't be, of course. Still, he could pass as a dead ringer for. ...

Taking a close look at the girl beside the man, he gasped. Were his eyes playing tricks?

"Teresa! Endicott!" If it hadn't been for Endicott, and the fact that he fitted with Teresa, Dunlee might have mistaken the girl for Mandie. But Mandie would not be traveling with Endicott.

"It can't be!" He gazed in astonishment.

Teresa wore a blue hat and veil and a long, sky-blue dress with white ribbon lacing in the front and at the bottom. She paused for a moment behind the coach and gazed toward the grandeur of the rough ridges of the gulch. Then she turned to the simple sod building, a far cry from the splendor and finery of her usual surroundings.

Why in the world would Teresa ever set out on a long, rough ride west?

Dunlee shook his head in sheer incredulity. Then he felt a sinking feeling in the pit of his stomach. Twelve years ago Teresa had left Hartman's ranch and Cimarron. Was she going back there? Somehow the suspicion settled over him like a dark cloud: she and the swarthy rogue of Ridgetop Manor had plotted some sinister intrigue. It had to do with Hartman.

He scowled and bit his lip. Here on the range men seldom saw a beautiful woman, especially a prize like Teresa. She could get whatever she wanted. It was disgusting that she might be here for a shabby motive. He moved the glasses, seeking a glimpse of her face within the thin veil. She was glancing northward in his direction, but he knew she could not spot him hunkered down behind a thick stand of sagebrush. He had been very careful to hold the glasses in the shade of some branches so that no glint of reflected sunlight would betray his presence.

Oh, but she was a honey! Despite her biting words of scorn in Virginia, he was swept with a longing to talk with her now. Perhaps time had softened her scorn. She could be candy sweet. He no longer was bitten by the old love for her, of course. In fact, he felt a deep sense of regret for letting his attraction for her blind him. But he would like to speak with her. He could tell her much about this land, information she could not learn from Endicott, who was himself a stranger to it.

Endicott! That man made it unlikely for him even to approach Teresa in peace. He was the ringleader, even beyond Pugley, in rigging a case to have

Dunlee slapped in jail. Or murdered under the pretense that he was trying to escape. Surely he must have some part in the efforts of Pugley and his gang to strip him of his money—and his life.

The solitary man watched the two walk to the station door. Teresa, as usual, was gliding with the smoothness of an eagle on a gentle Virginia breeze. Dunlee lingered beyond the sage, his horse concealed in a narrow, water-carved gully.

As he kept his vigil, he frowned. What would be his best move?

He did not think it wise to show himself to Endicott and Teresa. Something powerfully big must be in the air, some design he couldn't figure out. It had to be mighty attractive to lure them from their comforts in Blue Ridge Mountain country. As long as he did not know their intent, he sensed it might be wise to keep out of sight. He could follow them on to Cimarron—assuming they were headed there—and keep an eye on them.

At the same time he did not hanker to be trapped by Pugley, Trowling, and the other three. They might ride in at any time. Having been cheated out of his goal three times, Pugley's rage for blood would have fomented to a nasty pitch. The man would probably savor nothing sweeter than taking Dunlee alive. He would snatch at the chance to work Dunlee over with the bull whip he carried. Pugley would still be smarting from Dunlee's battering him into the grass that moonlit night in Virginia. Rank pride would be goading at him to exact revenge. And with four killers backing his hand, he would see that Dunlee paid the price if he caught him.

Then he had to reckon on the gunman, Choc Chenault. He might be in cahoots with Trowling and his new associates. If so, Dunlee would have a fight on his hands if he showed his face just now.

The two stage men led the horses to a water trough. One pumped water while the other brought a fresh team of four horses from the stable. Then they switched the harness to the new team.

In a matter of minutes, after a hasty meal, the passengers trooped back to the coach in the fading light of dusk. Then Endicott helped Teresa up, and he and the gunslinger climbed in. The driver spoke to the team and cracked the whip above the rumps of the lead pair. The horses quickly surged into a lope, and the coach bounded around a stand of cedars out of sight.

So, Chenault had not remained behind. That was a good sign. Perhaps he had no tie with Pugley, Trowling, and the other vultures.

Now it was high time to move. He led the black to the trough and let him drink. He kept a sharp lookout to catch any sign of the pursuers. His ears were alert to any sound—a horse blowing, the thud of hooves, the clatter of a stone kicked up. But he only heard the early barking of a coyote off in the wastes, and the flap of a night hawk as it flew up from a cedar tree.

He was still shaking his head in wonder over Teresa and Endicott showing up here. Then old man Harbin came out.

"Got the best grub between the Clifton House and Cimarron," the white-haired station agent said cheerfully. Then Dunlee really felt the hunger that gnawed at him.

"I could devour a steer," he grinned. "How are you, Harbin?"

"Oh, I know you. Dunn . . . no, Dundee . . . er, Dunlee."

"You got it. My family hailed from Scotland. There's a town called Dundee. But Dunlee it is."

"Yep. You come by several months back. Headed for Virginny."

"Harbin, I'm in trouble." He quickly explained about the five on his trail.

"Trowling's one o' 'em, eh? Makes sense. He's as ornery as a rattlesnake, an' doesn't need to be stepped on to be riled. I heard he was over in Texas. Tell you what. You fetch your horse 'round back an' put him in the shed. If they ride in while you're grabbin' a bite to eat, you can sneak out the back an' be clean away 'fore they know the diff'rence."

Harbin brought a bag of oats for the concealed black, then both men went into the station. Dunlee sat down on a chair in the dark bedroom back of the kitchen at the east end of the building, and dug into a huge bowl of warm stew. He knew that any men coming up suddenly might open the door and peer into the front station room where a lamp burned. They would see nobody but Harbin who came and went from the bedroom. They would not be able to see Dunlee in the back room.

"Been here nigh on seven years," Harbin commented. "But I never laid eyes on the likes of tonight. Man out here don't see no woman like that 'cept once in a coon's age. Headin' for Cimarron. Hope she comes again. Mandie von Ehrencroft. Beautiful woman, beautiful name."

Dunlee almost dropped his spoon. He fumbled to grab it in his lap. After gulping, his mouth full of stew, he wiped his mouth with his bandana.

"Somethin' wrong with the stew?" Harbin turned from the back door through which he had peered, being careful not to open it too far. Nothing stirred out there in the moonlit ruggedness to the north.

"No, no. Just thinkin' of a girl I knew named Mandie."

"They grow a lot of 'em in Virginny?"

Dunlee laughed, and went on eating.

"Said she was goin' to visit Shoat Hartman," Harbin rattled on. "He's invited her. Now I wonder. Can it have anythin' to do with gold? They's a rumor Hartman found gold, maybe lots of it, an' hid it somers on his place. Some been prowlin', greedy to find it."

Dunlee chewed thoughtfully. Gold . . . was that the angle? Gold . . . Teresa and Endicott. Well, if it was true about the gold, maybe it wasn't so hard to figure them taking the trouble of this long trip. Teresa would never put up with the privations of the wild Territory of New Mexico, never have anything to do with a rough-hewn, salty cattleman. Not unless . . . unless the lure was attractive enough to a gold digger's eye.

"Foxy, Hartman is. Got 'em all outfiggered. If'n he has gold, he never spends it."

"How do you reckon there's gold?"

"Man hit the bottle too hard over to Humbug Gulch at E-Town one night. Claimed he saw Hartman come onto a couple prospectors who'd shot each other. Hartman loaded the bodies in their wagon an' hauled 'em to his ranch. Figgered those prospectors must've found somethin', an' it fell to Hartman. They was a third prospector. He got shot to death, too. Seems the three might've come on somethin' big. Maybe like in '66 when those three fellers found gold heavy in their pans on Willow Crick. You know how their loose talk triggered the gold boom. Elizabethtown sprang up between the peaks of McGinty and Baldy, an' men swarmed there, to Michigan Gulch, Humbug Gulch. . . . Gold can bring out how lusty loco with greed men can be. The town's exploded with robbery, pillage, and murder."

Dunlee nodded. He had heard stories about the helltown not far to the northwest of Hartman's pass. As soon as those prospectors leaked the word of gold sparkling in their pans, men rushed to the vicinity of the discovery tree they marked, and staked claims. The town had taken its name from the eldest daughter of a surveyor, and the Aztec mine had proven the richest of the area.

"Anyhow," Harbin continued, "they's been some excitement. Some are out to wreck grief on Hartman to get at his gold . . . if'n he's got any hid."

Dunlee felt a surging elation for his friend Hartman. No man had thrown himself into the challenge more resolutely than Shoat to carve out a cattle kingdom in the untamed ruggedness of the southwest. The man had driven back redskins on the warpath, rustlers, horse thieves, wolves, and mountain lions. He had survived severe winters. If Dunlee could wish any man a stroke of sheer good fortune, Hartman was that man.

True, some misjudged the rancher. Too harsh, they said. But they did not know him close up. The men who laid their lives on the line for the brand knew their boss. They swore by him, called him a man among men, respected him as they did his friends Kit Carson, Lucien Maxwell, and Dick Wootton, who had become legends in the territory.

Yet Hartman had his enemies. They were rash, bitter men made foes by their own dark choices, men who sought concealment in outlaw strongholds from Fort Union soldiers, lawmen, and vigilantes. They skulked, nursing grudges for wounds from Hartman's guns or by his riders. Some had lost kin or sidekicks to the Hartman justice on the untamed frontier. The cattle lord's law had blazed from a heavy .53 calibre Hawken mountain man rifle, a Henry .44, a Colt .44, or a Winchester '73. And there were cases when his bare hands dealt it out.

Outlaws had learned to fear Hartman, even if his justice was not the sometimes vicious and overdone brand dealt out by the vigilantes of E-Town, who had formed to stop the criminal breed. Those citizens lashed out with the terror of lead pills and taut ropes.

Scarcely five minutes slipped by as Dunlee bolted down his food. The urgency spurred him to haste. He must steal away before Pugley's men pounded in. But the clock in Harbin's front room had just chimed eight when hoofbeats drummed in the gulch. Seconds later they thundered in the front yard.

"Yo, the house!"

Dunlee watched the old stage agent slip out past the bedroom door, the door drawn shut after him. Harbin gripped a Winchester '73. The sound of his bootheels on pine boards told Dunlee he was moving out into the yard to face the riders. Loud voices clamored for food and a place to stay the night.

"Feller on a black horse come by here?" That was the voice of Pugley. He didn't take long to voice his obsession.

"Had quite a number o' fellers the past few days." Harbin was matter-of-fact. "Seems some was on black horses. Who you lookin' fur?"

"Calls hisself Dunlee," Pugley pursued. He swung down, weary and disgruntled from the punishing ride. "Got a price on his head for murder in Virginia. Murdered three of our men between Fort Worth and here to boot. Dangerous man."

"Dunlee, eh? Feller came through here a few months back. Seems as how I do recollect. On his way to Virginny. You can put your horses in the corral. They's hay and oats. Got a batch o' stew inside. Stage folk left some. Come on in an' sit. Throw your bedrolls on the floor."

Dunlee liked the way Harbin steered away from Pugley's subject. Now he thought of moving out through the back door. But two of the men had walked around by the corner of the station near the bedroom to converse in low tones. The others led the horses out to the corral.

"Naw, he ain't here," one voice said. "We beat him. He's camped, hid out back there, but he'll be comin'. It would take us days to search out all those canyons. Here we can jest lay an' wait."

"May be." It was the voice of Trowling. "But I ain't so sure. I aim to take me a look around. First, that shed over there. Then the stable. If he's here, I'll git me some satisfaction 'fore Pugley gets his'n."

Harbin was quick. He set stew, biscuits, bowls, and spoons on a long table where stage passengers and crew had sat. In a jiffy he was bawling, "Come an' get it." The aroma of the stew overcame the hungry, weary men who tromped in from the stable. They rushed to the table like pigs crowding to a trough, not waiting for anybody. Dunlee could hear the rowdy voices and the slurping.

But Trowling and the other man had moved off toward the door of the shed, not five paces distant. They stood smoking. Dunlee had to act fast. They would spot the black and cut loose with a warning yell. He would be trapped between their two guns and the shooting irons of the three, cut off from his horse. His chances would be slim as the buck's in a box canyon with five hunters closing in.

He drew his Colt clear of leather, stepped to the back door, and eased it open enough to slip through. Then he barked sharply but not loudly:

"Make a move and it'll be your last."

Trowling put on the brakes as if he had suddenly seen the edge of a cliff. The other man did the same. Their right hands hovered near their gun handles, but neither liked the odds. They spun around, their mouths dropping open. Dunlee stepped out from the blackness near the wall, his gun trained on them.

"Nice and easy," he said. "I can drop you both before you clear leather."

They devoutly believed. Their hands slowly lifted into the air above their heads.

"Shore, shore," Trowling kind of grunted, after spitting his cigarette into the dust. He was scowling for letting a man get the drop on him. "We ain't makin' no play."

"Move over here, and step lively." They came

near the corner of the station and he had them drop to their knees. Then he stepped behind them, lifting their guns out of the holsters and poking them inside his belt. He frisked them for further weapons, coming up with a Bowie knife from Trowling and a derringer from his companion. These he stuffed into his pockets for the moment.

"Now, flat on your bellies. I'm gonna get my horse, and if you even make a move or a peep this itchy finger's liable to act up. I can punch the center out of a Bull Durham tag at fifty paces. Try me if you like, but it would be a losing gamble."

Dunlee brought the black and fastened the reins on a protruding log of the station roof.

The three hogs slopping at the table merely glanced up when Trowling and his companion stepped in.

"You're late," Pugley said. "They ain't much left now." All three of the men chuckled.

Dunlee stepped in, his Colt leveled. A spoon clattered out of a bowl. Pugley spat an oath, nearly choked on his mouthful, and started to reach inside his jacket. He decided against it, his right hand freezing in the air, still clutching his spoon. The other two simply gaped sheepishly. Their fingers spread out in plain view near their bowls. They gulped hard.

"Unbuckle your gunbelts slow and easy. Drop them behind you," Dunlee said. "If anybody flicks an eyelash too sudden, my finger's sure to get anxious. A man gets jumpy the way you've shot at me the past couple of weeks. Now, peel off your coats and drop them behind too."

Next, he pointed them out one by one and had them deposit any other weapons on the floor.

"Now, old man," he spoke harshly to Harbin, "you've been doing well tonight. You know what'll happen if you don't. Load those guns in a sack, and bring them to me."

Harbin grasped why Dunlee had spoken roughly to him. He didn't want these men to blame him for not warning them. A man with a gun in his back goes along. He grabbed an empty grain sack from a stack by the wall and loaded the guns with haste.

Not a man stirred. The two who had come in ahead of Dunlee leaned against the front wall, sullen and scarcely breathing. Their eyes were peeled toward the man with the gun. Pugley and the other two sat stupefied, not twitching a muscle. They were busy only with violent thoughts which their faces could not hide.

"Now, Pugley," said Dunlee, "I hanker for some explaining. You and your hounds came out here to rob and kill me. Clear from Virginia. Trowling an' his curs from Fort Worth. That's a long way. I want all the reasons, and I want them fast."

Pugley's block face was dark, hateful. He could have bitten railroad spikes in two. He cleared his throat uneasily. The muscles in his bull neck bulged and trembled.

"We want our money back."

"I won it fair and square. If you'd taken my money that night, you would've figured it was yours— no question."

"We needed it. We ain't never lost that much."

" 'We' means mainly you and Endicott?"

"Yeah. Then the murder. They found Mueller done in . . . your knife with blood on it layin' in the grass by the back fence. They's a reward out on you. Your runnin' an' everything . . . folks figger you done it."

"But *you* know I couldn't have, don't you Pugley? I was with you, Endicott, and the others. Then I lit a shuck for the von Ehrencroft's."

Harbin heard that name and glanced at him like a lantern had been lit in his brain.

Pugley blinked and cleared his throat again. He spoke with labored heaviness. "Well, I—"

"I left," Dunlee said slowly, "because someone broke into my cabin, stole my knife, and planted it to frame me. I knew you and Endicott and your bunch would lie through your teeth and swear I wasn't with you.

"And if that wasn't enough, someone could murder me on the pretense I was trying to escape. That would keep me from telling the truth to the good folk, who might listen. Isn't that the way it was, Pugley? Didn't that cross your mind?" He pressed the cold steel of the Colt mouth into the thick, hardened neck.

Pugley was breathing heavier. Beads of sweat broke out on his forehead like the silver heads of frost on a Virginia meadow.

"You know," Dunlee went on, his eyes watching the men carefully, "two men left the inn that night for a while—long enough for one to slip into town . . . long enough to kill Mueller, rob him, and ride back. Could be a man who made up a story he had stomach cramps and was stretched out on a couch where nobody saw him. And what if we have witnesses who recognized that man riding fast into town, saw him close by my cabin, where he could get the knife, saw him ride out a while later?"

Pugley stared at his bowl. He'd been ready to scoop out the last stew and fill the bowl again. Now all sense of hunger had fled. His stomach experienced other sensations. His fists were now on the table. He shifted them and leered in discomfort.

"Trowling," Dunlee went on, "you're a fool if you thick Pugley will share anything with you. And you're a bigger fool if you think I'll fork over money I took honestly in Virginia or won off you by riding that sorrel in Fort Worth.

"I'll be in Cimarron tomorrow, and you know about the outfit from Hartman's canyon. They'll be all-fired riled that you bothered me, prodded to come looking for you. Same goes for you other boys. Be thankful you haven't hurt me. That bunch would dog your trail to Robbers Roost or clear to Chihuahua if they had to. And they'd get you.

"Take my advice. Drop the whole thing before you're in too deep. This is my fourth run-in with some of you, and you haven't got the job done. It'll be tougher from here on. If I get any more 'roused I'll come after you myself, clean out the whole pack of you. I don't forget faces." He peered around, nodding as he made a special register of each countenance.

"Now." He directed his words to Pugley again. "Why are Endicott and Teresa out here?"

Harbin glanced over again. "Teresa?"

Pugley's eyes shot up, his face a study in surprise.

"What trick is this? They—they're out here? You gotta be pullin' my leg. They wouldn't—"

The snout of the barrel laid its agonizing menace at the base of his skull. He trembled with his former urge—to be thousands of miles from here.

"You know. Start talking."

"How in Sam Hill would I know?" he stalled.

"Because the two of them sent you. Then they got here about the same time. I'm losing my patience." One of Dunlee's hands grasped Pugley's sloping neck and pressed powerfully. The man winced.

"They just wanted to visit a man ... Hartman. Endicott ... wants you, wants his money back. The lady remembered the country from a few years back, came along to see it again."

The man could lie. Teresa, like Sheila, never wanted to lay eyes on the land again. Dunlee decided Pugley would lie all night. There must be more than that, and Pugley was afraid to spill it. He had a big stake in it and was too stubborn to jeopardize it. He was playing the odds that Dunlee was too good a man to squeeze the trigger unless a man tried to jump him.

"Whatever it is," Dunlee said firmly, "it won't work. They'll be two disappointed, shamed people. The same goes for you. If I see you again, I'll come shooting. They'll bury you like three of your gang already."

He backed to the door. "Your guns will be in the rocks on the south side of the stage road creek crossing, ten miles from here. The bullets will be at Swink's bar in Cimarron. Pugley, Trowling, come with me. Harbin, carry all your own guns out in the yard by the trough. Leave them where I can see them 'til I leave. If any of you take one step out that door you can expect to taste bullets."

He marched Pugley and Trowling out into the yard, tied the sack of guns to his saddlehorn, and swung up on the black. He made the two men turn all their horses out of the corral and start them west. The stage horses were left. Then he sent the men back to the station, rode over to Harbin by the trough, and let the black drink.

"Here's some money that'll more than take care of how I've put you out. I don't figure they'll bother you. If they do, they'll answer to me. Much obliged." He slipped three dollars to Harbin, who was standing between Dunlee and the station door. The men could not see.

"A man does what has to be done with that breed," Harbin admitted. "If they make a play for my guns, I've got a shotgun stashed where they won't think to look. I can get it fast."

So Dunlee rode out, driving the horses ahead of him. He moved them west on the Santa Fe Trail at least ten miles. Then he took to rocky ground where the men would be slowed up in tracking and finding them.

It was a comfort knowing the killers would not be riding hard on his trail, at least for part of the night. They were not likely to try to use the stage team, because those horses were spent after their pull that day. The ambushers would wait out the night, get some shut-eye, let the horses rest, then try to use them in the morning.

But Harbin, needing the animals for the next stage going north, would use his trusted shotgun and make the men hoof it.

Dunlee remembered a cave near the mouth of a nearby box canyon. It had a ledge trail providing an escape over the rim into rocks and brush. He drove the horses into the canyon where they would find grazing and where he could get to them quickly if wolves, a cougar, or a bear tried to molest them. He staked out the black just below in a place where he could crop lush grass, then unfurled his bedroll in the cave. From his vantage point he could hear anybody approaching from a good way off.

He tried to rest peacefully. But the thought of Teresa calling herself Mandie plagued him. Dressed as she was and fixed up that way, she looked a great deal like Mandie. Suddenly, he remembered being in the von Ehrencroft parlor gazing at a picture of Mandie. She looked much like Teresa in a certain pose. Besides, Teresa had studied acting and was skilled in applying makeup to look deceptively like the person she played. She knew many such tricks.

"Is posing as Mandie a scheme she and Endicott cooked up to deceive Shoat? Did Shoat really come on to gold, and send word to Mandie or me, and Teresa found out? Is this a play to get the gold? Did Endicott send Pugley and his men to put me out of the picture for stakes higher than just the money I won? Did he have to finish me so I wouldn't show up and spoil his plot?"

He lay hurting from these possibilities.

Hartman could quite naturally think Teresa was Mandie who had come home. He'd *want* to believe that. He hadn't laid eyes on Mandie or Teresa for twelve years, hadn't even seen a picture. They had grown up and changed.

Did Mandie know about this trip? Or had Teresa deceived her? That might work since Mandie was away at college some of the time.

Thoughts of Mandie flooded his mind; he tried

to visualize just how she looked, to see her eyes and long, flowing tresses, to imagine her voice soft and sweet in the Virginia air. Now he heard the melody of it as they walked together in the garden fragrance that last night. He wanted to hear more....

What would Mandie think of him, here in a cave in the wild country?

Dunlee's thoughts faded into dreams. He had to be riding before sunup, send a telegram from Cimarron that would reach Mandie. Get to Hartman to warn him. Go home....

7

Trevor Endicott stepped off the night coach and registered Teresa and himself at the St. James Hotel, one of Cimarron's finest. The place was run by Henri Lambert, a little Frenchman who had come to the U.S. on a sailing vessel from Nantes. He had cooked for Ulysses S. Grant and Abraham Lincoln, then made his way west cooking for wagon people on the Santa Fe Trail. He had quickly won a reputation as one of the best cooks in the Territory of New Mexico.

After breakfast the next morning Endicott and Teresa bought clothing to suit their plans. Teresa then wanted to catch up on her rest, bathe, and primp before lunch. That set Endicott free to walk about the place.

Cimarron was a small, dusty town sprawled south of the Cimarron River. Besides the Frenchman's hotel, dining room, billiard area, and bar there were only a few other scattered buildings, mostly one-story adobes. Endicott strolled across the street from the hotel to see the mansion of Lucien B. Maxwell. It had been built in the late 1850s. The house had become a stage stop beside the Santa Fe Trail.

According to the gunman that had ridden with Endicott on the stage, Maxwell was an intimate friend of Kit Carson, who had died six years back. He'd also been Shoat Hartman's friend. The three rode together in Fremont expeditions exploring the Rockies and traveling to California. Carson was a guide; Hartman and Maxwell were crack shots who supplied meat.

Maxwell married a daughter of the French Canadian Don Carlos Beaubien at Taos. Along with Guadalupe Miranda—a Mexican—Beaubien secured a land grant to this territory in 1841 from Manuel Armijo, governor of Mexico. The grant was later confirmed by the U.S. after its conquest of Mexico in 1846. When Beaubien died, Maxwell not only purchased the Miranda land but bought the shares of others in the Beaubien family. He had become a feudal baron, owning 1.75 million acres. It was the largest estate held by any man in the southwest.

"The Maxwell Land Grant," mused Endicott. "The man was a fool to sell out four years ago, even though he's got a good-sized ranch at Fort Sumner. He was just over fifty, and had it made here—a tremendous cattle and sheep ranch, the largest share of the Aztec mine that was the top gold claim near E-town, and some of the fastest race horses in the southwest.

"If I play my cards right, maybe I can rise to be greater than Maxwell."

Now that Maxwell had sold, agents from the Maxwell Land Grant and Railway Company were prying squatters off the land. Squatters' clubs had formed to buck the pressure with well-oiled Colts and Winchesters if necessary. The country was a hotbed

110

of mob fury and blazing gunfire as violent as the wild waters of the hills that tore canyons through the land. Soldiers from Fort Union were constantly on a peace-keeping vigil at Cimarron.

Only a few could claim clear title to their land— Shoat Hartman was among them. Hartman had not only ridden with Maxwell and trapped with him on the Columbia, Platte, and Arkansas thirty years earlier; he had not only helped him plant his stock-raising empire; he had saved his scalp in a death-defying rescue when a Comanche war party caught him in an ambush on the plains. In gratitude, Maxwell gave him a good strip of land, sold him more range at a low price, even let him in on beef contracts to the forts— Union, Conrad, Craig, Bascome. Hartman had a written deed that proved handy to except him from the land company's claims to land that was part of their deal with Maxwell.

Endicott eyed the two-story Maxwell "castle." With its Victorian furniture hauled by oxcart and mule from St. Louis over the Santa Fe Trail, it had long been as much a palace as Cimarron could boast. In its rooms were plush carpets, heavy velvet drapes, gold-framed oil paintings and heavy dark tables. Now it was in the hands of company men who had bought the Maxwell grant.

Another main building was the three-story stone grist mill where the federal government agent still had grain ground to ration to Utes and Apaches. Then there were George Bushnell's Beaufort Stables and his fortlike barn where Fort Union soldiers hung out when in town; a blacksmith shop; the National Hotel; Deputy Sheriff Dike Bellis's office and a new stone jail; Swink's Gambling Hall and Saloon; the *Cimarron News*; a shop combining services of mail, printing, and telegraph; and an immense stable area near the Maxwell House. Besides these, there were a few other businesses and scattered homes, with many broad, open spaces.

Endicott hired a man to ride out to Hartman's canyon with word that Mandie was in town. Then he sauntered into Swink's Gambling Hall. There, piles of money changed hands in faro, keno and roulette. Hot and dusty, he craved a drink to slake a raging thirst. Ordering the finest the barkeep could produce, he looked to the rear of the room for a card game.

These crude, poorly educated men of the southwest should be easy pickings . . . , he thought.

A swarthy, stocky Mexican under a massive sombrero remained at a table when three cowboys got up and tromped to the bar, losers. He flashed a toothy grin at Endicott, introduced himself as Malnardo, and invited him to play. Sitting down, the Virginian won a game, then lost. The cowhands who had recently left the table hovered near. Soon half a dozen men and a honky-tonk girl watched.

Endicott saw the gunman he had met on the stage come in and lean against the bar. The man quietly toyed with a drink, keeping an eye toward the card game.

The third game came to an end, the Mexican a big loser. Suddenly he lurched up in a rage, hurling his chair backward.

"Take your gringo hands off my money," he rapped. "That last card, you pull eet from the sleeve. The hand, eet cheats. Now feel the hand weeth a gun,

112

or geeve the money back and leave. Eet's the last time you weel cheat on Malnardo."

A faint smile pushed at the corners of Endicott's lips. It was an expression of cold contempt, of tolerating a lesser man, of gazing across at scum.

"My friend, I hardly know you. I don't wish to harm you. I would be pleased to have you reconsider. Allow me to buy you a drink, and sometime you can try again. I assure you, I did not cheat."

One of the cowboys who had been watching stepped back safely to one side. He broke a hush that fell upon the room.

"Stranger, did you say 'harm' him? You know who this is? Trig Malnardo! One of the best with a gun that's ever passed through." He glanced from Malnardo to the gunman at the bar. "You'd better apologize, fork over the money, and jest be thankful. That . . . or they'll carry you out to bury the same day you blowed in."

"No. No apologies," Endicott replied. Not a trace of fear disturbed the placid face. "It's simply a case of Mr. Malnardo making a small mistake. There's still time to correct it, and I'll be glad to accept that."

Malnardo stomped further back, spewing a loud, hissing sneer of disbelief across the table. His face flushed with the sting and fire of a man who raged over a double injury. He had a reputation. No southern dude was about to make him look silly.

"I don't make corrections where I see a man cheat." He spat the words through his teeth in disgust. "We'll settle eet weeth guns. Now, draw!"

Endicott's left hand already lay in his lap. He made a quick move with his right hand off the edge of the table toward his open coat as he shifted back, and toppled the table out of the way. Malnardo's hand, only inches from a pearl-handled gun butt, streaked over and up.

The blast of a gun crashed through the room, then a second shot. Men jumped back from the shock. Malnardo seemed to freeze for an instant, his face caught in a stare of utter shock, his frantic left hand clutching at his chest. His gun had cleared leather but swung up only halfway. His bullet, a split second behind the other shot, ploughed a thin furrow along the edge of the table top off to the right. His gun hand sank, and he staggered back, caught himself gamely, trying to bring the gun up again. Then he buckled forward on his face.

Endicott, in a blur of action, had half risen into a crouch. From his hands, which were together, a thin wisp of smoke licked upward and disappeared from the snout of a Smith and Wesson revolver. He watched Malnardo sprawl out on the dusty floor, his Colt .44 spilling free from relaxing fingers. Endicott's right hand placed his own gun inside his coat.

The man who had warned Endicott about his challenger stooped down and rolled the body over gently. A splotch of crimson widened swiftly on the gunman's shirt front. Right over his heart a small hole was obvious in the cloth.

A murmur of awe ran through the onlookers.

"It's a shame," Endicott said, shaking his head as he gazed on the fallen man. "We might have had a drink and forgotten the matter. I regret that he would have it no other way. I did not cheat as he supposed."

"That's the way I figger it, too." The gunman

from the stage had spoken from the bar. "I saw Malnardo gettin' a card from his own sleeve the game he beat you. He wanted to win bad, and got hotheaded when this game went sour."

"Thanks, Mr. Chenault," said Endicott, remembering the name from the stage ride. "Please, gentlemen, have a drink with me after we have taken care of the body."

A short time later, Endicott gathered up his winnings. He invited Chenault to join him for a drink at the table. He poured into two glasses. Others in the room moved away with a babble of voices to talk about what they had seen. They had never figured anybody could beat Malnardo—except maybe Clay Allison who ranched nearby to the northeast, or maybe Chenault himself.

"That was fast shootin'," Chenault said. Endicott smiled at a saloon girl who walked by the table, and lifted his glass. "Trig had killed at least ten men. Never lost 'til today."

"Once in a lifetime—that's all it takes. Now, Chenault, as I mentioned on the stage, we have come a long distance on our business. It is worth a lot to us if we're successful."

"I believe," returned Chenault with a twinkle in his eye, "I follow you. You're a plantation owner in Virginny. You bring along a lady who must be one of the finest flowers people this side of St. Louis ever saw out here. The way you both dress, the way she keeps herself and carries herself speaks of rich livin'. That takes money. Could it be Hartman's gold that pulled you here?"

The question was sudden. Endicott's poker face studied Chenault, and he sipped wine thoughtfully.

"I don't believe I mentioned gold."

"Ah, no. Nary a word. But gold has a habit of speakin' for itself, doesn't it? Men go a long way after gold, don't they? It was gold that drawed the crowds to Californy and to E-Town. I've made me a study of men for a good long spell, Mr. Endicott. I'd lay fifty to one I'm right in this case. You came because of gold."

Endicott wore a placid face. But inwardly he was grieved. He was a man used to doing the thinking. He did not like for others to think ahead of him.

"You really do have gold on your mind, Chenault. Is that all you talk about?"

"Not at all," Chenault smiled. He glanced knowingly at the saloon girl, and drew his tongue across his lips. "But I have given it a powerful lot of thought. That is, since I heard Hartman took the wagon to his place—the wagon with the gold."

Endicott set down his glass. A new alertness stole into his frame. He maintained the unperturbed face, but now his ears were ten times more perked.

"He took a wagon with gold?" The question was casual, low-key, as if a mere effort to carry on the conversation.

"You got it. Three prospectors got greedy over to Clear Creek. I figger one or more of 'em wanted to hog it all. They killed one another, but one was able to get on a mule an' make it to Hartman's ranch. He died there. Then Hartman rode back, found the wagon and the gold they'd collected an' fought over. I went an' traced the tracks myself. He hid the gold somewhere at his place."

"And you want it? Well, why haven't you just sneaked in and found it?"

"Not easy. Hartman's uncanny . . . got eyes in the back of his head. He sees all that moves. Got a lookout ridin' the ridge flankin' the pass where his headquarters are laid out. He can see most everything from up there . . . keep an eye on the whole pass an' a lot of country around."

"You have any idea how much gold he got?"

"Yeah, a lot of it. Three men known to be friends don't shoot it out comin' back to town like they done over no little pouch of gold dust. An' Hartman wouldn't be so secretlike less'n he had stumbled on somethin' big. Besides, I read other signs that tell me somethin'. Since that night I've noticed a tighter guard on the place, an extra rider swingin' in a loop all around. He's protectin' more'n just the ranch."

"But you don't know where he stashed the gold."

"No. But I figger I could get at it if the way was clear. Which it ain't now. His outfit's the toughest in these parts. I'd as soon face a detachment of Kit Carsons. Quantrill's guerrillas could've gone in there an' been shot to doll rags. If any got out they'd be packin' lead."

"Why do you tell me all of this?"

"Why? Let me shoot straight. I'm a man that finds out things I need to know. I happen to have a good friend—Trowling—a man you've never seen. Sent me a telegram from Fort Worth to Denver. He's throwed in with a man you hired to kill the man Hartman thinks of as a son. Hartman would leave a lot to that man if he died, and a lot to his daughter.

"Now, I know Hartman ain't laid eyes on his daughter in years. He thinks a lot of her. He'll fix her up fetchin' good. An' you figger to rake in something big, bein' her man.

"I peg you as a smart man. A man of opportunity. You don't hanker to wait 'til Hartman dies of old age. Me, I got men that can tear that place apart to get at the gold. First I can take care of Hartman, one way or another. His man Dunlee put lead in my arm about two years back, an' killed my partner. If Trowling an' your men plug Dunlee, I'll draw my satisfaction from Hartman hisself. You go along with me, we can both come out on top. You don't, I'll be comin' for you. Compared with me, Malnardo was slow. An' not as smart. I won't sucker into no trap with you holdin' a gun in your lap under the table."

Endicott chewed the inside of his cheek. He had thought nobody had seen he had been hiding a gun ready all the time.

Chenault knew.

"Do we understand each other?" Chenault was staring at him.

Endicott was shrewd. He knew how to manipulate others to gain his ends. He also knew how to make them disappear when they had outlived their usefulness. He had made several disappear. He might need Chenault and his men. All the better if Chenault was fast with a gun. Endicott would not try to buck that. He knew of other ways. Chenault fancied himself smart, but who was he but a country hick? He needed a good lesson on how the big boys do it. But that could wait 'til the opportune time. For now, why not scrape up all the manpower he could get?

"I think it could be to our advantage to work together," he told the gunman.

"Good, good. I've been scouting around the ranch, and I know the pass better than the back of my hand.

My men can whittle Hartman's outfit down one by one 'til it's easy to move in. I've got a man watchin' the ranch day an' night. Hartman will tip his hand sooner or later. Then I'll know where the gold is. Play it straight with me an' you'll come out good. Any double dealin' an' the best you get is a grave by a gully bank, with dirt caved in your face."

8

Dunlee reined the black in a grove of elms behind the corrals not far from Henri Lambert's hotel. Before heading for Virginia he had struck up a friendship with the squat Frenchman, a man in his midthirties. Now he looked forward to seeing him again. "Frenchy," as Dunlee had dubbed him, might know more than anybody about Endicott and Teresa since they had hit town. Dunlee had figured they would probably get some rest before proceeding to Hartman's canyon.

He gazed at the rear, upstairs windows of the hotel. Teresa might be primping in one of those back rooms, which afforded more privacy. She would also have a scenic view of the range stretching away to the east and south. Jerking his Stetson brim down to conceal his face from anyone looking out, he started across an open area with clumps of sagebrush and tall grama grass bending in a light breeze. His nostrils welcomed the leafy scent held in a moist prairie warmth, the smell of horses' hooves burning at the smithy's, and the tantalizing aroma of bread baking. Once he glanced up at the second story and caught a fleeting glimpse of a woman near a window. She was combing her hair as she stared off toward the rolling range behind him to the south. He ducked his head quickly.

It was Teresa!

Going in by a rear door, he saw Frenchy sitting in his small office. Dunlee could hear someone, possibly Frenchy's wife Mary, rattling dishes in the kitchen. The proprietor heard the bootheels and turned, recognizing him instantly. He beamed, pumped his hand with gusto, and asked to hear all about Virginia.

"I'll come in an' wear out your ear," Dunlee promised. "Right now I'm concerned about two people who rode in on the night stage—a lady named von Ehrencroft and a man named Endicott."

"Yes, they're staying here."

"Where is Endicott now?"

"He's over at Swink's. Hit town with a bang—I mean a real bang. Won at the tables, then Malnardo, the gunslinger, accused him of cheating. He beat Malnardo to his gun, and they carried Malnardo out to bury. Now Endicott's having a long palaver with another gunman, Choc Chenault—really going at it in a serious way."

Malnardo . . . Chenault. Dunlee wondered. How had Endicott beaten Trig to the gun and why would he be hobnobbing with Chenault? The man, among other things, was a paid killer. . . .

"Say, you know Endicott. And of course you know Miss Mandie," Frenchy said. "I asked her about you. She said you had left Virginia some time ago, that you were in Texas."

"Texas?" Dunlee took a cup of hot coffee Frenchy had poured for him and mused. The letter he had written would have let Mandie know he was in Texas. But Mandie was to keep that information secret. How did Teresa come to know?

"Why yes," Frenchy responded. "Too bad you left Virginia before Luke got there."

"Luke? Luke Savage? Luke . . . went to Virginia?"

"That he did. Hartman let me in on it. He sent him to bring you and Mandie." He savored more of his coffee, leaned back in a cowhair recliner chair. "Too bad about Luke. Fell real sick and decided to stay on a while 'til he's better. Told Mandie to come on with Endicott. He'll come later when he's able."

"Hmm." Dunlee was beginning to understand. Had Luke gone back there because Hartman was anxious to have Mandie come, urgent not to be denied? If Hartman really had gold, that could explain such an unusual trip. It might also be why he did not go himself but sent his most trusted man, the segundo. That might have been how Teresa and Endicott got wind of the gold—if there was gold.

But it just did not figure that Luke would stay on in Virginia. He was a breed of man who would come even if not well, simply gut it out. Even when ill, which was rare, he went about his work no matter how bad he felt. He would have to be seriously ill to stop in the midst of a job on which Hartman had sent him.

Well, maybe he was. Or was it something else?

"Frenchy, don't tell Ter . . . don't breathe a word to Mandie or Endicott that I'm here. I'll surprise . . . Mandie . . . a little later."

He took the black to Lambert's stable to be fed,

watered, and rested. The horse had more than earned his keep. Afterward he went to the Crocker store and bought several rounds of ammunition for his Colt and Winchester. He also purchased a couple of new shirts and two pairs of pants. Then he bought a bath, a haircut, and a shave. Having donned a fresh change of clothes, he carried the bag of ammunition he'd taken at Harbin's to Swink's and left it with "Lard" Guyser, carefully avoiding Endicott and Chenault. Dunlee asked Guyser not to mention he was back.

Then he strode back to Lambert's in his red shirt, black pants, and black Stetson. He knocked softly on Teresa's door.

"Who is it?" The voice was soft, touched with that thrushlike melody he remembered, that richness that made a man's heart leap to hear more.

"Dunlee."

"Did he hear a quick catch of breath beyond the door? A register of surprise? Or was he imagining it? If surprise, was it that of being caught off guard when she did not expect him to be alive? Was it the surprise of dismay, or of relief that he had gotten past the killers?

She opened the door and stood in a yellow dress. It had a blue bow at the waist and blue frilly lace around the neck. Her hair, a richer gold than ripened wheat, tumbled gracefully past her shoulders. She was stunning.

"Hello, Mandie." She did look much like Mandie.

She smiled, a strange smile in which he discerned a smugness of satisfaction. It routed the initial shock on her pretty face.

124

"Why hello, Marks. We meet again—a long way from Virginia. Come in."

"Yes, a lot different from Virginia."

The room was fragrant with the spice of her coiffure. "You should like this land . . . even if Teresa wouldn't."

"Oh, she would love it, too." Her voice bounded with enthusiasm, leaped with cheerfulness.

"The strange thing is your coming here with Endicott. That keeps Teresa apart from him for a long time. How did Teresa ever put up with that? I would think she'd be married to him by now. Or did the losses he suffered that night dampen her enthusiasm for him?"

He watched her closely when he got in that dig. It was meant to prick; he did not want to miss the reaction. Her eyes betrayed a slight, unguarded spark of irritation. His sword's point had struck to the quick. She felt it. She turned away to hide her feelings, and walked to a chair.

"You know," she said, still facing the wall, "Teresa may have more resource than you give her credit for."

"Yes, she has resource," he chuckled. He decided to shoot straight to the issue. "Resource so she could make herself up to masquerade as Mandie, . . . the deceit to try it. You know, you look so much like Mandie nobody would realize you were Teresa if he didn't know you both well. No use denying it. What's this all about, Teresa?"

She clenched her hands and paced across the room, gathering her wits a long time before replying.

"Why, Marks Dunlee, I should think what I do

is my own business." The defiance in her tone was unmistakable.

"If it were only you involved, I could agree. But when you pose as Mandie, others can be hurt—like an honest rancher who aches to see his daughter, like Mandie herself, like me. Then Luke."

She started to sit down but decided just to stand staring out the window. She straightened the dress on her shoulders.

"At least I can offer you a drink," she proposed. "Maybe we could be friends?" She moved to a dresser, her back to him, and lingered pouring drinks into small glasses. She brought one to him and stood gazing out the window at the low, hazy hills, blue in the distance.

"I think I will like this country. The blue hills remind me of the Blue Ridge Mountains."

Dunlee sat down and rested his arm on a table near the chair. Leftovers of her lunch with Endicott still remained. As he drew his glass toward his mouth he bumped a small pitcher. Some of his drink spilled in a tiny pool. He apologized for his clumsiness, and she replied graciously that it was all right.

Two small Mexican boys darted northward across the open area off to the side from the boarding house, armed with fishing poles. A small collie raced ahead.

"Oh, look, they're going fishing," Teresa said.

"Yes, they can catch some good ones in the river."

Then she asked about life in Cimarron and he began to explain. A short time later he looked back at his glass to pick it up. A fly had been dabbling at the edge of the spilled drink, but had fallen and was kicking its last, feeble spasms. Puzzled, he glanced to the glass. Teresa was still gazing out the window. Presently she stepped back toward her chair, momentarily turning her back to him. He flipped the contents out of the glass through the window. He hadn't sipped a drop.

She settled down into the chair, a finger toying with the strands of hair that tumbled to her bosom. Quickly she took interest in the empty glass.

"May I pour you more?"

"No." He smiled slightly. "That'll do the job. Now, back to this game about Mandie. You can't go through with this—whatever plan you have in mind. It can only cause heartache, maybe bloodshed. You know I'll buck it with all the fight in me. Hartman is like a pa to me. And he means a lot to Mandie. He's a man of iron will, because a man had to be tough to hold what he's held in a hard land. A weaker man would have crumbled long ago. I won't let you hurt this good man.

"And I don't want to see you shame yourself. Think of what you'll be throwing away. If it's Endicott you want, he's liable to end up crumpled in a pool of blood as a lot of others have out here, or a laughing stock. And how could you face those back in Virginia—dare show your face again?"

She looked down, bit her lip. Then she drew her lips into a resolute tightness, and tossed her hair back. Her eyes flashed sparks of fire.

"Marks, you do annoy me. Work against us and I can promise, you will be very sorry. Trevor has ways of dealing with people who get in his path. Now, you will excuse me. It's been a jerky, jolting trip. And the roads are one washout after another. I would like to rest before dinner."

He arose, noted a second fly that had kicked out its last efforts. He had never expected to thank flies. But now he did it silently as he moved to the door. How could the girl he had longed to marry stoop to this?

"Teresa, what happened to Luke back there?"

"Oh, him?" She averted his probing eyes, fished for words, then replied. "Too bad about him. He fell quite ill. Must've picked up something on his trip. It went on for several days, and the doctor could not determine just what was wrong. Mr. Savage was giddy, and didn't appear to be aware of what was going on. He couldn't walk without dizziness. He said he would come back here when he is able. I hope he is better by now."

"Where is he now—exactly?"

"Why, ... staying in a place not far from our farm. We would have had him stay right at the house, but he was adamant that he did not want to be a bother. So someone drops in a couple times a day to check on how he is responding."

"Does Whitehead know where he is?"

"Wh ...? Oh yes, of course."

"What did Luke say about you living this lie—masquerading as Mandie? Or does he suspect it? And does Mandie even know you came out here, that you're trying this?"

"Really, Marks, you test my patience. We will need to have a good, long talk once I've had the benefit of a full rest. But now, as I told you, I must get an hour or so of rest before dinner. Good-bye!"

"I'll go now, Teresa. But not before I say once again that you're in trouble. Way over your head, and the water's getting deeper all the time. This plan you and Endicott hatched will come to nothing. Hartman will have his Mandie. And his Luke. I'll see it doesn't work for you. Give it up—now!"

"Go!" She almost shouted it, her lips curling up in a seething fury. She beat at his arm with clenched fists. He backed out and went down the stairs. She was framed in her doorway, watching him. Then she stepped out to the railing above the lobby and followed him with scorching eyes until he had gone out the front door. Immediately she sped down the stairs and rapped on Frenchy's office door.

"I need to see Mr. Endicott right away," she told him. "You are such a kind man, I knew I could ask you to find him and have him come now." She favored the proprietor with one of her most winning smiles. Her big, pleading eyes and honeysweet voice produced a magical spell in Frenchy's heart. He hurried out into the street to find Endicott.

Dunlee, pausing by a window alongside Frenchy's, saw Teresa race down the stairs and turn toward his friend's office. Lingering, he saw Frenchy hasten away to please the damsel in need.

Was it poison, or just something to put me to sleep 'til Endicott could get rid of me after dark? He shuddered at his blindness. Under the spell of what he had felt was love, he had wanted this woman as his bride!

Their paid killers failed four times to keep me from coming back. Now the drink, number five. It just shows there's more than one way. Now their need to stop me is more desperate than ever. If I reach Shoat with the truth, their scheme crumbles around them. So they'll plot to finish me tonight.

His watch read 4:30. He had time to leave a telegram for Tom Jackson before old Dodd Lathrop locked up and shuffled home to his wife. Lathrop was there when Dunlee went into the office, a man past seventy-five, bent, wrinkled, and bespectacled.

As Dunlee strode away, he suddenly spotted Endicott across the street. Dunlee ducked behind a hipshot horse hitched to a post by a shop, so that he wouldn't be seen. Endicott pushed into Swink's place. He had hurried from the direction of Frenchy's, where he must have just talked with Teresa.

Why not just stalk in and invite Endicott to step outside? He could put it to him straight that he was on to his plan to have him killed. He could challenge him point-blank to a showdown here and now. And if he refused to draw he could tell Endicott to get out of town on tomorrow's eastbound stage, to forget about seeing Shoat. He could make it clear to him that he could choose that or face him before the stage dust settled. Decisive action would spare Shoat heartache and get rid of a schemer more poisonous than a rattler.

But he changed his mind when he peered in at Swink's. At a far table, Endicott was whispering something emphatically to a man with a revolver slung low on his thigh. Choc Chenault! The gunfighter was dressed in a red shirt, gray pants, and a gray Stetson. Something passed from Endicott's hand, hidden from Dunlee, to Chenault's.

Then Endicott and Chenault turned toward the front, and the watcher drew back out of sight. If he made a play now he'd have to face both men. That wasn't smart. Chenault was touted to be one of the fastest, deadliest men with a six-gun between the Staked Plains and Tucson.

"I'll wait," he told himself. "I'll see Endicott at the ranch. I can explain to Shoat all about this sorry scheme. He and his outfit will chase these deceivers out of the country so fast they won't hit the brakes 'til they reach Virginia."

He headed toward Lambert's stable, making sure Endicott and Chenault did not spot him. He'd throw his gear on the black and ride for Hartman's pass. He would not be surprised, judging by the attempts of Endicott's bunch the past couple of weeks, if someone took a shot at him tonight. And, based on the scene at Swink's plus Frenchy's words about Endicott jawing with Chenault, he suspected who would be holding the gun. A gun bought and paid for.

Astride the black, he skirted the corrals until he laid a good distance between himself and the stable. When he drifted into the deepening shadows of some young cottonwoods south of town, he threw a searching glance back. Someone in a red shirt and gray hat leaned against the rear corner of Lambert's livery. A claybank horse's head and neck were in sight beside the man, who held something in his hand. Probably a rifle. The man stepped back out of view. Dunlee moved behind the trees, dismounted, and waited. After a few minutes, he shrugged, remounted, and set his horse southward toward the pass and the Bar SH. It would take from two to three hours, but the black needed to rest, so he'd camp soon.

He made several irregular cuts in new directions to throw off anyone trying to follow, and that slowed him. Once he hazed half a dozen of Hartman's Durhams back over his tracks a ways. Then he veered off onto a rocky benchland laid out toward the southeast.

Behind him to the west was the broad, gently rolling rich prairie laid against the foothills of the Sangre de Cristo range of the Rockies. Strips of prairie darted in among the hills. Valleys plush with green grass stretched for miles between hills.

After riding higher ground for several miles, keeping shy of the skyline, he drew up in a place where he would be fortified by rocks as well as have a long view in three directions. He dragged his gear from the black and rubbed him down with tufts of dry grass. Throwing down his bedroll, he stretched out to get some sleep. His Winchester, ready at his side, gave him a measure of reassurance as he lay gazing at the star-dotted sky.

He planned to start out long before daybreak and get to the ranch early, before Shoat pulled out for town. And if Shoat left earlier, Dunlee could spot him on the road below and intercept him.

The thought of Shoat set his mind riding a new trail. He could imagine how Shoat had been anticipating the day he could see Mandie. At last the news had reached the ranch. Mandie was in town! The rancher's heart would have bounded into the heavens. He would not be able to contain himself for sheer expectation. Yet here Dunlee lay, intending to ride in to bring a dreaded word. He would throw a wet blanket over the flame of joy.

He would rather go up against the guns of Trowling and Pugley again than go in with news like that.

Scarcely five minutes slipped by. The black threw up his head, flicked his ears back toward the northwest along the bench, and issued a low snort. Dunlee was instantly on his feet by the horse's neck. He held the black's muzzle so that he would not nicker if another horse was approaching, and peered over a boulder. Sure enough, a horse and rider came on, moving slowly, about fifty paces below and cutting past to the southeast. In the moonlight Dunlee could make out a rifle cradled in the rider's arms. It was Chenault sitting the saddle. Soon the thud of hooves faded.

So, his suspicions were confirmed. Chenault was on the owlhoot trail after him. No doubt Endicott money fattened his wallet. He was piercing right on into Hartman range, probably hoping to catch Dunlee before he reached the pass. That, or slip in and bushwhack him at the headquarters. Come morning, Dunlee would need extreme care to pick his way shy of the killer's trap, to evade the stalker's cunning.

9

In the haze of predawn morning Dunlee threaded his
way in a semicircle. He hoped to give Chenault a wide
berth if he lurked in wait or slinked near Hartman's
pass. He had stayed alive by always doing the unexpected. It took longer this way, and so the sun was
half in view above the mountain crags by the time he
slipped in from the east to the ridge that rimmed the
pass on the north.

Once he caught a flicker of movement that might
have been a horse's rump and tail vanishing into brush.
It was several hundred yards away, back to the north.
He swung southward and skillfully used the cover of
brush and piñons, pausing now and again to listen and
watch for any sign of a man prowling in upon him.

Finally he approached the eastern mouth of the
pass, sticking to the ridge that flanked it on the north.
Below, a road wound into the canyon from the east.
A steep horse trail led off the tableland down into the
pass and intercepted the road. He meant to drop down
that way.

Suddenly a lineback dun swung squarely across
his path. It popped out of a nest of tall rocks about

fifty paces ahead. A rider had thrown a rifle up to cover him, and sat watching his approach.

"Coot," Dunlee yelled. "You old son of a gun. It's me, Marks."

"Well, I'll be a—." Coot Drescher never finished the exclamation. He lowered his rifle to the pommel, let out a wild whoop, and booted the lineback into a sudden start. He swept up alongside the black, hauled his mount to a quick stop, and grabbed Dunlee's hand in the warm shake of a friend.

"Didn't recognize you on that horse," he beamed. "Superb lookin' animal. But then you always was a good judge of horses. So you've come back. Shoat, he's missed you sore. This'll be a great day for him, you comin', then Mandie. He was rarin' to go. Pulled out in his buckboard two hours 'fore sunup to fetch Mandie."

"I missed seeing him on the road," Dunlee said with disappointment. "I kept off it. Had a man tryin' to trail me through the night."

"Who was after you?"

"Choc Chenault."

"Figgers. He's been layin' for a chance at Shoat, or any of us, since you plugged him in that brand-changin' affair. Maybe it was him, or some of his sidekicks, that kilt two of our men while you was gone.

"But as for Shoat, you wouldn't 'uv run into him on the road nohow. He was bound first for the west range. Wanted to see Curly over to the line dugout 'fore goin' on to town. Rustlers've been pickin' us a few at a time over there. Shoat's been shorthanded. He could jest spare Curly over there. 'Course, you know

Curly. I'd sooner run into a war party of Comanches than have to face him. He's a man takes care o' hisself."

"Yes," Dunlee agreed. "If Curly's riding the line the rustlers have a lot to worry about. But you know Shoat. He's got a lot of heart for any that rides for the brand. So he wants to see if Curly's all right."

A second rider emerged from the trail lifting from the road to the ridge. He came on to join them, a rifle laid across the pommel.

"Farr, this here's Marks Dunlee. This here's Farr Bucher. Farr joined up with us right after you pulled out. 'Fore I saw who you was I flashed him the signal from up here. He's come to back me."

Bucher was a stocky man in his midforties. He had prominent cheek bones and shifty eyes set in a pallid hatchet face. A thicket of dark beard climbed his cheeks, and an ancient, ugly scar slashed upward from his lower left jaw to his ear. Dunlee sized him up as a man who could bite heads off nails, an unfriendly soul, rougher than a cob. He picked up a distinct impression from the man's wolfishly hungry eyes and unsavory grunt. Bucher was disappointed he hadn't met up with trouble. His Winchester need not speak this time.

Dunlee remembered seeing that man somewhere, sometime. Was it in Texas or in this territory? He could not place him; it disturbed him.

"I'll spell you now," Bucher told Coot.

"Shore," Coot replied. "My stomach's scrapin' my backbone to get to breakfast." He started to ride off, then threw a message back over a shoulder to Bucher. "Keep an eye peeled for some coyote sniffin' on Dunlee's trail last night. Figgers to be Chenault. It's time we start bringin' in these gulchers draped over their saddles."

Bucher nodded and watched them ride away. His weasel eyes swept the terrain all about. Then he sent his horse bounding up into a nest of boulders to begin his vigil.

Over bunkhouse breakfast of bacon, beans, and biscuits washed down with coffee, Coot rehashed the situation at the Bar SH since Dunlee's departure. The newcomer listened in awe at the review of rustling, two punchers being gunned down, others shot at, strange riders flitting like ghosts. He scowled hardest at Hartman's close brush with a killer's boulder and a shot from a slope.

The men of the outfit were glad to see Dunlee. They also missed their ramrod, Luke Savage. Since two had paid with their lives for devotion to the brand and two had drawn pay and left in fear, the outfit was thinned to a bare minimum. Hartman had not been able to hire any new riders of the breed that suited him. He had to trust his men, and they had to know how to handle cattle *and* outlaws.

Still on the payroll were Curly Saxton, the daredevil who didn't know the meaning of fear; Huck Tompkins and Josh Tilling, hardworking men loyal to the core; Booger Towns, who could handle the job of two men whether busting broncs, riding the line, or dragging cattle out of mud bogs; Max Kinner, a roping wizard; and Farr Bucher, whom Coot claimed was too sneaky for a dry-gulcher to draw a bead on.

All the men were riding the range except Coot, Bucher, and Booger. Booger even now was riding a circle around the outfit's headquarters, hoping to flush out someone who didn't belong. He never roamed far outside rifleshot sound. If he heard any signal of trouble he would tear in pell-mell. He would be a fighting force to reckon with.

In the late afternoon, Bucher caught the sunlight in a bright signal he flashed from the ridge. Dunlee, waiting and laboring over the tough news he must break to a man who was like a father, saw the flash on metal. He thumped an old Indian drum hanging by tough, cowhide thongs from an oak peg on the front buckhouse wall. Coot, rifle in hand, hurried in from the corrals where he'd doctored a horse's leg.

"Someone comin' in. Figures to be Shoat bringing his company."

Dunlee proved to be correct. A moment later they saw the team and buckboard whipping up dust, darting into the canyon from the east. Hartman and the girl were perched on the seat together; Endicott was sitting on the other end.

Hartman hauled the trotting horses to a dust-swirling stop in front of the porch. He sprang down to lift Dunlee in a huge bear hug, overjoyed to see him. Endicott set Teresa down, and she favored Dunlee with the sweet smile that used to dazzle him.

Anything to make the act convincing.

"Oh, Marks, this ranch—seeing it again, and being back with Pa, why, it's simply snatched my breath away! Now, at last, we're all together. I do want us to make this a wonderful time."

Hartman's eyes shone with a sparkle Dunlee had never beheld in them. The man was flushed with a new color, brimming over with elation, alive with energy.

"Coot, this here's my daughter, Mandie, an' this is Trevor Endicott. We can thank him for bringin' her safe to us. You an' Marks will have to show our guests how we bust broncs tomorrow. Bet they never saw the likes of it in Virginny." He turned to the girl. "I guarantee you, Mandie, you never laid eyes on an all-around cowboy equal to Booger Towns. He'll be in later. Now Marks is back. He an' Coot are our bronc-ridin' champs. They ain't no bronc ever figgered how to throw them."

"Wait 'til you take a gander at the horse Marks fetched from Virginny," Coot said. Now that the talk was along his line he was regaining his confidence. He had been fumbling with his hat and blushing in bashfulness when the girl smiled at him. Never in all his born days had he seen a prettier woman, a lady with such class and elegance. He felt his heart pounding, like a Comanche drum. She simply stole his breath away. He turned before she looked at him again in his dusty, shabby clothes. His hands grabbed for luggage to carry in.

Hartman swept the two guests inside. Marks and Coot began to lug their things into the front room.

"Take Mandie's things to her ma's room," the rancher directed as his guests settled down on a blue sofa. "The gentleman will stay in my room, an' I'll be sleepin' out here."

"Oh, Pa," Dunlee heard the girl exclaim as he reached the bedroom, "you've still got this nice sofa. See, I remember it. Mr. Maxwell brought it out from St. Louis for you to give Ma, really special."

"Yeah, you remember. That's exactly how it was. Came over the Santa Fe Trail in a freighter's wagon, pulled by mules. Lucien an' I figgered your ma would like it, an' she did. But," he added slowly, "she didn't like the adobe house, the ranch an' the rough ways. Wasn't soft livin' like she grew up with in Boston." He gazed out a western window toward the trees and brush of the pass as it slashed on through the hills.

"Remember my eye!" Dunlee growled to himself as he stomped off the porch to pack supplies from the buckboard to the kitchen. "It's not because she's Mandie. Teresa could remember that for twelve years, or she rehearsed the right details with her mother before she left Virginia. Sure she'd come primed with 'memories.' Makes it convincing to Shoat!"

Teresa kept Hartman hanging on every word as the rest of the afternoon wore away. She seemed intent on not letting him out of her sight, not permitting him a time alone with Dunlee. Dunlee could not get to him. She brought out a bag of hard candy that Hartman raved about. Then she unpacked some gifts.

First she took out a picture album of herself, her sister (the *real* Mandie), her stepmother Sheila, and von Ehrencroft. There were also pictures of the estate.

Later she pulled out some books—one on Abe Lincoln, one on a history of horses, and others. She even produced a beautiful, hand-tooled belt for Hartman with a small replica of a ship set in the fancy buckle. Shoat's father had been a shipman, and as a boy Shoat had gotten a salty taste of life at sea. That was long before he hit the Santa Fe Trail. He was quite taken with the books and the belt.

"Now," Teresa finally said, "I'm going to prepare our dinner. And I insist, Pa, that you sit yourself

141

down in the kitchen and keep me constant company. We've so many things to catch up on."

Teresa was glad the lady who ran the boarding house at college had insisted that girls who stayed with her take turns cooking, baking, and doing household chores. With good teaching and a watchful eye on her, Teresa had learned well enough.

Hartman called in Coot and told him to go ahead with the chores, even the ones he normally did himself. Dunlee strode out to help. Coot showed him some of the new places where the hens were leaving their eggs, and told him there were four cows to milk and three calves to feed. It was not a job most cowhands savored, but it had to be done.

Coot went off to gather vegetables from a small garden near the house. Dunlee grabbed a milk stool, hobbles, and a bucket, and set about milking the Holsteins Hartman kept around to provide milk and butter for the outfit.

As he sat milking, his eyes combed the rim to the north, choked with trees, brush, and outcroppings of rock. Somewhere up there Bucher roved in deadly watchfulness, pursuing his vigil in solitude. He would cover points from which he could gaze down on the headquarters or in any direction across stretches of the range.

A nest of boulders jutting up almost due north above the corrals might furnish a lurking place for a rattler, even the human kind. It was a haunt Bucher would surely check from time to time.

Suddenly Dunlee's eyes were snatched to some fluttering doves. They lifted as if startled from a gnarled tree limb at the western fringe of those boulders.

Then Dunlee caught the sudden gleam of sunlight playing on metal. Peering intently from behind the cow, he caught the movement of a small spot of red between two boulders, then the vague gray of a hat. Again the sunlight reflected on metal.

Red? That was odd. Bucher was garbed in a black shirt and black hat. But *Chenault* had been clad in a red shirt and gray hat!

Chenault or no Chenault, the man was probably watching him in the corral and getting set to work his way down from the rim a ways for a closer shot. Or else he was figuring to try from about three hundred yards away, for the drop of a bullet from up there would give him added distance.

Dunlee got up and walked behind cows for protection. He casually bent over out of sight a couple of times, and reached the barn door. He poured the half bucket of milk into a larger bucket on a shelf, then went out the front of the stable, around the southwest corner, and into a gully that flanked it on the west. He meant to form a one-man reception committee for that bushwhacker.

Keeping under cover, he worked his way in a thin semi-circle up the steep ridge and over toward the boulders. A crow he had not seen flew up out of a small scrub oak, cawing loudly. Dunlee lay low for a time, hoping the stranger would not guess the reason for the crow's annoyance and slip away.

He took scarcely five minutes to ascend the ridge. Breathing hard from the punishment of a hard, fast climb, he bellied in to a spot with the boulders between him and the rim. Now ease up on the man and. . . . The snap of a dry twig off to the east made him jerk about. He caught a glimpse of a claybank horse with a rider in a red shirt disappearing into trees half a stone's throw away. They were moving as if spooked.

Too late!

He scrambled after the rider, Colt filling his hand, but could not catch sight of him again. He turned back, disappointed, and poked about the boulders. He found where the man had nestled in, and as he gazed down at the corral he whistled at his narrow escape. The distance from here was easily within rifle range. A skilled shot like Chenault could pick him off with one or two squeezes on the trigger.

Behind the boulders in the soft dirt beside a bush he stared at two sets of boot tracks. One set he had found in the dirt right beside the boulders. The other set revealed a slight hole worn in the right sole, about two inches from the front of the heel. The hole formed a rough triangle. He traced those tracks a few steps to the northeast, but lost them in some rocks.

So, Chenault and another man had a rendezvous up here. And within a strip where Bucher rode his watch. But why had Dunlee seen only one horseman retreating? He had heard the sound of only one horse cutting through the brush. He followed the claybank's tracks a ways and was sure of it.

He climbed back down to the barn and corral, absorbed with the foiled bushwhacking. Most of all he exulted that he had scanned the rim in time. Apart from that good fortune, Endicott and Teresa would be rid of his threat in one quick stroke—the press of a trigger. Hartman would have nobody to warn him—unless Luke could bring back word. And Dunlee did intend to warn Hartman, as soon as he could pry the rancher away from the magnet which held him.

Hartman invited all the men to come to his house for supper. Only Bucher would not be there at first, for he had to stick to his patrol. He would be relieved in a while and would ride in to join the party. The rancher was keyed for a very special celebration.

Teresa was the essence of candied sweetness. She had changed into another dress more befitting kitchen work. She used a batch of prepared dough for biscuits, slid a huge pan of patties into the oven of the wood stove, and laid beef steaks in a pan with thick sauce enhanced by spices she'd brought from Virginia. She had made three pies from dried apples, prepared a corn casserole, and even made a large salad from the greens Coot had brought in.

While bustling about the kitchen she had borne herself with grace. Her smiles to Hartman, whom she insisted should sit in the kitchen, had made putty of the tough cattleman.

Dunlee had come in a little while before supper was ready. As he watched the girl and heard the musical richness of her voice, he felt his own heart flip-flopping with strange emotions. She looked so very much like Mandie! The loneliness of his weeks on the trail west had left a void that cried for feminine company. The deprivations were sharp after enjoying the pleasant society that had spoiled him in Blue Ridge Mountain country. He'd stayed clear of the bawdy women many men resorted to. These were always available to lonely men with fat wallets.

Teresa's charm was intoxicating, downright enchanting. She looked so soft, fresh, and delicate. The spicy fragrance of her perfume and powder created an almost hypnotic effect. She had a baffling way of lulling a man into forgetting her bad qualities, even when he knew them.

He felt himself melting. He was as if under a spell, captivated by her tender, innocent-looking face and the rhapsody of her words. Dunlee got up, vacated the kitchen, and stood on the porch. He gazed long at the northern rim. Now it lay in a swath of darkness, a black mass set against a dark sky, lightened only by a silvery half-moon.

Endicott lounged on Hartman's big rawhide recliner. The tall estate man puffed at a pipe and looked off toward the rim, secluded in his meditations.

"Your man was up there tonight," Dunlee drawled. He leaned his frame back against the adobe wall near the door. "Spotted himself a good place to coil like a rattler in the rocks. Thought he could draw a bead on me in the corral. But I went up there and he turned tail and ran."

"*My* man?" Endicott sounded amused, but perhaps with a trace of wariness. Dunlee had caught him off guard, and he had spoken before he had clamped an iron grip on his emotions. "What's that supposed to mean?"

"Simple. It means the man you threw in with, the gunman you slipped the payoff to at Swink's yesterday. You know, after Teresa sent Frenchy to fetch you, and you went right back to the saloon. She'd just broken the news to you that I was still alive. Your killers hadn't finished me. Don't you remember, you both were worried I could wreck your little plot for gold?"

Endicott cleared his throat and shifted uneasily.

"The name's Chenault. Choc Chenault. He traces new brands on other men's cattle. Tried it against Hartman a few months back. I nearly shot his arm off, but he got away. I hear he's shot down around ten men in gun fights. Men are afraid to go up against him. When it pays he even takes to the coward's game . . . tried to bushwhack me. That would give you a free hand for your deceit.

"This Chenault, he came close to the end of his own career today. It's just a matter of time for him. Slinking around here like a lobo, he'll be caught. I'll get him myself, or one of the outfit will beat me to it. We make pelts out of lobos—even out of those they run with."

"You accusing me, Dunlee?" Endicott smirked.

"Simply stating fact, laying it on the line, Endicott. Your days are numbered. You could turn smart, take your pretty little she-wolf, and head out on the next stage. Spare you a lot of grief—maybe save you from the boothill. Stick around, prey on good people, and they'll bury you where the fourlegged lobos run. It's a sure plan for never seeing fair Virginia again. Out here at Cimarron and E-Town we don't have such genteel society. Men judge you for what you are. They speak their verdict with a gun. Or with rawhide stretched from a limb."

"I've taken about all I will from you," Endicott growled. He kept his voice low; he didn't want his words to carry into the house. "Yesterday I shot a man for mouthing hurtful words. Malnardo. Fancied himself hot with a gun. But he wasn't able to back his tongue. If the time comes, I can handle you myself.

147

I wouldn't need this ... this man you glibly connect with me.

"It may be fair to remind you. I have won many pistol shoots and more than enough duels to worry about any problems with a country hick."

"I'm afraid," returned Dunlee in a voice firm as steel, "you'll find gun fights out here a lot tougher than the tame duels you're used to. How was it you got the edge on Malnardo? Was it a trick, like sitting with your gun already in your hand in your lap?"

Endicott sprang up, his hand slipping inside his coat. Then, in a movement too fast and unexpected for him, Dunlee's left hand shot out. He caught the man's arm just above the wrist in a viselike grip, spun him off balance, and jerked his gun arm down. The gun clattered on the pine planks and Dunlee slammed the larger man back down on the chair's thongs. Endicott tried to get up, but two surprisingly powerful arms pinned him in place.

"Don't ever go after a gun like that again unless you mean to go all the way. You're lucky I was close enough to do it this way—and you're alive!" There was a cold finality in Dunlee's words. "Be thankful I have too much respect to spoil Shoat's celebration."

Endicott scowled and lay pinned. Then Dunlee relaxed the pressure and stepped back, scooped up the fallen gun, and emptied the bullets into his hand. He handed the weapon to Endicott and backed away, shoving the ammunition into his pocket just as Hartman pushed open the door and yelled, "Come an' get it."

The bunkhouse door popped open. Coot, Booger, and two others hurried toward the house. Endicott

148

pushed himself up slowly and slipped the emptied gun into its holster. He wiped the scowl off his face and went in past Dunlee.

Hartman had laid extra leaves into a table in the living room to make it long enough. Teresa had prepared a glorious supper. As they ate, Hartman sat at one end, she sat near him on one side, and Dunlee on the other side. Endicott was beside her, farther from the host, and the others filled in the rest of the table. Endicott said little. Hartman and the girl talked brightly about Virginia and the ranch.

Having a woman at the table with men was rare in the territory. The usual practice was for women to eat in a separate dining area, or to eat only after the last man left the table. Women were kept to their quarters; they were only glimpsed as they went about their chores. So it had been at the Maxwell house.

But Hartman had always wanted his wife to be at the table with him and the guests. He followed the land's custom only when he was away from home.

Coot finished early and rode up to the rim to spell Bucher, who came in a few minutes later and took a bench seat at the table. After the meal, Endicott produced a violin and played music such as had seldom sounded in these hills. Bending and swaying, he awed the men.

Later, Dunlee strode out from the porch behind the surly, shifty-eyed Bucher.

"Bucher, I need to jaw with you."

"Yeah, what about?" Bucher sensed from the tone that something was on Dunlee's mind.

Dunlee told him about spotting Chenault and climbing to the rocks as the gunfighter fled from his bushwhacker nest.

"I been seein' tracks," Bucher admitted. "He's clever as an old fox livin' off a chicken farm, though. Covers his trails careful 'fore you've follered him long. I slip back an' forth along that ridge, an' he must've sneaked in when he caught me away from that area. They's places a man can hide a horse where you'd never see him five feet away. Well, now, we're onto his game. I'll catch him dead to rights. Jest a matter of time."

Dunlee started to mention the second pair of boot tracks. But something held him back. He decided to nose around more on his own.

Bucher seemed in a hurry to get on to the bunkhouse, so Dunlee let him go. The patrol rider sprawled on a bunk and twisted up brown paper into a cigarette. He lit it thoughtfully and smoked.

Dunlee, having peered in at the door, closed it gently. He sat mulling over his thoughts on the bunkhouse steps, watching Booger and two other punchers out by the barn. Suddenly an idea ticked in his mind. He struck a match, lowered it near the dust where Bucher had walked, and examined the boot marks.

There it was, plain as day. The imprint in the dust showed a hole in the right sole in the shape of a rough triangle, identical to the tracks on the rim. He shook out the match before it burned his fingers, and sauntered back to the house.

He wanted to pry Hartman loose and lay the situation before him. It would be difficult to say things like he had to tell, but harder for Hartman. With his "Mandie" home and mighty sweet, he revelled in his glory. If Dunlee laid the truth on him now and could convince him it was so, it would be a painful letdown.

But Dunlee steeled himself. Bitter as the medicine was, it had to be given. Gently, yet firmly. Hartman would be better off knowing this "daughter" was a fake. He'd be glad to find out her chaperone was a deceiver who paid killers to cut down the man Hartman thought of as a son. And he'd be thankful to learn that one of his own outfit was in cahoots with a cold-blooded ambusher.

Hartman was talking with Endicott in the living room. Dunlee cut through the kitchen to the back, peered out the door, and saw Teresa. She had stepped out into the garden to enjoy the coolness of the evening. When she heard the door close behind him, she turned. They were alone, a little distance from the house, too far off to be overheard.

He was eager for clues about Mandie.

"You mind your tongue, Marks Dunlee!" He caught the sharp nervousness of her voice as he blocked her way back from the garden. The strain of playing a phony must be hard on her.

"Tell me about Mandie. How is she?"

"Very happy. Devoted to her college work. She's ... uh ... fallen in love with a man who has a law practice. He owns a rich estate outside of Richmond. The relationship sprang up suddenly, right after you disappeared."

"Really?" His incredulous tone was something Teresa could not miss. She glanced away, averting his eyes, even though he could not see her as well as he would like in the moonlight.

"Yes. She became very disheartened. That awful talk about the murder of Mr. Mueller. The evidence, they said, pointed to you. But she got over it. The man just swept her off her feet. Such a nice man, and good for her. I'm sure they'll be married."

Dunlee's mind reeled from the blow. But he tried not to give away his feelings.

"Whatever Mandie wants, I hope she'll be happy. She should have the best."

"She will. She was glad you were doing well, but decided against answering your letter. I suppose that was one book she felt would be better closed, not reopened."

Could this be true? he wondered. Or was this deceitful girl trying to plunge a dagger into him?

"I was doing well when I wrote," he replied. "But since then I've had three attempts on my life, almost a fourth tonight. A man was lining me in his sights when I saw a movement on the canyon rim. I went up to flush him out, but he got away fast."

"Really?" She was meditative for a moment. "You said a fourth time? You lead a charmed life, Marks. Do be careful. Who was involved in the other three incidents?"

"Pugley and his mad dogs."

"Oh? Pugley? Interesting! He and some of his crowd broke away from Trevor. Trevor feels they're a bad lot. He'll have nothing to do with them. Pugley is mad to get his money he thinks you took. He also feels you robbed and killed poor Mr. Mueller. And, he wants the reward out for you."

"Someone," he replied, "went to a lot of trouble to frame me. Knowing who wanted to get me, it isn't hard to figure out who. Pugley has come an awful long way just to get money he lost in a fair game. But what he wants most of all is me dead. That way he can feel it's a closed issue that I killed Mueller, and can convince others. That—plus the money—is a big incentive.

"But others want me dead, too. Take the killer on the rim. Somebody paid that man to get me. I think there's a bigger reason to get me than Pugley's money, or a reward, or to leave the murder rap on me. The reason I see is spelled g-o-l-d.

"You know, I didn't mention it, but there was even a fifth attempt to get me. Not by a bullet. It was a lot more subtle, more tricky. And I almost *swallowed* it."

He was aware that she tensed even though the darkness hid those beautiful, big eyes. He knew they were nervous, apprehensive. Just then Hartman threw open the door and walked out, his face a glow of fulfillment.

"Your escort, Trevor, is the likes of which I never saw," he grinned, shaking his head admiringly. Then he swept her into a big bear hug. "Mandie, Mandie! I never knew what happiness was 'til today. I don't want this ever to end."

"It won't," she smiled as she went back into the kitchen with him. "As long as you live, I want to be right here with you. And when you're gone—perish the thought—I'll keep this place just the way you want it."

Dunlee cringed at the lie. As long as he lived, eh? Just so the plot was that he wouldn't live long! And keep this place? Sure, Teresa, you'll run your nimble fingers through all the money you can get them on, then leave as fast as the stage will carry you—back to the whirl of fashion circles. Hartman's dreams will never change your plans.

Hartman was speaking again.

"The boys are in a trance over you, Mandie. They never laid eyes on a woman more pretty. I think they're afraid it's all a dream, just one of them fairy tales. They hope come mornin' they don't wake up and it'll be a—what's the word—a. . . ."

"An illusion," Dunlee supplied. "It isn't what it appears to be."

"Yeah, yeah, that's the word."

That night Dunlee found absolutely no chance to pry Hartman off by himself. Even when the Bar SH boss went out to look over his horses and cows, Teresa insisted on tagging along. She wasn't permitting him a minute alone.

"All right, Miss Beautiful." Dunlee scowled outside her hearing. He headed for the bunkhouse to turn in. "I can wait it out. I'll have my time with him."

He felt Hartman was safe until he revealed where his gold was—if he had gold. But once Endicott and Teresa figured they had it for sure, then what would the plot be? A drink prepared by special fingers serving a conniving mind, a knife plunged into the back, a heavy blow to the head in some hidden place, a bullet from a gun far off in the brush. . . ?

Dunlee slept with his gun in his hand and an ear turned to catch any creak of the floorboards. He was a light sleeper when he had to be. The way things had been going, with Bucher in a bunk nearby and Endicott in a bedroom across the yard, it was a time to sleep as light as a cat.

The next day he waited for a chance to catch Hartman. It never came. Endicott and Teresa skillfully took turns sticking to him like burrs. No doubt they were holding on until they could be rid of Dunlee. And they would expect that to be soon.

The Chenault way.

That night, as talk had almost died in the bunkhouse and Bucher was prowling the rim, Booger Towns said:

"Shoat an' me, we're ridin' over to Hangin' Tree Canyon come sunup. Gotta find where the rustlers are drivin' those cattle. They're just vanishin'."

Dunlee knew the canyon was on the west range. Curly was riding the line there, living in a dugout in a ridge bank.

"The woman and her friend traipsin' along?"

"Naw, Shoat laid down the law—jest the two of us go. Woman put up a fuss, but he stood firm as Wagon Mound Rock. Doesn't want to be slowed down, an' he ain't shore what we might run up agin. Can't be lookin' out for no skirt an' no dude. Two of our riders died over there."

Dunlee spoke to Hartman at breakfast while the two guests were seated at the table.

"I'll get to those broncs later, Shoat. Right now, I've got to ride into Cimarron. Got me some business. I'll see you here when we all get back."

That would have its effect on Endicott and the girl, he hoped. He thought he detected an expression of relief in Teresa's eyes as she glanced up from spreading honey on a buttered biscuit.

10

Josh Tillings remained near the ranchhouse, but the other men rode off to various points on the range. Even Bucher, who had ridden nighthawk duty along the rim, shrugged off "shut-eye" and headed out after breakfast. Coot was roaming the ridge.

Dunlee crested the ridge and set his horse to the northeast toward Cimarron. But he kept off the road, eyed the terrain ahead with devoted vigilance, and after a couple of miles swung hard back to the west. He waited in a clump of cedars for several minutes to see if anybody might be tailing him. Only a few of Hartman's cattle were in sight, grazing.

He could reach Hanging Tree Canyon in an hour if he pushed on at a steady jog. He'd get there soon after Hartman and Booger arrived, and have his talk with Hartman. How best to break such news puzzled him, and he rehearsed several approaches. But regardless of how he presented it, the message would be harsh as a bullet. He felt a sick, deep hurt within his breast for his friend and "father."

He emerged from a wooded area and started to skirt an open meadow of bluegrass and long-stemmed grama, where a small herd of cattle grazed. But he suddenly yanked the black to a halt in his tracks. Hastily he wheeled him back into the aspens. A rider was moving nearly a quarter of a mile ahead, crossing the meadow, entering a maze of rocks choked with sagebrush and juniper.

Bucher!

"Headed on a beeline toward Hanging Tree Canyon himself," Dunlee mused. Flanking the open strip but keeping under cover of brush, trees, and rocks, he followed. He had heard Hartman tell Bucher that he was to check up on the line rider on the east range. But that was the opposite direction from the way Bucher now rode. Something must be on his mind that cut against Hartman's interests.

Bucher drew up in a deep, sandy wash. He chose a well-concealed spot by the brush along the banks. Then he issued the call of a bluejay, keeping it up for several minutes at intervals.

As Dunlee peered out from a thick stand of piñons topping a knoll near the wash, he spotted a rider weaving through rugged terrain from the northwest. The horse and rider dropped down into the wash and apparently drew up for a rendezvous with Bucher.

Dunlee tied the black and worked stealthily to the lip of the wash, Winchester in hand. He lurked within twenty paces of the two, sprawled belly down in the tall grama. By lifting himself on both hands as if doing push-ups, he could peer over the grass and watch the two men.

The second rider was Choc Chenault.

Seeing the two together teased his memory. As

he cast about in his past, a scene drifted into his mind from a night at Uncle Dick Wootton's place in Raton Pass. He had been on his way to Virginia, and had stopped at the toll and stage stop that the famous Indian fighter Wootton ran. He wanted to collect on a loan to a cowhand he hoped might be there awaiting a trail herd.

Yes, it was all coming clearer now. A crowded room . . . a huge stone fireplace blazing . . . Wootton and his partner George McBride out collecting toll from a wagon train . . . Chenault with his left arm healed from the branding fire episode with Dunlee and Hartman. The gunman was sitting at a table with his back to the wall . . . a gambling game had just finished . . . a buffalo-robed hide tanner with money had fancied he could make a cleaning and was doing well until Chenault came into the game. Now the tanner pushed back, gave up his pile with the fallen face of a sore loser. His lips quivered in repressed rage, but he was careful not to mouth his feelings. Chenault's reputation was awesome. Quitting the table, he elbowed his way to the counter where drinks were sold.

Dunlee had watched while seated beyond a table near the front, where Chenault could not see him through another game that was in progress.

Several minutes had passed. The tanner had thrust three, now four jolts of whiskey down his throat. He was drinking too much.

"You was real good," a man beside the tanner said. "You shore had me beat, an' the others. Figgered you'd head on to Trinidad with a pile."

"Would've," the tanner scowled. "But what can you do with a man that hides cards up his sleeve?"

"Oh, you figger he cheated?"

"Yep." The tanner's mood was ugly. He sloshed more whiskey into his glass and swilled it, licked his lips, and set the glass down hard. "I know he did!"

A stocky man with a hatchet face and shifty eyes had slouched against a wall near the fireplace. Dunlee had marked him as a cougar watching for prey. Now he saw him move. His dark face, slashed by a scar, suddenly glowed with something more than the warmth of the fire and any whiskey he had guzzled. He pushed past a Mexican servant girl, nearly knocking over her tray of drinks. Dunlee, lounging behind others, saw him whisper low in Chenault's ear.

Chenault got up, stalked around the table with a bottle in his left hand. He set it down with a bang on the table.

"Gaskins!"

The tanner almost jumped out of his skin. Whiskey slopped on the floor from his refilled glass. He spun and gawked at the gunman.

"I hear you referred to me as a 'cheater.'"

"Me? Uh...uh..." The words seemed to harden into ice on Gaskins' thick tongue.

"Man who says that better be able to back up his words," Chenault barked. His tone was taunting, cocky. "That or he asks for a grave."

Others scurried to get away from the line of fire. A hush fell over the room. Blood was sure to be shed. The tanner was as near death as a cinnamon bear in the sights of Dick Wootton himself.

Gaskins, a huge man, blinked at the faces around the room. He did not relish being made to look like a fool. Pride prodded him. It burned its raging message in his whiskey-livened brain. He had the brute strength to maul the man who called him.

"You wanna fight?" His lips twisted in a lobo snarl. "Take off your gunbelt an' come to me like a man. What I do I do with my bare hands. Don't need no gun. I say if you're afraid to do that yo're not only a cheater. Yo're yeller clean through."

"I do my fightin' with a gun," Chenault said firmly. He took three steps forward, pausing scarcely an arm's length away. "I don't like to get all messed up."

Gaskins sneered. "Then I'll take yore gun away from you. We'll see how you do your fightin'!" He took a step forward confidently, grabbing for the gunman's right arm to manhandle him. But Chenault sprang catlike to the left, grabbed the collar of the buffalo coat, and rammed the man down. Gaskins plunged to his knees, and Chenault brought his right knee up against his chin with teeth-shattering force. Gaskins flopped backwards in a senseless daze, blood gushing from his nose and mouth. Sprawled on the floor, he writhed and groaned.

"Git him on his horse," Chenault rasped at two men he thought had come in with the tanner. "Take him away from the pass, an' tell him if I see him again I *will* do my fightin' with a gun."

Dunlee, now poised on fingertips in the grass, saw how fitting it was that Bucher and Chenault should meet like this. Their voices drifted in the morning stillness over the lip of the wash. But Dunlee could barely hear them. The words had something to do with Hartman, Hanging Tree Canyon, and cattle. Once the listener thought Bucher mentioned "Dunlee

161

... town." That would make sense. But he wasn't sure.

Chenault erupted in a torrent of oaths. Then he avowed, "I'll get him."

A red-tailed hawk swooped down and started to alight in a scrub oak near Dunlee, then flapped away, circling and screaming protest at his presence.

Bucher wheeled his horse, grunted loudly, and slapped a searching gaze along the side of the wash.

"Ah, it ain't nothin' but a silly hawk," Chenault soothed, a bit louder. "Screamin' at us. They's nobody else around. All I saw was Hartman an' one of his outfit goin' west from here, not comin' this way."

"Yeah, reckon yo're right. I'm still spooky after Dunlee near slipped up on you."

They settled down again to talking. A few minutes later, Bucher struck off to the east, and Chenault rode northeast, moving vigilantly. Dunlee slipped back to his mount and followed Chenault. The gunman went into a deep canyon and climbed its sloping southern bank until he disappeared behind an upjutting flat rock flanked by brush near the upper wall. In a few minutes he rode back out, put his horse down the shale embankment, and jogged on to the northeast toward Cimarron.

Dunlee, moving on foot, climbed quickly behind the rock and found a large cave hidden from below by the rock and overhanging brush growing out of the canyon wall. Inside the cave lay two running irons, ashes of a much-used campfire, and a lidded, iron strongbox from a stagecoach. In it were various foodstuffs. Around the floor of the cave were food wrappings, bones of cattle and venison, and tin cans.

Twenty paces back the cave opened out into a grassy basin an eighth of a mile across. Dunlee saw a bearded man perched on a rock whittling and looking away toward three horses cropping grass. He saw several piles of fresh cow manure.

Dunlee left the cave, returned to the black, and worked his way to the northeast. From a knoll he searched and caught sight of Chenault about a half mile away. He was headed toward town.

"Could be Bucher told him I was goin' to town," he soliloquized. "So he aims to set up an ambush. A man draws pay, he figures he'd better earn it. And Chenault doesn't agree on a gun job, then admit he couldn't handle it."

He turned the black and stopped following Chenault. He swung back in a half circle, avoiding the canyon where he had found the cave and on to Hanging Tree Canyon about three miles farther west. In the distance loomed the Sangre de Cristos.

Hanging Tree Canyon ran a couple miles in a southeastern slash, forming part of Hartman's western line. He had heard the outfit talk about the canyon's name. Shortly before Dunlee rode in from Texas, two men had been hazing stolen horses through the canyon when some punchers from the Lazy S ranch caught them in a trap. The riders of the outfit asked only a few questions. The proof they required was seeing horses from both spreads in the stolen bunch and recognizing both men as reputed horse thieves. Meeting at a cottonwood near the canyon's southeastern exit, they stretched the thieves' necks at the swinging ends of taut riatas.

That harsh justice was not as vicious as that which

the E-Town vigilantes could deal out. They had captured "Pony" O'Neil, wanted for murder, and not only lynched him, but shot his body to rags before they rode away.

Rustling during recent months had just about convinced the Bar SH riders that another necktie party was past due.

Dunlee came into the canyon and approached the hanging tree. A sandy bank loomed behind it. His eyes scanned the land for any movement. When he drew within a stone's throw of the cottonwood and the bank, Hartman appeared on the bank, and waved his hat in a friendly gesture. Then he led his horse from behind the bank to meet him.

"You were headed for town," he reminded Dunlee, obviously surprised.

"Yeah, Shoat. I'll be headin' there. But something was too important to wait." He swung down, wrapped the reins around a low limb, and relaxed on the grass at the foot of the bank.

"Well, you'd a seen me tonight anyhow, son. Must be powerful urgent."

"Sure is. I've been hoping to jaw with you ever since I got back. But the company's been so close that it had to keep 'til now."

"So what is it, son? You seen somethin'?" Hartman's mind was on rustlers, killers, and lurking riders flitting away like ghosts.

"Yeah. Seen a lot. An' wish it never happened. It isn't easy to say what I've got to say. Always had a powerful regard for you, Shoat. Your being so allfired happy an' me wanting you to be happy, well I don't like to slap a wet blanket on that."

"Shore, shore, son. Come on, out with it. No need to beat around the bush with me. Shoot straight." He was standing on one leg, the other propped on a decaying limb. Aroused to curiosity, he was peering intently at Dunlee.

"Well, brace yourself, Shoat. This won't be easy. It's about my stay in Virginia, and Mandie."

"Yeah." Hartman's voice was husky, a bit sad. "Mandie filled me in on the way out from town. You're in trouble back there, an' things aren't good between you an' Mandie like I hoped. Well, you know I'll stick by you, son. We'll try to work things out. Both of you show a little give an' take. . . ."

So Teresa had gotten in her licks first. And just as he had feared, she had filled Hartman's ears with another story. What would his story mean now? Would Hartman believe the soft-eyed, lovely faced girl with the golden hair and honey-smooth words, the girl he believed to be his own flesh and blood?

"Shoat," he said slowly, "I saw Mandie a lot of times. Her stepsister Teresa looks a lot like Mandie. I was so close to Teresa that I asked her to marry me. I know now, I fell hook, line, and sinker. All I could see was her beauty, all I could hear was her voice, like soothing music. But she was just seeing how far she could string me out. Then she dropped me because I didn't have the money Endicott had. I know now I assumed too much. Anyhow, it hurt, Shoat. But once I saw things as they really were I got over it fast. I saw Teresa was a gold digger, not a beautiful girl inside.

"Now I know it's Mandie who has the quality. She had been away a lot, and I let Teresa bewitch me."

"You're right about Mandie," Hartman affirmed vigorously. "Isn't she some lady!"

"I know you heard one side of the story on the trip out," Dunlee went on. "Now I'll tell you the other—the truth."

Hartman bristled. He was suddenly astir with questioning.

"The truth? Why I figger what Mandie said is true! She wouldn't lie to me. She told me you took it hard about Teresa an' wanted to lay hold on money. Then you turned up with a lot of money the night that man—Miller, no, Mueller—was knifed in his office. He had been robbed, an' your knife was picked up by the back fence. Had blood on it.

"The sheriff checked your bank account, an' you had withdrawn some they traced to a horse, this one here it must be. But that wasn't near the amount taken from Mueller. Then they found witnesses that swore they saw you sneakin' away from Mueller's that night by the back way. An' you ran. Mandie says she was all tore up over it. Then Luke got there with my letter, an' Endicott agreed to escort her out here."

"Shoat, I didn't kill Mueller."

"Well, son, I don't believe you did. That's jest the way that cockeyed 'evidence' looks."

"Thanks for the confidence. This thing has been twisted. That night I was at an inn several miles out of town. I went there to win some money in a gambling game. I had heard Endicott and a man named Pugley would be there. I figured I'd take Endicott, take him big, goad him into a madness to play for high stakes, and pick him clean.

"I wanted to flaunt that in front of Teresa, see her

change her tune, get me some satisfaction. It was pride, stupid pride. I was all wrong. Well, it worked. I cleaned Endicott and Pugley out. They plotted to ambush me when I left the inn. But I slipped out the back way and got clear while they were hunting me with guns.

"I rode right to Teresa, showed her the money. Sure as I figured, she did a switch. But I told her I wouldn't have her. You've heard the old saying about a woman spurned. She turned on me with seething hate. Then Mandie and I went walking in the garden, and she was sweeter than apple blossoms.

"We were there when one of the servants came burning the breeze. He said Mueller had been murdered. Endicott, Pugley, and the sheriff were searching for me. The deck was stacked. Endicott's crowd would claim I wasn't at the inn. I didn't have the chance of a cat in a kennel of hounds. Besides, a Negro friend of mine, Tom Jackson, overheard Pugley tell Endicott he'd do me in and claim self-defense while I was trying to make a run for it.

"That decided me. A live man on the run is better than a dead one in jail. So I lit a shuck."

Hartman kicked up sand and stood shaking his head. He was puzzled. He hunkered down, stirring a stick in the dust. Finally he looked Dunlee squarely in the eyes.

"If you say it, son, I want to believe you. I can't figger it all out. Mandie told me while we drove out that you fell from your horse an' got knocked senseless. After that you were never the same in the head."

Dunlee whistled in awe at the enormity of the lie.

"So she says you don't mean it, but your mind

gets things twisted. You see 'em just the opposite of what they are." Hartman was measuring him eyeball to eyeball.

"So that's how she and Endicott are covering up?" Dunlee gazed off at the rim of the canyon.

"I can't figger it," Hartman rejoined. "You tell me Endicott was dead set on seein' you done in. Yet he chaperones Mandie out here. That's a big service to me and to her."

"Endicott's two-faced, a lamb when it suits his plans and a sidewinder coiled to strike when he sees money or revenge." He told Hartman of seeing the Virginia plantation man in Swink's place with Chenault.

"You know our friend Chenault . . . the cow thief that got away that day after he meant to fry your hide with a hot iron." Hartman winced and grunted. Dunlee told of Chenault's ride over the moonlit benchland, later his nesting down for a bushwhacking, today his rendezvous with Bucher, then his stop at a hideout.

"Endicott with Chenault . . . Chenault with Bucher!" Hartman got up and stalked about. He stomped at the grama grass and drew his fists into tight weapons over and over again.

"There's no doubt in my mind. Endicott is paying Chenault to get rid of me," Dunlee said firmly. "And Bucher's in with Chenault and the other rustlers. But hold off on him. I want to see what he does for a while, without him guessing we're on to him."

"Tell me, why would Endicott come so far to get you?"

"That brings us to the big point this is all about," Dunlee replied. "Endicott's gotten used to big money.

He gets it, spends it, looks around for the next big pot. This time he thinks he sees a price big enough to go to extreme lengths. There's talk of you having gold hid away. Even old man Harbin at Lobo Gulch repeated things he'd picked up.

"You sent Luke to Mandie, and a letter with him. Is that right? Mandie's away at college, just comes home weekends or holidays. My guess is, Teresa got her hands on that letter. By the way, did it mention gold or striking it rich?" Hartman nodded and ran his tongue over his bottom lip meditatively. "My guess is, Teresa read that, ran to Endicott, and they hatched a scheme."

"Ah, but that can't be." Hartman waved it aside. "Mandie came right out. Teresa doesn't have anything to do with it."

This was where it would hurt. But even when a man cuts a bull worm out of an animal's hide and it hurts, it's for the critter's good. He can pour in ointment, and the cut will heal.

"Shoat, listen to me. Teresa's got everything to do with it. I saw Mandie and Teresa in quite a number of situations—the different ways they'd fix up their hair. A man couldn't help but be struck with how much alike they look. By primping and setting her hair like the other and with the right makeup, one could pass for the other to anyone who didn't know them well."

"What are you drivin' at?" Hartman was plainly agitated. He had gone back to his pacing in the dust. Dunlee arose also and cast about for words.

"Mandie," he said with quietness and tenderness, "is everything you think. You'd be proud of her, and she of you. She never would try to use you for any ambitions of gold digging, any get-rich-quick treachery. Mandie never even saw your letter, never got Luke's message. She's still back in Virginia, safe, I hope, but kept in the dark."

Hartman put on the brakes, uttered a gasp, and spun about.

"Son, you gone plumb loco?" He thundered the words with a swell in his voice that carried a good way up the canyon. "This here's crazy talk. It can't be. I know my Mandie. Yet you're tellin' me . . . that's actually Teresa back at the house."

"It doesn't seem to make sense," Dunlee granted. "But yes, that is Teresa with her man, Endicott. Birds of a feather. . . . She isn't the kind, sweet lady she puts on to be. She's got gold on her mind."

Well, maybe he wasn't the best for tact. But now he had it said.

The fist came up fast and caught him completely unprepared. It rocked Dunlee on his heels and dropped him back on the sand. He sprawled hard on his back and lay looking up at the tortured face glaring down on him.

"No man, not even my son, can insult Mandie like that." The rancher stood crouched, ready to take on the world. His hands were not clenched but hanging open at his side. Dunlee slowly drew his hand across his shirt to his jaw and felt of it gingerly. The whole side of his face and head were numb. The Bar SH boss packed a wallop, and he had jarred him through and through. Dunlee felt blood on his cheek from the inprint of the knuckles, and blood in his mouth. He had to turn his head and spit to keep from being strangled.

As his mind focused, he thought of the man hovering over him—rock-hard, enraged, yet singular for what he thought to be right. And lonely. He'd caressed a dream these past three days. Now a son had the effrontery to tell him it was a mocking nightmare.

Dunlee wiped his cheek and lips with his bandana, and mused on how he loved this big, hard, simple man.

"It's all right, Dad," he finally said. He knew his voice was shaky. "Does me good, real good, to see you still pack a lot of thunder. Only next time, lay it somewhere besides my jaw." Then he rolled over on his stomach and began to laugh, hiding the tears watering his eyes. He could hear Hartman relax. And after a moment the sovereign of the pass began to laugh with him.

"Dad," he finally said again. "What I said stabbed like a thorn. I'd have given anything to tell it so it wouldn't hurt. But I figured you'd pulled enough thorns out to know you can't avoid hurting if you're gonna help. The girl at the house is Teresa. But you'll like Mandie better. I guarantee it." He dusted off his clothes and walked to the black.

Hartman was just standing there, stroking his chin, apparently confused in the throes of an enormous struggle.

"There's Mandie and Luke," Dunlee said softly. He took the reins and slid a boot into the stirrup. "I sent a telegram before I left town. Now I'll see if an answer's come. You'll have the proof I'm not turned around in my head—least not 'til your fist landed. What we need to do is get the real Mandie out here, and Luke with her. See you tonight."

"You be careful, son. Chenault's sneakier'n a lobo. You'll know how to shake him, won't you?" He laid a big hand on Dunlee's knee after he had mounted. He stood motionless in the solitude of the hanging tree as Dunlee rode out.

11

Dunlee was careful to hide the black and slip into town without being seen by the wrong people. It was an hour past noon, and old Dodd Lathrop should be at his work. Lathrop ran the post office, the telegraph station, and a small print shop.

Dunlee approached the street through an alley two adobes over from Lathrop's. Intending to move right on to the office, he stopped and stepped back when he spotted two men loitering in front of the shop. One leaned lazily against the pole supporting the porch at one corner. The other sat slouched on the edge of the boardwalk porch. Dunlee recognized the man standing. One of Pugley's bunch. Then he identified the other as well from the incident at Lobo Gulch.

It was no surprise that they were stationed here. Endicott and Teresa, along with Chenault, must have ordered this to make sure he got no word from Virginia. And that prompted him to wonder about his own telegraph to Virginia. Had it even been sent? He mulled it over as he walked around to the rear door.

Lathrop, a bent and bespectacled pioneer in his

midseventies, was locking lead into a plate to print some handbills. He heard Dunlee's boot heels tapping on the stone floor and turned to peer over the rims of his specs. When he recognized Dunlee, and recollected that he had dispatched a telegram, he wiped his ink-blackened fingers on his apron. The visitor sensed that the silver-haired townsman betrayed a reaction of dismay. Lathrop's eyes dropped, the furrows on his forehead tensed, and his lips and cheeks drew tight. Even his words were strangely high-pitched.

"Eh, you've er . . . come about the . . . the wire. I . . . uh . . . uh . . . let me see. I've got it right up here in the box." He led the way to the small front room of the shop, slipped behind a desk littered with what seemed like five years of business, and fumbled through some papers in a box tray. Apprehensively he glanced out the lone window. The two men were there, but looking the other way, their backs to him. His face registered relief. He spied the sheet he wanted and pulled it out. "Eh, yes, this is it." He held it out to Dunlee and leaned on the desk, glancing again toward the street. His manner was fidgity.

The words addressed to Marks Dunlee read:

Mandie and Endicott visiting father in Cimarron. Savage still sick. Tom Jackson.

He read it again. His face tightened into a frown.

Lathrop's mouth dropped open as he kept an eye on the window. Boot heels tapped on the porch, and they heard the door being jerked open. Dunlee instinctively stepped back into a corner behind the front counter.

He could not be seen from the other side of the counter unless a man leaned forward over it and looked to the left. His gun came into his hand as he waited.

Lathrop quickly stepped around his desk and moved to the counter.

"Old man!" The voice boomed from the doorway. It was loud and angry. "I saw you through the winder. You try changin' that message an' you know what'll happen." Dunlee heard a sharp, cracking sound. The speaker had snapped a stick in his hands. He saw Lathrop jump in fear, then steady himself against the counter. His wrinkled face drained of its color, and he looked sick.

"I . . . I know."

"All right. Best you remember real good."

Boot heels rapped on the boards again, the door banged, and the man was outside.

Lathrop sank wearily on the edge of his desk, shaking like a leaf.

"They threatened your life," Dunlee said in a low voice. "Or was it your wife, too?"

"It was her," he admitted weakly, finding the window again as if wondering if he would see those eyes peering in. "They said they'd break her neck. An' if I went to the sheriff, they had men that would come later an' break the missus like a stick."

"I'm sorry. I'll have a man stationed with a gun in the stand of piñons in front of your house. Right away. And I'll see they don't know you told me the truth. Now, where's the *real* message?"

"They took it." Lathrop fumbled out the words. "And they made me send a second copy of the phony message to the Hartman ranch by a messenger this

175

mornin'. It was to go direct to Hartman or his daughter—no one else."

"Uh-huh. And what did the real message say?"

Lathrop motioned him into the back room where they could not be seen if the men gazed in at the window.

"It said a woman . . . Mandie it was . . . would come immediately. She'd be with a man . . . a Jackson feller. She was . . . er . . . lookin' into the matter of a man . . . Luke. She said he . . . uh . . . disappeared. She feared foul play."

Dunlee asked, "Did the men say anything about plans to stop Mandie and Jackson when they come?"

"Oh, eh, one of 'em jest laughed and said . . . let's see . . . uh, yes, it 'twas like this: 'It looks like we'll take a ride up close to the Clifton House and wait for the stage.' Then he said he'd have to go hisself for sure. Said he always savored the looks of that woman, an' he could hardly wait."

Dunlee winced.

"Was he one of the two out front now?"

"No, he was shorter, eh, built solid as a butte. Looked tougher'n any Texas bull. Meanest face I laid eyes on in a long spell. Had a bull whip poked in his belt."

"Roe Pugley!"

Dunlee assured Lathrop again that he'd throw a guard on his place. Then he ducked out the back way and made sure the men out front did not see him. Yanking his broad brim down to hide his upper face, he bent a little to disguise his walk, and went off cautiously behind the few adobes to Frenchy's.

Frenchy was hunched at his desk, figuring in a ledger.

"Sure," he responded. "I can get you jest the man. Tad Cottring. Busted up his leg when his horse fell on him. Jest hobbles about town. Needs the work, doesn't fear anything that moves, and is a good shot. He won't mind sittin' a while, and he's tough as bull hide."

"Cottring, yes, I remember him. I hear tell he can hit anything that moves with his rifle. And he's a man to ride the river with. All right, he's our man. Take this money and tell him to post himself day and night in the piñons in front of Lathrop's house. Since there's a hill back of the cabin he can even spot anyone coming over it from the rear or the sides. And let Mrs. Lathrop know he's there, but tell her nobody else is to know except her and her man. Nobody. See that Cottring understands that, too."

"Only one else that'll know is me," Frenchy grinned. "Been cravin' some excitement. I'll be taking food and coffee to Cottring. Can even put in some guarding myself. And if I hear a shot, I'll be over there with my buffalo gun to back Tad."

"Pugley and his killers are riding up somewhere near Clifton House to grab the lady and her friend off the stage," Dunlee said. "I figure they'll use some trick. But I'll be there, too."

"They're stayin' in rooms here an' takin' meals out front," Frenchy informed him. "I'll keep my eyes an' ears open. Maybe they'll let some word slip. If so, I'll get the word to you right away."

Dunlee knew he could count on Frenchy. He slipped back to the black and rode warily in a circle to the southeast, shying far from the regular road to the Bar SH. Chenault would be on the prowl to earn his pay with a well-placed rifle shot.

12

Back in Virginia, the events of the past days were hard to figure. It was some time before Mandie, Tom, and the sun-darkened plainsman, Luke, began to understand what had happened.

For Mandie it began innocently enough. But it quickly became mysterious when Tom rode over and compared notes. Soon it turned into a real puzzler. Luke began to grasp what had befallen him after more than a fortnight in a dark place encircled by a tangled web of trees, brush, and vines. But, as by a working of providence, what was hard to figure began to clear up. Soon it was as plain as the sun at noon.

Mandie rode home in a carriage driven by one of the servants. He had explained that Whitehead—who usually met her in town—had been sent by Miss Teresa on an errand to Richmond. The servant also told her that Miss Teresa had gone away on a trip. Mr. Endicott had gone with her. As soon as Mandie arrived at the house her mother Sheila gave her the details.

Teresa had received a letter from a former college friend who now lived near Boston and was very ill, imploring her to come and help. Trevor, having relatives in the Boston area, insisted he go as her escort.

Fine, Mandie told herself. And she went outside to gather a rose bouquet from the garden.

Tom was fishing at the creek when a livery man from town drove by in a buggy. Alongside him sat a stranger, steadying a suitcase pressed against him, going west toward the von Ehrencroft's. The livery man came back alone within a half hour, so Tom knew he had time to go to the von Ehrencroft's but nowhere else. The stranger had stayed. The thing that struck Tom was that the stranger's broad-brimmed hat looked exactly like Dunlee's. Tom figured he'd ask Whitehead who the visitor was.

Tom had received a letter from Dunlee, which was inside an envelope addressed to the blacksmith, Buell McCoy. The letter had come from a place in Texas. With the letter was a second one addressed to Mandie, which Tom volunteered to carry to her. Since she was not yet back from college, however, he entrusted it to Whitehead, whom he knew would keep his trust. He cautioned him to see that only Mandie knew about it.

Within a day Pugley and three other men up and left. Pugley had placed another man in charge of his farm and mentioned he might be away several weeks. But Tom did not know where the boss was going. He didn't care. That is, not until a short time later.

Tom had scribbled a brief letter in his poor penmanship to Dunlee and mailed it to a Mr. D. Smith in Fort Worth, Texas, in care of the proprietor of a hotel. Not wanting to be seen mailing the letter, he loitered a few minutes outside the post office, watching the postal agent in his office. When he saw him busy at a desk, looking the other way, Tom tiptoed in and dropped the envelope quietly through the slot. He left just as silently.

A few minutes later Tom was looking at a window display at a leather goods shop nearby when a man spoke to him. He turned to see the postal agent, a short chubby man with a thick stand of whiskers and a cigar stuffed between thick lips.

"I see you're writing to someone in Texas."

That took Tom aback. He was sure he'd evaded the postmaster's eyes. He shifted uneasily, gulped awkwardly, and fumbled a weak "Me, suh?"

"Yes, you. Oh, now I recognize you. You work for a man named Pugley. Sure. It figures. You must be writing to him. Texas . . . yes, that's where he was going. Rough country."

"Texas, suh?"

"Why, sure, boy. You know that."

"Ah, . . . I . . . yes, suh. You'se a smart man. You knows he went dere?"

"Of course. Heard him ask the station clerk Conway the cost. I was there when he bought the tickets for himself and his men. Must be an important trip, four of them going like that."

Tom was dumbfounded. The agent shook his head at the expression on his face, muttered something like "The cat's got your tongue," and shuffled on up the street to more intelligent conversations.

"Texas," Tom murmured. Dunlee's letter had said "Texas," and that's where he had just mailed his own letter to Dunlee. Why had Pugley gone there on this sudden trip? Pugley had rarely gone on long trips.

Tom sank down on a bench near a fountain, and plunged his face into both hands, absorbed in thought. Could Pugley have gotten wind that Texas was where he could find the man he wanted to destroy? That would be enough to spur him to such a trip. But how could he have found out? The only people who knew were McCoy, Mandie, and himself . . . and Whitehead.

He went straight to Buell McCoy.

"No," the smithy said. "I ain't breathed a word— not even to my wife."

So Tom rode to the von Ehrencroft's. Whitehead came out to talk with him.

"Yes, Tom, I gave da letter straight to Miss Mandie when she done come home."

So Tom spoke with Miss Mandie.

Yes, she had received the letter from Dunlee but hadn't told anyone. She asked Whitehead if he might have mentioned it. He swore that he had not, then left to finish some chores. Mandie turned to Tom.

"Why, Tom? What's this all about?"

Tom told her about Pugley heading out for Texas with three men. He added that he'd heard Pugley vow to Endicott that he would kill Dunlee to make it look like he was trying to escape.

"I see." Her face was solemn at thoughts of such murderous designs. "I remember Marks saying he had won all that money from Trevor and Mr. Pugley. He mentioned they plotted to keep him from leaving the inn safe and sound. They wanted the money back.

"Whitehead brought us news that they were with the men coming to arrest Marks. Marks felt that the evidence that seemed to incriminate him was a frame-up. I believe that. I am astounded that Mr. Pugley would want to kill him. It sounds as if he were trying to cover up, to make it impossible for Marks to talk."

"Yessum," Tom replied. "Mistah Dunlee, he didn't kill Mistah Mueller. He left da inn an' done rode straight heah. Mistah Endicott an' Mistah Pugley, dey came on to town. I believe dey stopped by Mistah Dunlee's cabin outside town, broke in, an' took his knife to make it look like Mistah Dunlee done did Mistah Mueller in. I went by Mistah Dunlee's cabin after I heard da ruckus at Mistah Mueller's. One of his windahs was all busted in. Someone done crawled through it."

"Well, you could tell this to the sheriff," she said.

"Ain't no one gwinna believe no black man," Tom responded. " 'Sides, what Mistah Endicott says is what most folk gwinna believe. Least dey do if dey knows what's good fo' dem."

"Maybe Mister Pugley did go to find Marks," she concluded. Her face looked pale. "Oh, I do hope he sees them before they see him. He would know what to do. But how could they have found out where he is?" She leaned back on the porch railing, her fingers caressing a honeysuckle branch. Then she thought of something. "I'll send Dolcie out with orange juice for you. I want to go check on something."

Later she unlocked a drawer of her dresser and took an envelope from a stack of letters. For a long moment she examined it. She had made a slit in one end to remove the letter when Whitehead had given it to her. Now she carefully opened it the regular way, loosening the sealed flap. As she did so she noticed a small part of the flap underneath which had pulled a portion of the envelope with it, where the glue had not separated neatly.

"Hmm. I didn't do this," she murmured. "How . . . ?" Then she studied the underside of the flap more closely. There was more glue than she had seen on most envelopes. Then something else caught her eye. It was a small pinkish smudge impressed by a finger. The hue looked like rouge from a woman's face, perhaps rubbed on a finger by touching the face.

A woman had pressed the flap down, perhaps holding it while spreading a thin but wider than usual strip of glue. That would make sense if a person was resealing the envelope.

She went to Teresa's room and found some papers on top of her writing desk. Shuffling through them, she came across similar faint pinkish imprints. When she sniffed the smudges she caught the same fragrance. Then she saw the bottle of glue pushed back in a corner of the desk. She spread some on a paper and compared it with her envelope. Why would Teresa . . . ?

She returned to the porch.

"Tom, do you have the letter Marks wrote you?"

"Yessum." He handed her the envelope. She examined the inner side of the flap. The strip of glue was much narrower and straighter than on her envelope. While she was studying this she heard Tom say to Whitehead:

"A few days befo' Miss Mandie done come home, I sees a gentleman in a buggy wid da livery man, comin' out dis way. But when da buggy come back da gentleman he ain't deah no mo'. You folks must've had a visitor."

"Umm," Whitehead nodded. "You means Mistah Luke."

"Luke?" Mandie asked, looking up with a puzzled expression on her face. Dunlee had mentioned a Luke fondly to her several times, and she even remembered something dear about a Luke when she had been a small girl. She knew of nobody else by that name who might be coming here. "Who was this, Whitehead? Was someone here to visit while I was away?"

"Well, I'se done spoke out of turn," Whitehead said. "Miss Teresa, she done tells me not to say nothin'. She said you would only be powerful disappointed he done come an' went away an' you didn't see him. I hopes Miss Teresa won't be angry at me."

"It's all right," she reassured. "Who was this man Luke? When was he here? Where did he go?"

"He said his name was Mistah . . . let me see . . . ah, yes, Mistah Savage."

"Luke Savage. Why, that's the name of a friend Marks knew on the ranch where I lived as a small girl."

"Yessum. He done come a few days 'fo you come home. He was askin' fo' you."

"Well, why didn't he just wait, as our guest?"

"He did, Miss Mandie. He wanted to see you real powerful. He done come on an errand just to find you an' Mistah Dunlee. Miss Teresa sent me on a trip to Richmond. She made me promise I wouldn't breathe a word about dis to you. Now I done broke dat promise. Anyway, when I done come back Mistah Luke was gone. Your mother told me he dis up an' decided to go back home, early dat mornin' 'fo you returned."

"What? Why, that's incredible. Just a few hours

before I was to come, after he'd waited several days, and he came to see me? It doesn't make sense."

"How did he leave?" Tom wanted to know.

"Miss Teresa told your mother Mistah Endicott drove him to town early dat mornin' in his buggy."

"Hmm." Tom scratched his head, puzzled. "I was fishin', then workin' near da road all dat mornin'. Only buggy I saw was when Mistah Endicott an' Miss Teresa went by about da middle o' da mornin' toward town. Da next buggy went by was de one comin' from town with you, Miss Mandie, late dat day."

"I just don't understand," she said. "Where did Mister Savage go, and why did he leave, so suddenly? Why, in the first place, did he travel all that distance to see me? He *must* have come on an errand for my father, since he works for him."

"Yessum," Whitehead agreed. "Right after he done come in da house, Miss Teresa asked me to show him around da place. We was lookin' at da orchard an' he said he had a letter he must give to you. Didn't dat letter explain?"

"Letter? Nobody said anything about a letter for me. It must be he left it. An oversight, I'm sure. I'll ask Mother."

A little while later a servant drove Sheila von Ehrencroft back from a visit to another estate. She alighted from the carriage, an attractive woman in her late forties. Her hair was the hue of golden wheat stalks, her eyes blue as the Roanoke River. Mandie met her eagerly at the porch and accompanied her into the living room.

"Mother, a Mr. Luke Savage came to see me. Why didn't you tell me?"

"Ohhhhh ... that?" Sheila caught her breath, taken by surprise. She gestured with a white-gloved hand as if to put the matter away. It was of little consequence. "Mr. Savage came to see Mr. Dunlee, I think, and simply wanted to give you regards from your ... from Shoat Hartman. I felt he was uncomfortable here. The ease and the fineness of things nearly swept his breath away. He had existed in such crude ways. I gathered that he became fidgity because he wanted to see Marks Dunlee, who was no longer in the area. He grew impatient to get back to the wilds."

"But he brought a letter especially for me," Mandie persisted. "And he came such a long distance. I should think the trip must have been very important."

"Oh, I don't think anything Hartman or his men do is of much importance," Sheila sniffed. "I'm sure he simply made it appear important at first. You know, it would afford him a convenient reason to justify his calling on us. At least that's what Teresa surmised. She talked the most with him. I had several meetings with the Ladies' Guild that week and was hardly ever around. The morning he left I slept late and Teresa said she saw him off."

"The letter—where is it, Mother?"

"Oh, yes. Teresa said he gave her a letter before he left. She said he told her it was simply a greeting from your ... from Shoat Hartman. Since he was coming so far to see Marks Dunlee, Hartman wanted him to leave the greeting for you, too. Teresa said she put the letter in your room. Do you suppose when Dolcie dusted it may have been inadvertently laid aside? It might have gotten mixed into those old journals at the edge of your desk that Dolcie threw away. I asked Dolcie to put them in the incinerator the day she cleaned your room, before you returned. Several letters were right near them."

Mandie did not find the letter. She asked Dolcie, who was peeling potatoes.

"Yes, honey child, I seed da letters—all three of 'em," Dolcie replied. "I says to myself, I'se needs to put a ribbon 'round dese so'se dey's sho to be right here when Miss Mandie come. Dat's what I did."

"I found three letters with a ribbon. There must have been four. Is it possible you brushed one over in the journals that were thrown away?"

"Oh, mercies no, Miss Mandie. Dey was jest three. 'Sides, I went through all those journals 'fo I threw 'em out to see if anything might be stuck in 'em. Even shook 'em out good, one by one."

Mandie sent back to Whitehead and Tom, who were looking at some horses in a corral.

"Whitehead, we can't find the letter. Mother said it was only a short greeting from my father. Mr. Savage mainly came to see Marks, and was only taking the occasion to pass on a greeting to me."

Whitehead's forehead wrinkled.

"What is it, Whitehead?"

"Oh, Miss Mandie, I jest don't know. Dis jest gets mo' an' mo' complicated. Mistah Savage done tells me he's been on da road many days jest anxious to see you. Yo' father gave him strict orders he must see you fo' sho. Da letter was very important. It had to go to you, not to nobody else, no mattah who. He said no team o' horses could drag him away—not 'til he talked with you."

Mandie leaned on the corral poles, trying to reconstruct that day she came back. Several things had happened that day. Luke Savage made a sudden, mysterious decision to depart without seeing her. Yet her father had sent him all the way from the Territory of New Mexico to see her. And he left the very day he would see her. Then, when he left, Tom had not seen him go past, even though Tom was working near the road where he never missed what went by.

That very day had Teresa departed with Endicott on a trip to Boston to see a friend close enough to ask for her but one Teresa had never mentioned. A day or so earlier Pugley had left bound for Texas—possibly to try and grab Marks Dunlee.

The thought of Pugley leaving made her think of Endicott, a man close to Pugley and a man who badly wanted Dunlee. She didn't trust Endicott, despite Teresa's enchantment with his dark good looks, flash, and power. Perhaps it might help to go to town. She might verify where Endicott and Teresa had gone.

Teresa. Could she have pried into Mandie's mail, learned where Dunlee was, and passed on the information? It was hard to imagine, but Teresa had harbored a raging scorn against Dunlee ever since he told her he wouldn't have her.

To town, then. She could even find out if the station agent remembered a Mr. Savage and where he had gone.

13

The darkness of early morning was still flung across the grandeur of the Blue Ridge Mountain beauty. Luke Savage strode out on the von Ehrencroft porch. He gripped his valise. A man long in the habit of rising early, often riding nightwatch over a herd, he thought it nothing unusual to be up long before daybreak.

That beautiful sister of the woman he eagerly awaited had said that Endicott would be by before the crack of dawn. He would get Savage settled in a cabin they were letting him use. It was not far away.

Luke was glad to get some breathing room, free of all the company and the etiquette with which he felt awkward. He had been fearing he might make some big slip and be embarrassed. The lure of a cabin by himself, near good fishing, was powerful. He appreciated Endicott suggesting it. That man had some good qualities after all. Luke would be content to wait there, to take a long, carefree stroll in the woods, and do some squirrel hunting as well as fishing until evening. Then Teresa would send a buggy to fetch him back to dinner and Mandie.

Trevor Endicott already perched in his buggy, waiting. Luke also liked that. The man was punctual. But there was something ominous in his dark, mysterious countenance for which he did not care. Another man was with Endicott. He was at least six inches taller than Luke's six feet, and prodigiously muscled. He had the most apelike mug that Luke had ever looked into. And he'd seen some ugly ones. He towered on a rear bar of the buggy, his enormous hands clamped to the back of the seat. Luke clambered onto the seat next to Endicott with a simple "Howdy, you shore don't keep a man waitin'!"

The master of Ridgetop Manor reined the buggy horse east toward town for a mile or so, then cut south on a narrow, rutted lane through a cotton field. A jostling half hour later he guided the horse down off a gentle knoll into a glen where Luke saw a cabin thickly surrounded by trees and choked by brush. The place didn't look much used, but he liked the out-of-the-way situation. He had often been thankful for solitude.

They tromped inside. Endicott poked a fire into life in the wood stove, and heated water for coffee.

The ape, named Porsen, was hulking outside the door, leering at some wood that needed chopping. Endicott stirred coffee in three cups. He kept his big frame between the cup and the door.

An hour later Luke lay stretched on the bunk in a deep sleep, knocked out by the drug in his coffee. Endicott had wheeled the buggy away, but Porsen was out front chopping. A heavy iron bar set deeply in a thick doorpost assured the huge ax man that the sleeper would not be coming out even should he awake and try the door. There were no windows in the cabin walls. From a hole high up in the middle of the thick oak door Porsen could peer in and see if the man for whom he was responsible still sprawled on the bunk.

Several days later Luke awoke. He lay in darkness puzzling at a gleam of light from the door. He had a befuddled remembrance of that gleam. His arms swept out in a broad stretch and one of them struck something. He heard the thud of an object on the hard dirt floor and the sound of spilling liquid.

Vaguely he recalled food. Then he remembered that he had been eating from a bowl beside the bunk. He lay for some time trying to put things together, puzzling over where he was and why. He felt weak; it seemed as if a hundred blacksmiths were pounding anvils in his head. In the midst of the ache, nothing made clear sense.

Eventually some swirling thoughts formed. He fumbled in a pocket of his britches, found a match, and lit it by drawing it across a round wall log. As the light flared, he blinked, shut his eyes, and dropped the match when it began to burn his fingers. Reaching for a second match, he lit it and made out a kerosene lamp on a table a few feet away. Feeling a sensation of weakness and swooning, he sat up, managed to rise to his feet, and stood swaying as if ready to crash back into the bed. Fighting gamely, he stayed up and staggered to the lamp. With hands that seemed all thumbs, he got the wick burning after what seemed an hour.

Luke had no idea where he was. He recognized nothing about this place. But, appreciating the light, he sank back on the bunk and sat with his face cupped in his hands. His thinking gradually cleared a little. Then he stared at the food spilled across the dirt. Some kind of stew with potatoes and meat, he told himself. A spoon lay on a wooden box by the bed. So, his arm must have knocked the bowl off the box. Slowly it came back to him that he had eaten food from the bowl once, twice, many times. He dimly remembered eating in darkness.

Had he been ill? Was Shoat taking care of him? Was this a line shack? No, he didn't see a thing that was familiar, and he knew the line shacks.

He glanced again at the food. A hungry rat was acting confused in the dirt near the stew.

"Like me," he murmured. "Dizzy." But as he watched the miserable creature flop down in sleep, it dawned on him that the food had done this to the animal. He got up again and staggered to a bucket of water and a cup on the table near the lamp. He drank deeply to slake a raging thirst, and realized he was ravenous. Searching about, he found part of a loaf of homebaked bread, tore off a huge chunk, and began to eat. All the while he stumbled about the room, the movement seeming to clear his head and make his step more sure. He tried the door, but could not budge it. Bolted on the outside! Why would . . . ?

He stared out the door from the small hole and saw a path climbing a knoll, cut by recent wheel ruts. He stood there a long time, and in his mind's eye the picture of a buggy came back. He rode in that buggy. Another man drove, and a third man hovered behind—a huge man.

Endicott . . . Porsen.

But when was that? This morning? He felt his

face and brushed the coarse growth of many days. A man who shaved daily when he could, he grimaced, appalled. Then the sensation struck him of how dirty and itchy he was, how smelly he was, as if he had not had a bath in days. The thought occurred to look at his pocket watch. But he found it run down.

Slowly the situation came back. He had come by stage coach and by train to Virginia . . . come to see a lady . . . Mandie . . . and a man . . . Dunlee. But he could not remember having seen them. He could not figure that out. He had come to see them, and here he was in a dark cabin, filthy . . . locked in!

"Have I been drinkin' . . . been on a big drunk for days? No, I never drink like that . . . it can't be. . . . But how . . . ?"

He remembered not whiskey but coffee. He had been sipping coffee. Endicott and Porsen had held cups too. He could not remember seeing them go. But there were dim recollections of eating off a crate, lying on the bunk, of seeing a big man stalking about now and then, but mostly what seemed like a long night of tossing. . . .

He paced back toward the bunk, saw the spilled food again, and the motionless rat.

"Somethin' put in the food," he thought. "Makes 'im dizzy, . . . makes 'im sleep . . . makes *me* dizzy. I—I been sleepin' for days. But why am I cooped up here . . . locked in like a jail? Nobody should do that to me."

He found an old wad of wrapping paper and raked what he could of the spilled food into it, then wrapped it. Spying a pail under the bunk, he remembered using it, recalled being ordered to use it. . . . Ah,

Porsen, the ape. He dropped the wadded paper into the pail and recoiled from the stench. Then he set the bowl back on the box near the spoon.

Walking about had helped. He was getting his wits back.

"Good thing I knocked over that food," he mused, "or I'd have eaten it an' been asleep again. I would never do that, sleep an' never shave. This is all wrong. Those men don't want me to leave. I've got to find Mandie! I was supposed to see her an' have dinner. I have to get out of here!"

One of Hartman's warnings drifted back to mind. Don't trust anyone you don't know. Deliver the letter direct to Mandie. Yes, the letter right there in his pocket. He felt but realized his coat was not on. Then he saw it hanging with some other items of clothing on wall pegs. Quickly he slipped his hand inside and into the pocket. The envelope was not there.

Hearing steps approaching, he doused the light with great haste and lay down. After a while, he heard Porsen come in, listened to his heavy steps approaching the bed, and saw out of a corner of a half-closed eye that the ape gripped a pistol in his right hand. He was taking no chances of being jumped. Luke would need to remember how careful the man was.

Porsen picked up the dish, grunted his satisfaction, and busied himself rustling up grub. First he gratified his own stomach, and took warmed water for coffee from the kettle on the stove. Eventually he scraped food into the bowl. Luke noticed that he dragged a bag out of a pocket and spilled some of the contents into the food. Then he stirred the food and brought it over to the box, again gripping the pistol, ready.

After a long time of puffing on a pipe and pawing an old, yellowed magazine, Porsen came over and clamped a lock on Luke's right leg. Then Luke remembered feeling the clamp at other times and pulling himself out of bed on one leg awkwardly to use the pail under the bunk.

Now he was totally sure of his situation. The clamp, fastened by a chain to the iron bar at the foot of the bunk, was proof enough. He was wasting his days in a prison.

Porsen shook a bedroll to full spread on a pile of straw across the room, laid his pistol by the wall for an easy grab, blew out the lamp, and crawled onto the blanket. Luke waited until he was snoring with the ferocity of a Scottish gale, then dumped the food into the pail.

The next morning he feigned a sound sleep as Porsen set more food on the box, unlocked the clamp, and left the cabin. Going to the door, Luke peered through the hole. Porsen was trudging up the knoll away from the cabin. So he set in motion a plan that had been forming as he lay sleepless most of the night.

He stuffed Porsen's bedroll under his own blanket to take on the shape of a man in the vague light from the door hole. Then he got a skillet with a black bottom that might look like a patch of dark hair on the pillow, half covered by the blanket.

Then the wait began. It seemed Porsen would never come. Finally, Luke heard the big, heavy feet. All morning and much of the afternoon he had sat on a chair near the door fingering a chunk of firewood. His ears had perked at every sound, birds chirping, a donkey braying far away, cows bellowing, a squirrel scolding some intruder, a large bird fluttering from a tree, and locusts singing.

Porsen peered in through the hole. Then he opened the door, leaned forward, and peered at the bunk more carefully. The fuller light streaming in showed his rifle thrust ahead of him, poised for quick action. He stepped in, rifle in one hand and two rabbits dangling from the other. Still wary of the bunk, he started to tromp across to the table near the stove.

Quick as a cat Luke pounced. He rapped his captor hard alongside the head. The guard's knees buckled and he crumpled heavily to the floor as an ox would collapse when struck between the eyes. Luke snatched up the rifle, set it near the door, and relieved Porsen of the pistol poked inside the belt. He tucked it down inside his own belt and dragged Porsen's massive body to the bunk, clamping both wrists to the end of the bed. He flopped the hulk on the bunk and used a rope he'd found slung over a nail to bind his feet to the other end of the bunk. Powerful as Porsen was, he would not be going anywhere for a while. A good, long while. Luke even ripped the man's shirt off, knotted it, and tied it around the thick neck to form a gag.

Luke put on his coat, took his suitcase, the bag from which the coffee and food was "doctored," and the rifle. He bolted the door behind him. After a while his eyes became accustomed to the late afternoon sunlight, and he headed over the knoll to cut across the fields. His head was clear about the direction he must take to hoof it back several miles to the von Ehrencroft's.

He had to find Mandie. And he must get back to Hartman.

14

Tom and Mandie hurried back from town, agitated by what they had just learned. The train agent had remembered the arrival of a man meeting Luke Savage's description. But the agent said he had never returned and purchased a ticket to leave. And yes, he remembered Trevor Endicott and a beautiful woman.

"Sure, sure. You mean the two who started on that trip west? I told them to go on to St. Louis and from there on west. They can reach Denver, then Pueblo by rail now, then get a stagecoach."

So it wasn't Boston after all.

"I remember Marks talking about a friend of his in Cimarron. Frenchy," Mandie told Tom. "I'll wire him. He'll know if Trevor and Teresa have come there."

She was troubled about why the two would take this trip. What could be their motive?

She stepped up to the counter at the telegraph office.

"I am Mandie von Ehrencroft. I'd like to. . . ."

"Oh, yes, Miss von Ehrencroft," the heavyset, middle-aged agent cut in eagerly. "Imagine you pop-pin' in like this. I have a telegram just came in, had your name on it. I just got back from runnin' it over to Buell McCoy. Here, I have a copy of it."

She took the paper, saw it was from Marks Dunlee, and read swiftly.

> *Endicott and Teresa arrived. She posing as Hartman daughter. Scheme for wealth he found. Hartman sent Luke to bring you. Treachery evident. Find Luke and rush to Hartman. Will meet.*

She held a gasp below her breath. Her heart was pounding from the shocking words. But showing outward poise, she smiled at the agent.

"Please say nothing of this to anybody," she requested softly. "Nothing!"

"I won't, Miss. My job is to relay messages, not gossip about 'em."

As she stepped from the office she breathed a sigh of relief. Marks was safely home from Texas. Pugley and his thugs had not been able to stop him, if indeed they had gone there after him. The way things had been shaping up, she was certain they had.

They found McCoy shoeing a horse. He handed Mandie the telegram he had planned to take to Tom after quitting time. As they rode homeward, she said to Tom, "This is so hard to believe. But the pieces keep fitting together. I cannot imagine how Teresa could get entangled in treachery like this. I fear something awful has happened to Mr. Savage. They've taken him somewhere to keep him from reaching me. It's clear that they have not wanted me to find out and spoil the plot. We've got to find Luke. Then I want you to go with me, with us, on a long trip west."

Tom hurried the horse down the lane toward the farm and approached a small clump of willows a stone's throw from the farm yard. A man with a dark, bearded face stepped from the trees, one hand lifting a rifle and the other clutching a valise.

"Hold up there!"

Tom hauled the horse to a stop, fearing for Miss Mandie. Then he realized from the man's big, broad-brimmed hat that he might be the man he had seen go by in a buggy toward the von Ehrencroft place.

"Miss, I'm Luke Savage. You . . . could you be Miss Mandie? You look a heap like Miss Teresa."

"Yes . . . yes, I'm Mandie. Thank God you're safe, Mr. Savage. We feared—."

"Miss, I'm right glad to see you. Came a long way for this moment." He swept off his Stetson and bowed. "Mighty sorry I look so dirty. Some men kept me locked up, an' drugged me to keep me sleepin'. I must 'pear worse'n a steer jest dragged out of a mud hole. I'll get cleaned up, then I'll look tolerable."

"Oh, do climb in," she beamed. "You look wonderful, just being safe." He stepped up behind the seat and steadied himself with one hand while the other clung to the rifle and the valise.

"Miss, I had me a special letter your pa sent you, but those men taken it from me . . . Endicott an' Porsen. They tricked me the mornin' 'fore you were supposed to get home."

"Oh, my, you've been locked up more than three weeks!" She was indignant.

"Yes, Miss, haven't ever had so much sleep in my life."

"It's terrible, but it fits other things we've been

slowly finding out. The letter, do you know what it said?"

"Never read it. But I know what it was about." He hesitated until he had stepped off the buggy and helped her down. Tom drove on to the barn, leaving them alone near the porch. Then he briefly told her how much her father loved her and what he had confided.

Well, that explained Dunlee's telegram. The best Mandie could piece things together, Teresa and Endicott had found out what was in the letter and formed a treacherous plot to get the riches.

"Well," she said to herself, "I knew Teresa was quite a schemer. But this goes beyond the wildest thing I ever imagined she could do. I am so ashamed for her."

Mandie sent Whitehead and two of the farm hands armed to take Porsen to the sheriff. Luke bathed in lilac water, shaved, and dressed in clean clothes while Mandie packed.

In town, Mandie reported Endicott's and Porsen's crime to the mayor, an old friend of her family. He assured her he would make sure the sheriff threw Porsen in jail and held him. A bit later the three travelers were winding toward St. Louis.

In her heart, Mandie relished the thought: from the Blue Ridge Mountains to the rugged range east of the snowcapped Sangre de Cristos. She liked it, and she treasured the reasons why.

Her father was there. And Marks Dunlee.

15

Shoat Hartman rode alone down the slope from the north ridge to the ranch headquarters. He had split up from Booger about three hours earlier as they came back from Hanging Tree Canyon.

"Go on in," he had said. "Me, I want to do some scoutin' around. Better chance not bein' seen if I'm alone. Maybe I'll get lucky an' sneak up on one of the critters that don't have any business here." But he had seen nothing that looked suspicious.

Hartman stripped the gear from his mount, and sent Booger to the house. He was to tell "Mandie" he'd be in after he gave his horse a good rubdown and mended the cinch on his saddle. Hartman wanted her to fetch more of the dried apples out of the cellar. He had a craving for apple pie.

Nearly an hour later Hartman headed for the house as the sun dipped low toward the peaks of the Sangre de Cristos. He had reached the porch steps when Booger's yell from the pasture halted him.

"Rider on his way in."

Hartman wheeled to catch the signal Bucher was flashing from the ridge. A visitor had gained the rim rider's approval to enter the pass toward the house without a rifle slug somewhere between his head and belt buckle.

Teresa and Endicott came out on the porch to join the rancher. Hartman soon recognized one of the townsmen, Zeke Hester, who ran errands for Dodd Lathrop. Zeke came into the yard and swung his horse over by the porch. He leaned down and handed Hartman an envelope. It was a telegram.

"It's for one of your men—Dunlee."

Hartman invited the messenger to stay for supper and spend the night. He mentioned the apple pie, and Hester's eyes lit up with new life after his wearying ride.

A few minutes later, Dunlee set his horse to the trail down off the ridge and soon strode to the house, glad to be at the end of the long, hot ride. Hartman handed him the unopened envelope. Dunlee leaned against a pole of the porch, reading the message. He folded it grimly, and stuck it in his shirt pocket. He glanced at Teresa, who was eyeing him, a faint smile flickering at the edges of her lush lips. Triumph seemed to dance in her face, as if she knew what was in the telegram and felt vindication.

"It must not be good news," she spoke up, her tone different from the look. "You seem so forlorn."

"Depends on who's judging," he shrugged. "Here, you might as well read it."

He handed the telegram to Hartman, who read it as Teresa eagerly crowded up to his elbow to scan the contents.

Hartman finished and looked at Dunlee. It was a long, searching look. He seemed to be debating within himself. Then he shook his head approvingly at what he had read, and turned his eyes on the woman beside him. Her smile was one of immense delight, her eyes flashing in confidence.

"Well, at least that's clear," she said. "Rest yourself, Pa. I'll have supper ready in just a little while. The apple pies should be well along by now. You're going to like them!"

The next day Dunlee busted broncs. Part of the time Teresa took in the action, watching between corral poles. He gave her quite a show with those snorting, squealing, pile-driving horses. He figured she was hoping one of the wild string would toss him on his head and break his neck.

Dunlee kept a wary eye on the northern rim. Between broncs and when he had fought a bucker to a standstill he scanned the outlands for any sign of Chenault. A man can live with a sharp consciousness about a hired killer slipping about his deadly game. But he had an idea that what he'd made clear to Bucher before he headed out for his patrol might get some results.

"Bucher," he'd said within the hearing of Hartman, Booger, and the two guests, "a bushwhacker laid up in them rocks the other day tried to line me in his sights. If he gets back up there and takes a shot at me while I'm working broncs today, I won't come after him first. I'll come after you. If I do, you'll wish you never drifted into this territory."

"Them's tall words, Dunlee." Bucher glared resentfully out of his beady eyes. Dunlee had seen a kinder sentiment in the eyes of a hissing diamondback.

"Not as tall as the job I'll do if you let him through to take a crack at me," Dunlee promised. "The way he slipped in there, a man could get the idea you were working in cahoots with him, looking the other way."

"You ain't got no cause," Bucher snarled. He lifted his hand to his gun butt. But hardly had his fingers come to rest on it when he found himself gazing into the gaping barrel of a .44 that had seemed to leap effortlessly into Dunlee's hand.

"Next time you lay a paw on that gun when I'm trying to get your attention," Dunlee drawled with icy coolness, "you'd better be ready to go all the way. There's only one thing I can figure when a man reaches for a gun like that."

Bucher stared at Dunlee's gun, took his hand away from his own shooting iron, and crossed his arms.

"Forget it, Bucher," Hartman cut in gruffly. "Light a shuck for the ridge. If you need to cover that strip twice as careful as before, do it! I want this prowlin' around stopped—now!"

Bucher nodded, cast a wicked eye on Dunlee, and spun on his heels to get his horse. As he forked the mount and took off for the rim rocks, he was sizzling mad. But he was also perplexed. How could Dunlee hit the nail on the head the way he did? The man was coming too close for comfort. He would have to figure a way to speed up things without it reflecting on him.

Teresa was awed by Dunlee's handling of the broncs. They were a savage breed trapped in a box canyon that slashed the grassy range to the south.

They could buck and twist and snort with more fire than any horses she had ever seen. She was amazed that a human being could stay astride, and this cowboy clung like a burr. He rode them out to a jaded standstill.

The last of the string Dunlee was working took him up on a mound in the corral in the final efforts to dislodge the rider. Marks felt the bronc's pitching growing weak, then brought him to a standstill facing the house. He glanced out over the ranchhouse to a hogback beyond. In a sweeping look he caught sight of a burly figure slipping furtively over the hump, then dropping from view. Hartman was going out there alone. Perhaps he was going to look at some gold.

A half minute later, as Dunlee still sat atop the motionless mustang, he spotted Endicott crawling over the hogback. The man was obviously trying not to be seen following the rancher.

Teresa had grown weary of the struggles in the corral, and loathed the manure dust drifting her way. Besides, she was disgruntled at not seeing Dunlee dumped. She went back to the porch and began fanning herself and leafing through a catalogue of feminine fashions.

Dunlee abandoned the bronc he'd gentled and made for the barn. Once out of sight, he waited 'til he was sure Teresa was not looking, then slipped out the front door. Crawling into the brush by the wall, he worked his way as quickly as possible through brush and trees to the far side of the hogback. There he scanned the tracks of the two men.

A few hundred short paces behind the hogback

the blunt south ridge of the pass jutted up after a gradual slope and a couple of low shelves. The entire terrain was thick with brush and trees. A man on foot could move about without even being seen from the north ridge, if careful. This side of the pass was also strewn with many boulders.

Hartman, he thought, might be slipping away to his hiding place. If so, it would not do to let Endicott follow him to it. Suppose this unscrupulous man found the treasure which had lured him all the way from Virginia. Then he could bash Hartman's head in, hide the body, and move back at a convenient time to pack out the wealth. There was no trusting a man who plotted with Pugley to kill Dunlee, who led in some foul act against Luke, who was scheming a dark treachery with Teresa, who had probably hired Chenault to strike him down, and whose men had threatened poor old Lathrop and his wife. Endicott was already in so deep that he might regard murdering Hartman as a small thing.

When Dunlee was almost to the base of the ridge wall, he spotted Endicott about a hundred paces east, crouched low, working through brush with his eyes to the ground. Then, as Dunlee studied the tracks of Hartman while hunkered down out of sight, his face burst into a pleased smile. The boot marks told his well-trained eyes that Hartman had started east but backtracked over his own prints. The impressions in the dirt in one place showed that the soles of his boots had come down twice, the second time a shade off the first, slightly enlarging the mark. Hartman had sneaked off to the west, and had thrown Endicott off to the east.

He saw Endicott move out of view beyond some rocks, then hurried west along the ridge in search of Hartman. Unfortunately, the ground grew rocky; there were various places where Hartman could crawl over large rocks, leaving no trail.

Yet Dunlee's training as a cavalry scout helped him. He picked up the path from signs most men would miss—a dried aspen leaf crushed as if by a boot, a small rock loosened from the hard soil around it, a small dried twig of a young cottonwood broken and bent westward at elbow height.

He passed a small cave in the base of the ridge's bluntness, and noted several other crevices in the rocky wall. Nobody lurked there. Finally, after he'd gone a couple of long stone throws from the spot where Hartman had fooled Endicott, he paused to lean on a high upjutting boulder. He was at a loss to find any further sign of his friend's movement.

"At least he's shed of Endicott, and safe," he muttered. He knew that from where he paused he would be able to spot the Virginian if he came this way. And he would not be seen himself.

It was here that he was swept by an awareness of how weary he was. The harsh pounding on the broncs for several hours had left him somewhat drained. So he sank down on a slash in the boulder and rested. He would be content to let Hartman go his way as long as he could interpose between the man and the schemer.

As he relaxed, he reflected that a man could climb astride this boulder and gaze down a slope—through a break in the aspens, cottonwoods, and brush—and have a commanding view of the house. His eyes would hurtle a couple of deep arroyos bewhiskered with brush.

He mused at Hartman's story of a raid a far-roving Comanche war party had made a few years back. Shoat had sent Mandie out through a tunnel from the basement of the house to hide in a cave he'd previously shown her. Sheila had been with her, but fainted dead away just outside the end of the tunnel. Mandie had gone on to the cave, and later had stood on her tiptoes on a high rock, watching the Comanches ride away. After the shots of the defenders driving off the braves had been stilled for a long while, she started back and met her father coming for her.

Could this be the high rock? Maybe. But if so, where would the cave be?

As his eyes examined the boulder and various large rocks nestled into a pile with it, he noticed a nearby pile of crushed, dried leaves. What arrested his attention was a light indentation like the arc of a plate, a heavy plate, neatly pressed upon the leaves. What could have mashed those leaves into that unusual shape? The toe or heel of a boot would not make that big an arc. He looked around, mystified. Then he noticed a ruggedly circular plate of rock about four inches thick and nearly three feet across. It was lying amidst other rocks.

Something caught his eye . . . a thin spray of cigarette ashes entrapped in a narrow fissure of the plate. A man had paused here. The burnt tip of his cigarette had cascaded down. His eyes studied the rest of the slab. This led to a larger discovery. The upper left edge of the slab was smoothly rounded; it was just the right shape to match the impression in the leaves. Someone had lifted this slab and set it down on the shelf nearby, crushing the leaves in that form.

Why would anyone pick up . . . ? On a hunch, he jumped up, his heart pounding. Grasping the stone firmly, he lifted it and gazed into a gaping fissure large enough to admit a man on his hands and knees crawling down into the nest of rocks.

Dunlee set the stone down, dropped to his knees, and lowered himself head first into the opening to take a look. Reaching back, he fished several matches from his pocket and struck one on the rock wall beside him. He started to crawl farther down. Suddenly he saw a flicker of light dancing on the wall of rock below him. He first thought it was sunlight slipping in from some other opening. But then he sensed that it was the light of a lantern playing on the area below. At that same instant something brushed his chin, clutched the collar of his shirt, and jerked him down into the depths of the cave.

A mumble of shock had only begun to rush to his lips when he felt a slamming sensation on the side of his head and went limp in a horrible blackness.

His mind gradually cleared, and he opened his eyes. He was aware of a throbbing in his head. But the blackness had fled. There was light, and he blinked. Now he became conscious of a lantern flickering on a rocky floor nearby, smelled the oil, saw a man's boot, a leg, then the form of a large hulk hovering close.

"Easy, easy. How'd I know it was you? You were working the horses. Then you come crawlin' in here. . . ."

"Shoat!" He looked up sheepishly into a face etched with dark lines of concern in the pale light. He sat up, his own face twisting into a wry grin, despite the throbbing in his head. "Something about my head you don't like? That's twice in two days you busted me."

"Sorry, son. Purely sorry." Hartman's voice was soothing as he pushed his head and arms through the opening and set the slab back over the entrance to conceal the cave. "I suspected I had me a coyote. Been a lot of two-legged ones slinkin' around. Lookin' for treasure."

"One of them from the house," Dunlee jerked a thumb eastward.

"Now hold on there," Hartman reproved, settling his frame against a wall of the cave to sit and rest. "If you're speakin' of my guests. . . ."

"I am," the newcomer returned firmly. "I saw Endicott stalking behind you over the hogback, acting real careful. His intention was plain. But he didn't read sign on you backtracking, so he went off east. He'd like to know real bad where the cache is. If he located it, I don't think your life would be worth a worn-off boot heel."

"Marks, those are strong words. Like your words at Hangin' Tree yesterday. I've been givin' that some thought. It doesn't come easy. I thought the telegram last night set things straight. There it was, plain, from Virginny. It's Mandie we got here. And that man's a friend of Mandie. It jest don't make no sense to keep harpin' on that same string."

"Shoat, listen to me. That telegram was just what Endicott and Teresa want you to believe. They've thought of just about every angle. Here, take a look at this." He handed the true telegram from town to the rancher, who held it over by the lamp. Then his mouth sagged open and his eyes widened with new perception.

"Hmm!"

"Yes," Dunlee said emphatically. "The real Mandie's on her way. Luke and Tom are with her. I know it's all hard to believe. Endicott's a slick operator. He lays his plans with a lot of care to cover all the details. He's got Teresa with him in this about as deep as she can plunge. But she could go deeper if she killed for what she's after. I wouldn't be surprised now if she would stoop to that.

"Those two don't know I got my hands on this telegram. They slapped a guard on the telegraph office, threatened Lathrop with breaking his wife's neck. But I sneaked in the back, took this right out from under their noses. Last night I wanted Endicott and Teresa to think they had things just the way they planned. If they feel safe, thinking Mandie won't reach you to upset their scheme, they won't resort to anything more drastic. At least I hope not."

"Mandie won't reach me? What do you mean by that?"

Dunlee explained that Pugley and his men knew of Mandie's true telegram and were planning to take her off the stage near the headwaters of the Canadian River.

Hartman's brow furrowed into deep, dark lines in the dim light. He groaned and spat angrily into the far shadows.

"Don't worry," Dunlee reassured him. "I'll go a lot farther than the Clifton House and beat them to it. Even if I have to go all the way to Raton Pass I'll take Mandie, Luke, and Tom myself, and bring them back here safe."

"You're a good man, Marks. I trust you. You're the finest son." He paused, shook his head. "Mandie bein' on the way, this one we got here is Teresa like you been tellin' me. But how . . . how can she look so all-fired like my Mandie?"

"There's a whole world of tricks we never learned," Dunlee replied. "You learn a lot at acting school where Teresa trained. I saw a play once about George Washington. The man acting out Washington's part was the spitting image of the picture of Washington."

"It's uncanny," Hartman shrugged. "I've asked her things about the days here when Mandie was little. She gives me answers only Mandie would know . . . exact things, places, people."

"She's put in some work," Dunlee agreed. "Those things could be memorized. Mandie may have talked a lot about her days here. Or Teresa got hold of a diary. Or she pumped Sheila.

"One other matter I didn't mention to you yesterday at the canyon. We got too busy about other things. On my way over there I saw Bucher heading west. I followed. A few miles east of the hanging tree he met up with Chenault. They had quite a long talk, mighty friendly. They were talking cattle.

"Bucher turned back to head east as he agreed with you. But I tailed Chenault. He led me to a cave in a canyon wall, and I saw running irons, a man sitting guard, and plenty of space to run in cattle, maybe twenty, thirty head. They could cover their tracks, hold them there a while, then shove them on some night."

"Good man. We can smoke out that rustlers' nest." Hartman's eyes blazed with fury.

"That we can do, now that we know where to strike. But I'd advise waiting 'til we can catch them with some cattle. It's just a matter of time 'til they hit again. Our big move now is to get Mandie here safe. After that, if Pugley and his crowd head back we can get the whole bunch in one swipe."

"Makes sense," the boss admitted.

"Is this where you've got the treasure stashed?"

Hartman gazed steadily at him for a moment. "I can tell you, Marks. Yes, it's here, or not far from here. If anything happens to me, it's best you know. Back here."

He motioned to the rear of the cave, swinging the lantern to hurl back the darkness.

"I found a tunnel—natural waterway from some of the big rains. Runs back of this cave an' comes out down near the side of the barn in the gully by that old scrub oak, down beneath its roots at the rocky bottom of a bank. I found a way to plug it off so the water doesn't run through it.

"The gold is buried in pouches wrapped in heavy burlap about every five feet in the silt floor of the tunnel, startin' about ten feet from the oak and workin' back this way from it. Nobody knows about this tunnel. The long grass an' brush hangin' down the bank over the oak's roots keep it hidden."

He showed Dunlee a rock in the bottom of the cave's back wall about three feet high and a couple feet wide. "I wedged this in here against the other rocks an' dirt. Brush an' grass about cover it over. Takes a strong man to work it out and move it aside. No one else on the ranch could budge it alone—not even Booger. And who would suspect it opens into a long tunnel? Actually, though, I can leave this end as it is an' crawl in from underneath the oak."

"Endicott could get help to move it if he suspected," Dunlee replied. "But then, he'll never even find the cave. And if he did, how would he guess what lay behind that stone? It's a secret only the two of us know."

"Where do you reckon Endicott has wandered by now?"

"No place near here, I hope." Dunlee hoisted the slab at the entrance a trifle to press his ear to the opening. For a while he listened intently. Sparrows chirped in bushes and on overhanging tree limbs. A ground hog's industrious work digging a few feet away from the nest of rocks told him Endicott could not be near. So he lifted the plate and set it to the side quietly.

"I'll scout around and see if he's up this way."

"Good. I'll be along after a while."

Dunlee laid the slab back into place across the other rocks and edged out from the secret cave. He had assured himself that Endicott was not close by. Working his way farther westward, he made sure he left no signs of being here. His aim was to circle and go in toward the barn.

About a hundred and fifty paces to the west he decided to lower himself over the lip of a rocky bank from a shelf where he walked. Seeing a clump of scrub oak not far from the edge, he ducked under a branch and grabbed another branch to let himself down over the edge to an outjutting ledge a few feet below. Beyond that it was another ten-foot drop to the sandy bottom of the gully. He could go down slowly.

Just as he was bending to go under the limb and over the edge he saw a movement out of the corner of an eye. It was quick and blurry. He felt something hard rap him a grazing blow alongside the head. All he knew then was the fleeting sensation of darkness closing in, as if a lamp had suddenly been snuffed. His fingers slipped off the limb, and his chest struck the lip of the gully wall. Then he was falling away into emptiness.

16

Dunlee blinked, staring at the sand and sagebrush beside him. He moved his left arm and grimaced from a stab of soreness. He groaned and gingerly felt his arm. The sleeve was almost ripped off, wet with blood. He looked at several gashes on his exposed arm, then became aware of pains in his shoulders, chest and hips.

He slowly picked himself up. More jolts of pain racked his frame.

He had been sprawled at the sandy bottom of a deep, twisting gully. His denims had been laid bare at the right kneecap. Gazing up at the gully wall, he saw the overhanging branches of a scrub oak. Then his mind, still foggy, vaguely recollected his head striking something hard . . . or something hard clouting him.

He leaned against the slanted side of the gully and let his senses clear. It occurred to him to feel for his gun. It was still in its holster, secured by the thick, tough leather thong. His hat was gone. Then he located the Stetson snagged in the branches of a sage bush on a narrow ledge a few feet below the rim of the bank. As near as he could guess, his plunging body had hit the cushion of that bush before tumbling another ten feet through tough catclaw. He found a long oak branch lying in the gully, and shook the Stetson free.

Looking up had required him to squint into the sun, and he realized that it was about noon. He'd been sprawled unconscious for a couple of hours.

Hearing the swish of steps in the soft sand, he spun around and flicked his thong loose to fill his hand with the .44. Booger strode around a turn of the gully. The ranchhand's mouth fell open in astonishment.

"What in thunder? You tangled with a mountain lion, Marks? Shoat sent me out to round you up. Never expected this."

"Guess I didn't either," the banged-up man admitted sheepishly, limping to meet him. "Somebody . . . I didn't see who . . . clubbed me by that tree. I took quite a tumble, worse'n biting the dust from any bronc."

Booger whistled. "I never knowed any bronc that could dump you. Yeah, I can tell where you landed. The brush broke your fall or you'd uv made a regular crater. Good thing, or you'd be worse off. We've got to patch you up, then I'll scout around up here. I'm hopin' there'll be tracks. Then we'll see."

When Dunlee limped in, Teresa and Hartman looked up from a conversation in the living room.

"Oh my!" the girl exclaimed. "One of those savage horses finally got the better of you."

"Beggin' your pardon, Miss," Booger put in quickly. "No horse in that string's gonna bang Marks up like this. A two-legged bronc did this. But we'll get him." His words held a forceful resolve.

220

Dunlee swept past them and jerked open the door of Endicott's room. The man was not inside.

"What do you mean, barging into Trevor's room?" Teresa burned him with wide-eyed indignation. She thrust herself between him and the doorway. "A gentleman doesn't do such a thing."

"Well, now, isn't that a fact!" Dunlee replied. Sarcasm sharpened his voice. "Come to think of it, there's a lot of other things a gentleman doesn't do. Like busting a man from behind, spilling him down into a deep gully, counting on him being dead."

"Marks," she said reprovingly. "That is not like you, blaming a man rashly. Trevor could never...."

"Why don't you sit down an' let Shoat look at those bruises," Booger suggested. "Whoever the coyote was, I'll come onto his tracks. They'll tell us what we need to know."

"Thanks, Booger." Dunlee dropped wearily into a chair of taut rawhide.

If any man in the outfit could read signs as well— or nearly as well—as Shoat or Dunlee, it was Booger. The cowboy had worked with Utes, even spent several years as an Army scout. He was a cunning tracker.

Hartman, who had sat listening, asked Teresa to heat water for bathing the wounds.

"Anyway," Teresa rejoined before going to the kitchen, "Trevor has been here at the house or out by the corrals."

"Oh, you've had him in sight all the time since I was forking those broncs?" Dunlee queried. Hartman had begun to peel away his ragged shirt to look at the arms and shoulders.

"Yes," she replied. Hartman glanced at her

thoughtfully. Then she went to poke wood in the stove and get a fire going. It would take a while to get water heated. She came back and winced as she saw the ugly gashes and dark bruises.

Hartman studied her from his crouched position, and she spoke.

"Trevor couldn't have been the one. He would never strike from behind. And he would not attack one of Pa's friends. With all the mysterious riders sighted near the pass, long before Trevor came, there should be an obvious explanation."

"When everything comes to light," Dunlee said as he peeled up his pants leg to reveal a dark bruise on his right leg, "the explanation will be obvious, as you say. We'll have the man dead to rights. And by all rights he ought to be dead!"

She flashed him a look of razor sharpness but bit her tongue on something she was about to say.

Hartman told her she could find bandages and antiseptic in a box in the kitchen. She brought them and began to lay them out on a table nearby. Then she brought hot water and watched Hartman bathe the wounds and apply the antiseptic with gentle hands.

"Now, Mandie, you go to your room or outside for a while. I'll look at the rest of him."

"Surely, Pa." She smiled and went out of the house. Endicott was now perched atop a cedar pole taking long drags on a cigarette. She joined him.

Booger came in after a while. He nodded to Hartman, who had finished his nursing work and was rocking with a scowl on his face.

"No tracks. He covered up real good."

Dunlee groaned his disappointment.

"Couple of things, though," Booger added. "Back of the scrub oak, a boot toe had pressed agin the bark of a dead limb lyin' on the ground. The boot mashed through the soft bark. It had a broad toe, wider than most of the boots you see around here. Bucher wears wide-toed boots. So does Endicott.

"Somethin' else . . . a small, stub branch close to the limb you must've been reachin' for by the bank. It was snapped almost off recent as today, jest hangin' loose. My bet is, his sleeve snagged on it as he came at you. The sleeve might have a snag or tear."

"That's sharp work," Dunlee returned. "Don't breathe this . . . to anybody."

"Much obliged, Booger. We can all keep our eyes open." Hartman seemed strangely detached, his thoughts ranging far and deep. Booger went out to scout farther around for tracks. He led a zebra dun out of a corral and put his rig on while Endicott and Teresa talked with him.

Dunlee raised up on an elbow and glanced out the front window across the room on the north.

"Teresa's talking with Booger. Three to one she's turning on her charm. Trying to entice any word out of him on what he found. Booger, he won't say. You can count on him." He settled back to rest as Hartman continued to gaze toward the corrals. Finally, Hartman sauntered out to doctor a cow.

Lying there thinking about the morning's events, Dunlee suddenly got an idea. Teresa knew the details of Mandie's early childhood because Mandie had told her all about it. Or . . . she'd studied Mandie's diary. Mandie had mentioned that she had written a lot of things there.

On a hunch, Dunlee limped to Teresa's room. He left the door slightly open so he could see past the open front door out to the corrals.

Her suitcase sat on a table. He found it locked. Given a little time he could open it, but he decided to check around the room first.

A hasty check of the dresser drawers turned up nothing. The drawer of a small lamp table proved the same. He glanced toward the corrals again, saw Hartman talking with the two. A search of the closet was unsuccessful.

Then his eyes fell on the bedspread. It was slightly wrinkled, with a faintly noticeable impression from a body. Teresa had lain on the bed since it had been made that morning. He looked around for any reading material nearby but found only the fashion catalogue she had brought from Virginia. He lifted the mattress and felt beneath it. Then he checked the floor under the bed, and slid his fingers beneath the pillows.

Again he checked the scene at the corrals. Hartman was taking some salve to doctor some cuts on one of his cows. Endicott and Teresa were following, for he had emphatically motioned them to come along. Teresa glanced back toward the house and walked along with reluctance.

"She's worried at me being in the house alone," he surmised with satisfaction. It did him good despite the hurting in his limbs. "Maybe . . . maybe she doesn't want anyone to get ideas about looking in here. What is it, woman, that you're fretting about?"

He let his eyes rove around the room as he paced about, racking his brain for a place to look. A place that might turn up something interesting. The floor

creaked a bit. Then he saw it . . . an almost impercep-
tible rise near the edge of the bearskin rug under a
small table over along the wall by the closet. He lifted
the edge of the rug by the wall. His fingers closed on
a flat, thick object. The diary!

Mandie's name was on the cover. As he leafed
through it he saw entries dating back many years.
Then he saw a bookmark, and checked the pages
there. As his eyes scanned those pages, they stopped,
went back, and read a second time.

> . . . the Indians came to kill us and steal our horses.
> I saw lots of them. Pa had three rifles and some
> other guns. He was shooting. Some of our men
> were shooting Indians from the bunkhouse. The
> way they yelled was awful. Ma and me just lay
> on the floor where Pa said to. Then the Indians
> went away. Pa said they would come back. He
> yelled for me and Ma to go out through the cellar
> to the cave he had showed me. I could show Ma
> where it was, and we could hide. . . .

Dunlee imagined Mandie as a little girl, scrib-
bling down the events she had just witnessed. The
entry went on to describe how they had run to the
cave. Hearing the Indians returning, Sheila had fainted
just inside the cave entrance. Mandie had covered her
with dead brush, then had run to the other end of the
tunnel.

Mandie's description of the tunnel's location was
precise. Anyone who read it could probably find the
hiding place with little effort. Dunlee frowned.

He was about to place the bookmark back inside when something else caught his eye. In the margin next to the reference to the cave was a small pencil check. He held the open diary up to the sunlight coming from the window, and noticed that the page bore impressions left by something sharp—perhaps a woman's nails thumping the paper while she was deep in thought.

Dunlee looked out. Nobody was approaching. Satisfied, he paged through the diary looking for other pencil marks in the margin. But no others were there. He closed the diary, pushed it back under the bearskin, and left Teresa's door closed as before.

He lay on the couch and picked up *The New Mexican*, a newspaper that Hartman had brought from Santa Fe. But his mind was full of his new discovery. It all made sense. Teresa had snitched Mandie's diary. It was loaded with personal information to help her play her little game. Her gold-digging instinct had led her to the entry mentioning a cave . . . a place only Mandie and her father knew. He was sure Teresa suspected that place to be as likely as any Hartman might choose to hide gold. But not knowing where that cave was, she had alerted her partner. He had watched for a chance to follow Hartman . . . to the exact place or close enough to narrow the search.

Dunlee believed Endicott was the one who had rapped him on the head. He was certainly the prime suspect. But whoever had done it had probably looked down into the gully and figured the victim was dead. Or he had been frightened away before he could climb down and finish him off. And so he had slipped away fast before Hartman might see him up there.

If the man was Endicott, he must have passed near the cave. Then he had seen Dunlee coming. The fact that Dunlee had left his broncs to come out to meet Hartman might cause him to wonder. Had Hartman told Dunlee where the gold was? Well, if Endicott suspected Dunlee knew, his fear of Dunlee spoiling the scheme was more important than the chance that Dunlee might lead him unwittingly to the cache. Bashing out the life of the man who knew Teresa would be all-important. It would insure the ongoing of the deceit. Perhaps the opportunity that presented itself was too choice to let slip through his fingers.

Dunlee decided to urge Hartman to post a hidden lookout along the southern ridge, just west of the pass. The lookout location might be kept secret from all except the guard, Hartman, and Dunlee. As sorely as Hartman needed his few men for other work, that move might prove invaluable. If Hartman or his waddy should catch Endicott snooping over there it could be highly embarrassing to the Virginian. And it would open Hartman's eyes even wider.

Dunlee's priority now, however, was to meet the real Mandie and to fetch her back. Her sudden appearance, coming as a shock to Teresa and to Endicott, would provide the great clincher. Then the deceivers would not be able to leave fast enough.

He heard footsteps on the porch planks, and twisted about to look at Endicott and Teresa. Teresa held her man's coat draped over one arm. Endicott, who nodded and smiled coldly, wore pointed boots. Dunlee distinctly remembered he had worn broad-toed boots that morning that had left tracks south of the house.

Dunlee spoke casually to Teresa. She was moving toward her room.

"Something happen to the coat?"

"Oh, no." But he detected a slight catch in her voice, as if taken by surprise. "I just need to brush it. Things get a bit dusty out by the corrals, you know."

"Sure. They get torn, too. A rip, a snag, or a button popped off."

"Oh, no problem with that here." She hastened into her room. Almost instantly she was back at the door. "Why, of course, I do remember. Your shirt—it's torn. I'll mend it after supper. I should have offered earlier."

Endicott ignored her and stalked into his room.

Dunlee's advice about a guard made quick sense to Hartman. He assigned Booger and Coot to take turns patrolling the strip of the pass close by. But they were to make rides a half mile or so west now and then so as not to pull the attention of Bucher and the rest to the one small area of the murder attempt.

Still sore, Dunlee handled lighter work the next day. Luckily, he was walking with only a slight limp, and his cuts would heal beneath the new sets of bandages.

A rider came from town early that evening. It was Zeke Hester, with another telegram for Hartman.

"It's for your daughter, so I was told," said Hester.

Teresa opened it in front of Hartman and Dunlee on the porch. "Well, it's no secret," she smiled after finishing it. She passed it on to Hartman and he in turn to Dunlee.

All well here. We miss you, Mandie, but stay long as you desire. Concerned that you are safe and happy. Teresa.

"Interesting move," Dunlee whispered later to Hartman when the two were alone. "They're running scared that I might persuade you otherwise. Tricks like this are supposed to make them look just right."

"Yeah. Doggone it, even if she's not Mandie, she's been the spice of my life since she got here. I never was treated so nice in my life. It ain't easy to wait this out. Still, I'm game. I don't like bein' made a fool. I'm hankerin' for Mandie to get here. We can have this thing out, bust the lid wide open. When do you leave to meet the stage?"

"If I leave in the mornin' I'll get there in plenty of time. They'll come by train to Denver, then on to Pueblo, in the Colorado territory. Then they'll get the stage through Raton Pass, and on to the Clifton House. I can watch the stage road but go a bit farther than the Clifton House, where Pugley's bunch will be. There's Willow Springs where the driver always pulls up to give the horses a drink and a short breather after coming from Wootton's toll road through the pass.

"I'll be hid out and able to see through my field glasses if our people are there. Luke, he'll probably hop off to stretch his legs the least chance he gets. He'll be easy to spot.

"Pugley and his sidekicks will make their bid somewhere just north or south of the Clifton House. I figure they'll be disguised. Tom Stockton's in charge at the Clifton House. A good man. They won't try bucking him and his men. If I can beat them to the stage, I'll have a good start to get into the rough country to the southwest. With Luke and Tom along we'll make it back all right. I'll need five horses. One'll be a packhorse for their baggage."

"How'll I explain your bein' gone?" wondered Hartman. "Ah, I'll just say you're deliverin' horses for me. That's what you will be doin'—deliverin' 'em to Luke an' the others. But nobody else needs to know the whole story."

"No, they figure they have *us* fooled. We're not supposed to know Mandie's on her way. But they want the gold, and they may decide this plan of Teresa posing as Mandie is too slow. If they switch to some quicker way to the gold, a way that involves killing, Endicott won't hold back. And Teresa, with the lure of gold dust in her mind's eye, may not balk very long at it either. You'll have to be ready for anything. I'd keep most of the men close by.

"One thing'll help. Put Coot on the ridge tonight, not Bucher. And let Coot know I'll be leaving mighty early. I'll ride toward Cimarron, then cut back east once I get into rocky country. I can lose anyone that tries trailing me."

"Works jest right," Hartman nodded as he heard Teresa coming up from the cellar. "It's Coot's night to ride guard up there anyhow."

17

Dunlee spent a day and a half on the trek to the crossing. The distance of nearly fifty miles was, in Cimarron language, "just a little piece." Still, he was weary of handling four extra horses through rugged, ascending country. There had been many stops and vigilant precautions to avoid riding into trouble with wandering Utes or Apaches or even far-ranging Comanches from the Oklahoma Panhandle who would be greatly tempted by the fine horses. He picketed the animals in a hilltop glen well-hidden by aspens, ponderosas, spruce and heavy brush. From there he could gaze down the slope and across a meadow a half-mile to Willow Springs. With his field glasses he would be able to see the stage moving along a ridge road a mile away before it descended to the springs.

He hoped he could pass the time quietly without having to wait too many days for the right stage. A coach would come daily. He had arrived on Sunday, late in the afternoon.

Stripping the gear from the horses, he gave them all a good rubdown with tufts of the plenteous grass on the knoll. Then he dug out some jerky, got a fire going beneath limbs that would spread and dissipate the smoke, and heated water. The meat—combined with coffee, fluffy dried biscuits, and berry preserves—tasted good.

As he lay on his bedroll gazing up at the limbs and blue sky, he was thankful. Much of the sharp soreness was gone from his body. Even so, he was dead tired from the trek.

At the Lobo Gulch station Harbin had set venison, pinto beans, and coffee before him. Then the old man leaned his elbows on the table and talked with a disapproving shake of his head.

"They shore was here. Five of 'em. Same bunch that was here before, jest one different. Pugley did most of the talkin', then Trowling. They said a lot in low tones I couldn't catch. Kept glancin' like they didn't want me to come up suddenlike an' hear. Whatever it was, it was bad."

"You say they did mention goin' to the Clifton House?"

"Yep. Couple of 'em was laughin' about some women they hankered to see. Bad women, moved in somers near Stockton's stop to lure trail crowds. Goodnight an' others have trailed a lot of cattle through, as you know. Pugley jest grinned an' said, '*Them* women you can have. Jest save the special one for me.' What are they plannin', Dunlee?"

"Trying to take a woman and two men off a stage," Dunlee replied between bites. "If they got their hands on them. . . ." He winced and drained the coffee cup.

"I've seen mean ones in my day, but Pugley and Trowling are as low-down as they come. Pugley can cut a man like a meat cleaver with that whip, and he's bloodthirsty. Besides, he's the foulest scum with women. Trowling's only a step behind. They lay their paws on whatever they want. You'd find more mercy in a drooling timber wolf slinking in after a tender calf."

Dunlee lounged on the hill. He hoped he had outsmarted the five who had passed the stage station ahead of him. They should be an hour's ride or so behind him now, waiting somewhere near the Clifton House . . . he hoped. Probably they would make their try shortly before the stage reached the Clifton House, or shortly after it left. Or they might plan to distract Stockton, who ran the House, long enough to grab the passengers.

The Barlow and Sanderson stage wound its way along the ridge road down from Raton Pass and on to Willow Springs. As Dunlee played the glasses on the coach windows his face twisted in disappointment. He'd have to wait for the next stage. He watered the horses at a creek and picketed them where they could graze on the lush grass. Then he ate wild berries and read a copy of *David Copperfield*, which he'd bought on his way from Virginia.

The next stage was late. He waited anxiously, his glasses lifting again and again to the farthest spot where he would catch a glimpse of it. The wait was beginning to wear at him.

Then, when the driver was nearly an hour behind schedule, Dunlee detected a movement between some blotches of aspen and riveted the glasses on the area. It was the red stage. The driver was keeping the four horses at a lope, trying to make up some of the lost time.

233

Training the glasses on the windows, Dunlee strained to make out a clue. At this distance, and with the vehicle moving, it was hard to tell. Some of the dust whipped up by the horses' hooves drifted back in puffs that obscured his sight of the window. Once in a while, harder-packed stretches of the road cut down on the dust. Dunlee thought he saw a woman's dress and hat, then a man's arm pointing from a window.

Two people . . . maybe more. The coach veered almost directly toward him and came on toward Willow Springs. Something within him whispered this was it. Having saddled the horses just in case, he now mounted the black and rode toward the springs. He kept well hidden by trees and brush, and threaded his way with vigilant eyes to all sides. Others too might be watching the springs area.

When he was a few hundred yards from the stage he saw a long arm pointing at a buck darting into the brush. Then he saw the face of a man leaning out a window.

A black man! Tom Jackson? It certainly looked like him. The driver hauled back on the reins to bring the foam-flecked horses to a stop.

Mandie had been talking with a middle-aged woman who had also gotten on the stage at Pueblo, having in tow a small, cotton-haired boy.

"I'm Lenora Stowers," the woman smiled. "This is Billy, my son. He's five. We're going to join his father, my husband. He'll be waiting with a wagon. He's a fur trapper."

"Oh, a rough trip but a short one," Mandie returned the smile. "It's nice to meet you, Billy. You'll soon be a young man."

"I'm already a young man." The boy was emphatic. "Pa knows."

"Are *you* going far?" Mrs. Stowers inquired.

"Not much farther. To Cimarron. We've come from Virginia ... such a long journey, by train to Denver, then Pueblo, and now by stagecoach." She introduced Luke and Tom, then seized the siderailing when the violent coach bounced her against the ceiling. The driver had vowed to make up the time lost fixing a wheel on Dick Wootton's rugged trail through Raton Pass. He was blistering the road like a rabbit a jump ahead of a flash flood.

The conversation lagged as they became absorbed with the scenic grandeur. Mandie also was preoccupied with other thoughts.

Could there be an attempt to grab them off the stage? It made sense, for the plotters had already taken drastic measures in Virginia. And Dunlee's telegram had sounded ominous.

Mandie was quite worn down by the ride from Pueblo. All the things she had remembered from a seven-year-old's experience of travel were nearly unbearable now: the dust that seemed to coat her with thin grime from head to toe, the jolting and the lurching, especially on the rocky stretch through Raton Pass, the foul language of the driver and shotgun guard when they forgot ladies were near.... Her ankles and knees ached from bracing herself endlessly to keep from being pitched into somebody's lap. Her legs, feeling cramped, would welcome a chance to stretch.

The driver, a jovial and decent man on the ground, seemed transformed into a madman once exalted to his throne of authority above. She wondered if her headache would ever subside, her stomach ever feel settled again.

"Just bottle me and serve me for jelly—with a dash of dust for flavoring," she had laughed to Luke and Tom after the wheel was fixed and they bounced on through the toll road Wootton had cleared. They had been forever fetching her bandanas or cloths, dampened and cooled from canteens to bathe her face and arms. They were standing up to the trip better than she. Luke, however, had bragged that she was a good traveler compared to many he'd witnessed on his trip east.

"Tomorrow we'll see your pa an' Dunlee," Luke said presently. The stage careened wildly around a curve, and she was amazed for the hundredth time that the wheels stayed on. "Just down there," Luke pointed, "we'll stop at Willow Springs. Water the horses an' give them a short breather. I'll get us outta here for a couple minutes, even if the driver howls."

Grateful, she looked forward to the opportunity to walk about, to dip her feet in a stream from the springs, to splash water on her face and bathe her neck. The thought drifted in the midst of her headache that she should be thankful for her blessings . . . Dunlee was not around to see her now!

The coach streaked down the slope, and the springs seemed to swing across the terrain to meet them. Then the stage lurched to a halt, the body rocking on the thoroughbraces. Luke hit the ground even before it had stopped. Tom stepped down, too, suddenly cut loose with a tremendous whoop, and went berserk with excitement.

"Mistah Dunlee! Mistah Dunlee!"

Mandie turned in the seat, felt her breath catching in her throat, a strange sensation leaping up within her breast. What on earth could Tom mean? He couldn't mean. . . .

Luke was dragging a rider off his horse, a familiar-looking black horse, and giving him a tremendous bear hug. Tom was grabbing his arm, beside himself for joy. Then the rider looked toward her. She gasped an exultant gasp. Dirt or no dirt. . . .

"Marks!"

He tore loose from the two men and grabbed her waist, lifting her gently to the sandy, deep-rutted roadway. He held her close for a moment, and she could not fight back the tears.

"You . . . you came to meet us!"

"Told you I would. Came to fetch you home. You've had enough of this coach. Your seat is a saddle from here on."

The driver, a weather-beaten man with a chaparral of long, dark whiskers, took in the scene. He grunted approval, once assured all was well. The shotgun guard, having dropped to the ground, went over and doused his face.

"Luke," Dunlee said, "take the black and fetch the horses from that hill yonder." Luke grabbed the reins and swung up. He was elated to hit the saddle again. He tore off across the meadow at full gallop. In three or four minutes he was back leading the other horses.

"When you get to the Clifton House, or somewhere close," Dunlee said to the driver and guard, "you'll find five men wanting to do harm to this lady and her escorts. They're a mean outfit. Just forget these passengers were on the stage." The men nodded. Dunlee stepped over to the woman and the boy.

"Ma'am, I hope the rest of your journey will be pleasant. There's a mean bunch dead set on jerking this lady and our friends away from the stage. We'll be obliged if you don't let on that these were on the stage."

"Why, yes," Lenora Stowers agreed. "If she says it's all right."

Mandie assured her all was proper, and Mrs. Stowers' face took on a firm resolve to help. Billy, temporarily free from her grip, turned from watching Luke and Tom strap valises on the pack animal.

"Mommy, is this a holdout . . . I mean a holdup?"

"No, no, Billy. Just a man who came to take our friends home on his horses. It's all right." He endorsed that with a pleased look, and pressed closer to her, a bit sheepish.

The driver, anxious to be off, popped his whip with a loud crack above the rumps of the lead horses. The team surged forward and the coach sloshed free of a stream, spinning water with it. In seconds it was racing far away.

Dunlee briefed his friends on the plot. They grasped why he had met them so far from Cimarron.

"I know you're tired," he said gently to Mandie, "and I wish I could let you rest a spell. But our best bet is to lose ourselves deep in the hills by sundown. We can rest where it's safe."

Mandie understood. No complaints, though she

looked like a faded rose. She was game to do what had to be done. Dunlee saw in her more of Shoat than Sheila.

He touched her chin with a gentle finger and smiled. "At a time like this, you respond just the way I had you pictured. To be made of Shoat Hartman stock is something. I mean something!"

He hoisted her into the saddle of a dark bay, then swung up into his own saddle. Bringing the black alongside her, he led off. Luke and Tom brought up the rear, Luke handling the packhorse.

"Our aim," Dunlee explained, "is to strike out due west. After a while we'll cut south, where we won't leave tracks. Try to throw off any trackers . . . at least enough to put them farther behind."

Three hours later they had pierced far into the shadowed hills. Many valleys, mesas, and tortuous canyons—as well as clumps of trees and brush— would make it difficult for anyone to find them.

Anybody but the uncanny Trowling, he thought grimly.

As the sun was sending the last flickers of golden light to the slope east of them, Dunlee stopped the party in a deep basin overhung by ponderosas and surrounded by brush. He felt this place would be safe for the night. There were some good lookout points to hear any riders approaching.

Luke shot three rabbits. They roasted the meat and ate eagerly. Dunlee pulled some stale biscuits, dried apples, and berry preserves from his pack and shared these. Luke had bought some hard candy in Denver, and he took it out for all to enjoy. The horses fed on knee-high grama and drank from a pool in the rocks, fresh from a heavy shower that morning.

Dunlee spread out a blanket for Mandie on a mattress of leaves. He unrolled other blankets to keep her warm against the chill of the night. Her bed was beside the steep bank of shale and rock, overhung by thick brush that formed a natural canopy against rain. Above that, the limbs of a ponderosa spread out a greater roof.

"You all get some sleep," Dunlee urged. "I'll be on guard for a while. Then I'll roust you, Tom. After a couple of hours you give it over to Luke, then get some more rest yourself. Luke, we want to be up by four so we can be on our way. Get a fire going and heat coffee. We'll eat light tomorrow, but we'll manage on hardtack, biscuits, berries, and wild onions. We can't risk any shots to get meat, since they draw attention. Maybe we can club a wild turkey."

He glanced toward the girl in the dim light of the dying fire. Already she had dropped into a sound sleep. Good. He climbed up to the lip of the basin, and sought a rock beside a ponderosa trunk. Propping himself against the tree, he sat for a long time, listening. He didn't expect any of Pugley's group this soon, but Utes and Apaches might be prowling. He'd known them to slip up on a camp in the most remote places. The mounts would be a prize.

The horses cropped nearby. Watching these sensitive animals, listening for their reactions to night sounds, was a big help. The longer he waited into the night, the better he felt about the safety of his group. An owl hooted from an aspen across the basin, and a coyote barked its sad sentiments in a nearby haunt. Once he saw the dark form of an antelope flitting through the brush on a hillside.

He wondered how successful the stage men had been in hiding the fact that Mandie had been on the coach. If Pugley did not realize she had been on that coach, tomorrow would be safe. If he had found out the trick, his killers would be combing the land for sight or track of their prey.

And if they found them? His group would be up against it, outnumbered five men to three.

18

The driver brought the stage to a dust-swirling stop at the Clifton House on the Canadian River. Climbing down, the shotgun guard flung open the stage door and reached to help the young boy down, then his mother.

A man in buckskin stepped up to greet the two passengers. He swept up the boy in one arm and flung the other around the woman, who came eagerly into his welcoming embrace.

Two men crowded right behind him, peering in at the three seats of the empty coach. Their faces were hard and unshaven. Low-slung guns rode their right thighs. They threw disgruntled glances from the coach to the shotgun man. One discharged a huge stream of tobacco juice toward the rear wheel of the Concord and grabbed the guard by the shoulder as he started to turn to go into the House. The three-story place now served the stage line but continued to cater to roundup crews, trail hands, and trappers. Stockton had established it in 1867.

"We're 'spectin' a young lady an' two men," the man grated as if spitting out nails.

"Well, they ain't no such here, you can see," the guard returned. His jaw set firmly, his voice definite but not unfriendly.

"Hey, Jib, what is it?" asked a stocky man who seemed built as powerful as a bull. He had just crossed the street from the stable. The way he spoke left no doubt that he called the shots for Jib and his companion. A curled bullwhip was mounted on one hip, tied with a thong in its holster. Beneath it a revolver with a polished wooden handle was slung at his thigh.

"They ain't here," Jib flung back over his shoulder. His voice was heavy with irritation.

Pugley's eyes raked the guard up and down.

"You seen a lady from Virginia an' two men? Maybe they stayed over to rest up at Pueblo?"

"No, ain't nary a lady an' no two men that stayed over," the guard replied firmly. "All's we do is haul passengers. We don't make 'em appear."

"You don't say?" Pugley sneered. He was irritated by the long wait and lack of success.

The boy, set down on the ground by his father, turned with a flush of importance to the men. He stood up to the guard.

"Don't you 'member? The lady and the men got off at the springs when the horses drank," he blurted. The guard had plain forgotten, and he could save the day!

"Billy!" his mother reproved, grabbing to put her hand over his mouth. It was an instinctive reaction. She glanced up into the leering face of the bullwhip man. He had planted both feet in the dust and was eyeing her as a cat that has just trapped a mouse.

"Afternoon, ma'am. That there's quite a boy. Now, tell us all about it. All about it."

"Why, I . . . I. . . ." She groped with a fluster of thoughts.

"Mommy, you know the purty lady with the black man and. . . ." Billy was saving the day again! Why couldn't these grownups remember better, or just come out with it?

"Ahh!" Pugley's bellow was triumphant. "You're doin' good, boy. Now, ma'am, beggin' your pardon, but I'm losin' my patience. You fetch me that information about the lady and the men. I want it now!"

"Here, now," the woman's husband cut in. His face flashed with an impatience of his own. "A man don't speak to my wife that way."

Pugley scarcely noticed him. He simply brought his massive arm up in a sudden swing, caught the man's jaw with the back of his hand, and knocked him sprawling on his back. Stunned, the man shook his head and struggled to come to his senses.

Lenora Stowers gasped. Drawing her hand to her mouth in consternation, she knelt to help her man. The guard started to bring up his gun on Pugley, but two men shouldered up, grabbing his arms and jerking him back.

Pugley glowered down at the woman. Then he pressed his fist against the throat of the guard. Another of his men blocked the path of the driver, who had started to back the shotgun man.

"Now," Pugley thundered, "you cough up that information fast, or you'll wish you had."

"Go to blazes." The guard had fire in his eyes.

The two men slammed him back against the door, which banged shut.

"No, stop it," Mrs. Stowers shrilled. "This has

gone far enough. The woman got off at Willow Springs after the pass. A man met her and the two with her. He had horses."

Pugley erupted with a deep-throated curse, and spat into the dust. His face burned with fury at the sting of being outfoxed.

"What man? What'd he look like?"

"They called him Dan . . . no, Dunlee. He rode a big black horse." Mrs. Stowers felt cheap, sick, and disgusted with herself. But she wanted to be away from this scene, to have her man clear of the destruction she feared these men would wreak on him if he reasserted himself. She rationalized that the young lady and the men were too far away by now to be in danger.

"Hey, Max, you need help?"

Pugley and his men spun about to see Tom Stockton and two men from a trail-herd bunch appraising the situation from the doorway. Stockton raised a shotgun, and the cowboys each held a Colt .44 trained at the troublemakers' stomachs.

"No, he don't need no help," Pugley growled. "We got what we wanted to know." He and his men stomped toward the stable where saddled horses switched at flies. A minute later their horses' hooves droned northward toward Willow Springs. Pugley halted the men a minute up from the House.

"Dunlee's got a big start," he yelled. "But we can head him off. He won't know we found out. He'll be workin' his way west somewhere northwest of here. That lady ain't up to travelin' long, so they'll stop for the night. Jib, you ride due west—fast. Sweep the country for sign of 'em. The rest of us will head northwest, spread out, an' cover a big strip."

Jib Slackett rode off, the other four watching him go.

"Let me make one thing clear, boys," Pugley said. "Do whatever suits your fancy with the others. But deliver me Dunlee an' the little lady—alive. Hear me ... alive! They's a bonus of fifty bucks for the man that spots 'em first. I've got special plans for them two."

They saw his fingers curl about the stock of his whip. The sign had Dunlee written all over it. They already knew what he craved of the woman ... but they were unlike most men, who honored the code of the west. They didn't care.

After two hours of steady travel through the early morning, Dunlee glanced at the rim of the sun peeking over the blue-shadowed western peaks. It was six o'clock by his watch.

He rode ahead, probing the terrain for any sign of Indians or others. The way birds act can alert a watchful man, as can the movement of a deer, a mountain goat, or a wild mustang. He knew he had to be prepared for the worst.

He had to assume that the whipmaster had somehow found out about his move. It wasn't likely, but a vigilant man stays alive by being ready. And if the bully from Virginia had gotten wind of the trick, he would figure the group's head start and count on Mandie being able to ride only a limited distance into the night. He'd probably thrust his human bloodhounds west and northwest. They'd spread out over the land, peering from ridges and knolls commanding wide expanses. They'd scan the gullies, the buffalo wallows, the trees, and clumps of brush.

Dunlee swung the black around and threw up a hand to halt the group.

"We're going on due south," he announced. "I know how to zigzag through by way of hills, canyons, and draws where they won't be liable to sight us from one of the hills. I'll scout ahead to check things out. Tom, you follow a couple stone-throws back. Luke, you come with Mandie about the same distance behind Tom. Keep your eyes open every second."

Two hours later, much further to the south, Dunlee waved Tom on. Together they waited for the others to catch up.

"Pugley's men are farther south, if they're on to us at all," he said. "Least that's how I figure it. We'll rest here a few minutes. That'll give me a chance to meander over to that butte and study the country for miles around."

He rode off, keeping his mount to the high brush as much as possible, halting now and again to scan the butte with the glasses. He had wrapped a bandana around them to prevent the sun from gleaming on the metal and giving away his presence. That morning they had all torn strips from blankets to cover any metal on their rigs that might reflect the light. The men let their shirts hang loose to hide their belt buckles, guns, and cartridge belts. Dunlee had stuffed his spurs in his saddlebag.

An antelope suddenly scurried up from the brush ahead of him and bounded across the prairie circling the butte. Dunlee lingered in a deep arroyo, flanked by steep walls and overhung by brush. He climbed to a spot where he could probe the butte again. He was now only a couple hundred paces off from the northwest corner. The butte jutted up at least two hundred feet.

Nothing moved . . . nothing except a prairie dog scratching out sand on a ledge high up along the rock base of the butte. Then he heard the rattle of a rock tumbling somewhere up there. A startled dove fluttered up along the far height of the butte. Dunlee studied that area. In a rocky niche high up, he thought he saw the shape of a man's hat, a dark gray. Then it moved, pulled out of sight.

He got the black and went on cautiously, using the tall brush to shield him. He was sure he'd seen a hat, perhaps taken off and laid on a rock while a man let his head cool off in the shade.

He led the black close to the wall. Then he tied the reins to an aspen.

Inside a hollow of rock that jutted up more than twenty feet, stood a claybank horse. It had been left at the base of a cavelike seclusion in the butte, and was waiting on three legs, tail switching. Dunlee saw a steep pathway up through a crevice, and understood how the man had climbed near the top.

This was an excellent chance to get the drop on one of Pugley's searchers. He could force the man to go along with his own group. He pocketed a fistful of stones he might use as diversions later, and stealthily climbed the path.

He was two-thirds to the top where he believed the man was stationed when he heard a sudden creak behind him. It was like the sound of new boot leather being bent. Too late, he twisted about to gape into the barrel of a Winchester '73 not ten feet away. Behind the rifle was a wiry man wearing a dark-gray Stetson. He was flattened against a sloping rock wall within a side crevice Dunlee had not realized was there.

Intent on reaching the top unheard, he had expected his enemy to be lurking somewhere above.

The man's face wrinkled in a wicked grin. Two huge buckteeth protruded over the man's lower lip like tiny upside-down buttes.

"You're obligin', friend," the captor gloated. "You jest earned me a bonus. Reach down real careful an' fetch your gunbelt over here. One wrong move an' you've got a long way to drop."

Dunlee recognized him as one of the men he'd disarmed and set afoot at Lobo Gulch that night.

"Been itchin' for a chance at you," bucktooth said, and cackled. "Maybe I'll get my chance after Pugley's had the turn he craves. He spoke first for you. Wants you real bad. Wants to do some cuttin'— the bullwhip kind."

"Good thing we split up," Dunlee drawled, as if greatly relieved. He did not know if the man had spotted the others with him. "At least all you get is me. The others will be safe, like we figured."

The man's face tightened just a bit. Dunlee sensed that the words had hit home. His captor had not spotted him with the others.

"We'll see," the man said in a low, threatening growl. "First, you lay down, head pointin' down, across that slab of rock. Stretch your arms in front of you." When Dunlee complied, the man cautiously hunted for a shoulder holster or any other weapons. He pulled out a Bowie knife.

Then the outlaw followed him down to the hollow in the butte where the claybank waited. That's when he struck Dunlee with his pistol butt and dropped him unconscious on the rocky floor of the aperture.

19

Luke hunkered down on a rock near the ravine, well-hidden from the butte by the branches of a piñon.

"He's checkin' things out," he told Tom and Mandie. They rested in the shade of the bank below him, refreshed by the coolness of sand they had dug up. "He went around the butte on foot. He'll be back around directly."

A few minutes later he sprang up.

"He's givin' us the signal to come on over an' join 'im."

Tom crawled up and saw the figure standing a few feet up on the northeast face of the butte, waving them in with broad sweeps of his hat. The black hat, blue shirt, and black pants were clear enough.

"Sho 'nuff," the black man nodded. "He skinned up high an' saw all's clear. Ah feels bettah already."

They started out, riding straight in, and saw Dunlee bringing his black around the butte to the south side.

Luke and Tom swung down near the hollow in the rock, while Dunlee, half-hidden behind the black, was apparently adjusting his cinch, his hat brim down and a rifle cradled in his right arm. They were coming around behind the rump of the horse when the rifle swung up. A voice barked a command. It was neither Dunlee's voice nor Dunlee's face.

"Reach high!"

Luke stopped in his tracks, his mouth falling open in shock. Tom uttered a groan, and they both flung up their hands as they felt a sickening feeling in the pits of their stomachs. They were in trouble now. Bad trouble.

"On your knees, facin' the woman!" He stripped them of their guns, then made them belly down in the sand while he searched for other weapons. He also kept his eyes on Mandie, who sat as if petrified in her saddle. She was frightened by this man and what the capture meant. But she was more fearful for Dunlee. Where was he? Had the man struck him and let him plunge down that face of rock? Left him bleeding? The knife handle jutting from the leather case on the man's hip sent shivers through her.

When the captor had laced Luke's and Tom's hands to their saddlehorns with rawhide thongs, he bound Mandie's. Then a surge of relief shot through her when he went inside the rock hollow and brought out Dunlee. He was dressed in other clothes, the shirt still hanging open. Mandie bit her lip when she saw blood on Dunlee's hair and neck, but thanked God that he was alive. Judging from his groggy stagger to the black, she surmised that the man had clubbed him.

She shuddered. Her mind flashed back to her childhood, when Comanche braves whipped through the ranchyard raising blood-curdling yells. That same sense of terror shot within her now—the fear of what would happen if the raiders won. Now, this evil-looking man had already won. She groaned. She had paled at accounts of what befell women who came under the power of ruthless men. Or, for that matter, what happened to men who were taken.

They sliced southward in a beeline, their captor bringing up the rear. His ever-threatening rifle rested across his pommel.

As the black bore him onward across the miles, Dunlee's mind cleared. But his head still throbbed. A man of unusual prowess in the cavalry, known for his skill in stalking Indians or scouting their land without being entrapped, he had let himself be outmaneuvered here. And these friends, as well as Hartman, had counted on him.

A cold sensation, akin to terror, ran through his frame. As far as he could predict, Pugley and his cohorts would never risk turning them loose. In their lust for a cut from the gold, they would never let anybody free who might be their downfall. They would attend brutally to every detail.

And Mandie. . . . Besides abusing her by ruthless force, they could use her on a ransom offer in exchange for gold. This was the kind of leverage they had been waiting to find. Endicott could always arrange for it to look like the outlaws had grabbed Mandie. Teresa could conveniently disappear for a time, and Hartman might think she was Mandie. Or, if Hartman's eyes were fully open to the truth by now, and he knew it was in fact Mandie the outlaws had, all the better. Endicott could demand the gold, luring Hartman to some spot where he could meet him. And Hartman would turn over the gold because he loved Mandie so dearly. Then Hartman would die.

Dunlee felt fully responsible for their trouble. If only he had anticipated the trick this outlaw hit upon. He reminded himself that self-accusation would get him nowhere. It wasn't the first time he had failed. And he had gotten out of other tight places, often aware that the good Lord was at his side. He had to set his mind on a positive trail. He had to think, to pray, to reason things out, to look for a way that would work. Or it would be the last time he would ever fail.

Pugley had asked his men to rendezvous at a deeply-gouged canyon running west and east. The descent dipped into a broad, sandy wash slashed out through the land by rushing floodwaters.

They found a large cave there, above a broad ledge, shoulder-high to Dunlee astride his horse. There were signs that men had used it long before. Strewn about were rusty tin cans, tobacco pouches, a broken pick, and the faint remains of old fires.

The four prisoners were bound hand and foot and kept against the back wall of the cave, about fifteen feet from the face of the canyon wall.

Pugley and Trowling met and hunkered down on the shelf, greedily sizing up their catch. Pugley had just shelled out fifty dollars to Jib, making good on his bonus offer in a flush of prosperous celebration. The night before he had smarted from the sting of defeat. Now he savored the thrill of a conqueror. Never had he felt so high; he had Dunlee and Mandie in his hands. The other two did not matter. . . .

Pugley had often lain awake at night scheming to have Dunlee at his mercy like this. He would never forget the night Dunlee had wrenched the whip from his fingers and smashed him into the grass. Since then, Dunlee's escapes from Pugley's clutches and his stripping away the horses and guns at Lobo Gulch had driven the whipmaster to an insatiable craving for revenge. The sweet taste of it was now beginning to leave its savor.

As for the girl, out here in the lonely wastes amidst men of this raw breed, he could do all he desired. Back in Virginia, he had long followed her with lingering eyes.

He might have to answer to Endicott in the end. But out here he answered only to himself and his own impulses. He was king. If anybody questioned him he had the brute force and meanness to back it up. Even Trowling, a man of the gun more than of savage strength, knew he was the leader. Trowling had backed down a couple of times. And so Pugley answered only to Pugley.

An idea was now forming in his brain. He need not even answer to Endicott, come the final reckoning. . . .

"There they be," Trowling gloated. "Ain't she a sweet honey! Ow-eee! An' your man Dunlee . . . he don't look so tough. Jib brought in all four by hisself alone."

"Naw, he ain't so tough," Pugley scowled. A devilish meanness was aflame in his eyes and twisting his mouth. "After supper comes the fun. We'll strap him to yonder cottonwood," he said, jerking a thumb toward the floor of the canyon to the east. "An' Rube, you ain't never saw a man take the toughness out of another like I'm gonna do. When I get done workin' him over, he won't even be able to crawl—not even whisper—for mercy. Not that I'd give him any if he did."

"That's powerful hate. What about the other two?"

"Them?" Pugley's tone was one of contempt. "That one, he's a no-count nigger. I left him to look after my place, an' he run off out here. Workin' agin me! He won't be goin' back. Won't be goin' nowhere. He's one nigger that's done for.

"The other? He's runnin' with Dunlee, ain't he? That's enough to deserve the whip. But you men can have 'im. Jest finish 'im. Plug 'im, drag 'im, or stretch 'im from yonder limb. Makes me no matter. All's I want is Dunlee . . . after that the little honey."

The two drew immense pleasure from speaking their minds within earshot of the prisoners. They wanted to gloat over the reactions. Dunlee and Luke afforded them none. Their faces betrayed no emotions. Tom stared straight ahead, his eyes showing no sign of panic that would heighten their joy. But he was all churned up inside.

Only Mandie, who had seen little of violence since leaving the ranch long ago, was shaking. And though she fought bravely, tears coursed from both eyes down her peach-tinted cheeks. Dunlee heard her soft sob, and his lips drew tight.

"After supper, like I said," Pugley repeated. He patted his whipstock, and fingered the curls of the leather. They were as ominous as a rattlesnake coiled on his hip. "That deer Lasko shot has been skinned an' supper's roastin'. First we'll have a feast, then the fun."

He laughed coarsely at the prospect, and Trowling with him. Then they slouched away to the fire.

"Luke," Dunlee said in a low voice, "we can get out of here. You'll find a thin knife blade in a pocket along the inside of my left boot. Back up here, an' you can get your hands to it."

The ramrod breathed a great sigh of relief. His own thoughts had carried him back to Cimarron. He'd been remembering a special woman, wondering how she would deal with him never coming back. And right when the chance of a lifetime lay before them. . . . Now he rebuked himself for drifting off into self-pity. He needed the grit of Dunlee, the cool to think of a way.

"An old habit," Dunlee spoke again. Luke turned his back and fumbled at the boot. Since his wrists were tied behind him, it was difficult and painful to stretch the fingers into position to get at the blade.

Then Trowling's boot heels thudded on the shelf and Luke writhed away against the wall, as yet unsuccessful.

The outlaw sprawled back across a rock, took out some makings, and spun up a cigarette. He kept blowing smoke and letting his eyes drift time and again to relish the girl.

Jib came to spell Trowling. He, too, stared at the girl. After a while, however, it grew dark. Luke got into position to take out the blade under the cover of darkness. Then Pugley yelled.

"Hey, Jib, get 'em on their feet. Bring 'em down here now. Go help him, Gorse."

So they were seated near the fire on a fallen cottonwood limb. One of the men untied their hands, and covered them with a shotgun as they ate. Generous helpings of venison between slices of dry bread were passed out with coffee. Tin cups had to be shared.

As they ate, the men razzed Dunlee. They were hooting and hollering about the fun coming up.

"Here, have more meat," Gorse offered. "We want you nice an' satisfied. Once Pugley here gets at you, you ain't gonna be too satisfied." They savored that one with loud cackling.

Dunlee declined the extra food. Gorse wanted to stuff it in his mouth, but Pugley stopped him.

"Lay off, Gorse. You'll have plenty to enjoy later. Jib, saddle up an' take a message for me. I mean now." Jib gulped down the last of his food, chased it with some coffee, and went to slap his gear on a horse. Securing directions from Pugley, he rode out. He would inform Chenault or Bucher about the capture, and the message would get to Endicott.

"Take your boots off, Tom," Dunlee whispered, then asked the same of Luke. They looked questioningly at him but complied. He, too, removed his, and thrust his feet toward the fire.

"Hey, what's this?" Gorse demanded.

"No big thing," Dunlee replied matter-of-factly. "We always did it in Virginia. Makes the feet feel good after sweatin' in boots all day. Anybody knows that."

"Shore, don't do no good for the noses, though," Trowling put in, wrinkling his nose.

They went on talking for quite a while, some still stuffing. Finally, Pugley banged down his tin cup.

"Tie their hands behind 'em again," he commanded. "All 'cept Dunlee."

The leader stood up, took his whip loose, and aimed it at his cup set on a rock near the fire. His aim was dead center. The cup leaped off the rock into the sand.

"Lace him to the cottonwood, belly in," Pugley ordered. "Stretch his arms around the tree." Three men jerked Dunlee to his stocking feet and led him to the tree about fifty paces away, within the outer pale of the firelight. With ropes, they lashed his arms around the trunk, then each leg separately to the base of the tree, knees in. One of them roughly ripped his shirt off, leaving only shreds of it hanging to his arms.

All this time Pugley kept cracking his whip, getting his arm limbered.

Luke glanced at Mandie. She was horrified, scarcely able to believe her eyes. Pugley was inhuman. Then Luke slid down to the ground near Dunlee's boots. As soon as the men's attention was diverted. . . .

The men strode back from the cottonwood, and Pugley walked toward Dunlee, dragging part of the whip in the sand. As he cocked his arm, the three stood near the three prisoners by the fire, eager to gaze on the spectacle.

Luke's fingers found the boot and felt for the hard line of the blade. Ah, there. Tom stole a glance at him and edged over to help hide his movement from the men. Mandie saw what they were doing and prayed the plan would work. Her eyes darted around the circle of the fire to two rifles leaning against a bush, butts in the dirt, not ten feet away.

The whip cracked against the naked back. It drew blood from the ugly gash it cut. Dunlee's body stiffened, trembled, then slowly relaxed. But he did not give Pugley even the added pleasure of a groan.

"What'll it be, Dunlee?" Pugley hissed. "One for every step you made me walk from Lobo Gulch? Or one for every dollar you took off'n Endicott an' me?"

He laughed coarsely. Ah, this was his night. "Think you could mess with Pugley an' get away with it, eh, Dunlee?" The whip was poised to explode again against the bleeding flesh. The cocked arm was ready to punctuate that wicked laugh.

"What'll it be for you, Pugley?" Luke shouted. The four men wheeled to gape into the barrels of two rifles in the hands of Luke and Tom. "Will it be one bullet for every lash you planned to lay on him, or one for every time you've tried to do him in?"

Trowling sputtered a curse. He started to let his hand paw at his pearl-handled gun, then thought better. Gorse and Lasko stared from the two rifles to Pugley, then back, and grasped the hard facts. All of them slowly lifted their hands skyward.

Pugley gazed as if stupefied. His whip hand was still poised but remained in the air as if made of marble. His lower lip curled down in a vicious snarl of disgust.

"That's a good pose. Hold her right there, an' don't give or take an inch or I'll blast you out from under it," Luke rasped. "Get that other arm up there, too. Quick!"

Luke felt carefully to slash Mandie's thongs, never taking his eyes or gun off the men. "Now," he said to the girl, "go cut Dunlee loose, and take him his rifle. Walk way out around those skunks."

She fled to Dunlee and went to work on the ropes.

"See here, we can make us a deal," Pugley whined. He started to take a step toward Luke.

Trowling had been inching back toward a fallen limb that was almost as thick as his body. He suddenly flung himself into a dive for it as his hand streaked toward his revolver. Luke shot him through the side as he dropped, and Trowling was dead before he hit the ground. Gorse saw the blurred move of Trowling and reacted on impulse, pawing for his gun, too. Dunlee, swinging about free and triggering the rifle Mandie had carried to him, hit Gorse in the chest and Tom's shot slammed the outlaw in the neck. He pitched backwards into the dust and lay still.

Pugley and Lasko kept their hands up, staring at the aftermath in stunned disbelief.

Dunlee rubbed his wrists and legs where the brutal riatas had gripped him. He swung his rifle on the two remaining outlaws. Now the odds had changed—three men against two. Mandie's hand felt soft and gentle as she took his left hand and led him back to the fire. He could feel the lash furrow in his back. Every step was painful.

Tom scurried to relieve the two live outlaws of their guns, then collected the weapons of the fallen men. He tied the hands of Pugley and Lasko behind them.

"It takes a low-down breed to stand behind a whip an' cut a man up when his hands an' feet are tied," Luke rapped at Pugley. "How good are you without those advantages? I'm gonna find out." He began to roll up his sleeves.

"No, Luke!" Dunlee cut in. "It was me he whipped. I have the privilege coming. Mandie, I want you to go sit on that shelf over there, with Tom. You won't want to watch this."

"Please," she replied. "I've watched fights before. I'm a big girl. I'd rather stay."

Pugley rubbed his fists when Luke untied his wrists. A glint of smugness began to shine in his eyes. Confident of his brute strength, he figured satisfaction was coming back.

"The other time you caught me with too much drink in me," he sneered at Dunlee. "You got in a lucky punch. This time, I'll mess you up in the front to match your back."

Dunlee remembered talk about Pugley winning some fights in Virginia, one in a challenge against a name boxer. But Dunlee had learned some things about boxing while in the cavalry.

Pugley swaggered in and flung a right with sledge-hammer force. But it never found its mark. Dunlee simply ducked under it and came up with a powerful right of his own. It caught Pugley squarely under the chin, lifted him off his toes, and flopped him like a bag of potatoes flat on his back. He lay sputtering, spitting blood from loosened teeth and cut lips. Shaking his head to clear it of a heavy fog, he came up on an elbow. Then he hauled himself up, rocked on his feet, and stalked around Dunlee more warily.

He shot a left jab that glanced off Dunlee's cheek, then bored in with a right. It landed on his opponent's chest and pounded him back a step. Then Dunlee threw a straight left that crunched Pugley's nose. Pugley shook his head like a maddened bull, wiped his nose on his sleeve, and surged in swinging. Dunlee stepped outside the intended blows and brought his left hand crashing into his foe's jaw. The punch was hard enough to fell a normal man . . . but Pugley was not normal.

He staggered back a couple of steps, winced as if

stung, then returned hammering for Dunlee's face. Dunlee sidestepped, and found Pugley's chin again with a rock-hard right, followed with a left jab to the jaw, then another right. Pugley grunted and flopped hard into the sand. This time he just lay sprawled out, knocked senseless. Or senseless as usual, but this time quiet about it.

Mandie came over and took Dunlee's arm.

"Come now, let me bathe that awful cut." He noted that she was surprisingly calm after what she'd just witnessed. Perhaps it was because she felt the same as he did. Pugley had needed to be knocked down several notches.

Tom had thrown more wood on the fire against the chilling breeze from Baldy and the Sangre de Cristos. Now he sat helping Luke guard the two outlaws with a rifle poised on a knee. Pugley, hands again tied behind him, sagged with his back to a log, chin drooping on his chest. His face was badly battered.

A few minutes later, with hot water ready, Mandie tenderly cleaned Dunlee's back. Then she took salve from her valise and applied it to the savage stripe. She bound the wound with gauze.

"You're different," the patient remarked. "Not like some of the eastern ladies that come out here—leastways when they first get here. You're not just made for the parlor but for the wide open spaces."

"Meaning . . . you approve?"

"I do!"

"Well, after all, I was born out here. I went through a Comanche attack. I've seen men die. I've learned to tend cows and calves that are sick or hurt. You learn fast when there's no one else to do it. You can't just sit back and watch."

"You mentioned the Indian attack," he said. "Did you know your diary is missing, with your description of that raid?"

"Why, yes. I couldn't find it when I was packing for the trip." She was puzzled. "How do you know that?"

"Teresa has it. She's been posing as you, and every little trick helps the masquerade. She's making that play with Endicott for your pa's gold. You know how gold can turn people's heads. The diary tells her what Mandie would know. I found it in her room. Had a marker at the page about the hidden cave, even put a pencil check beside it."

"This is so hard to believe," she said. "I know Teresa has a scalding hate for Pa. She's never forgiven him for beating her father into the street. But that was a fair fight. I never dreamed she would go so far."

"She's in it deep now," Luke spoke up. "Endicott had me drugged, an' his ape Porsen held me prisoner. I figure he'll try anything now to get at the gold. An' Teresa's in it all the way with him."

Dunlee explained Endicott's scheme for Pugley and his men to murder him, and how this had failed four times. He even mentioned Teresa's clever attempt to drug or poison him.

"I bet I know where Teresa got that idea," Mandie said. "One of Henri von Ehrencroft's sisters was suspected of using poison in three or four cases. They never could prove it for sure, but she had to leave because of the talk."

Dunlee told them about Endicott's attempt to bash his head in, and the plot to manipulate the telegraph operator.

Mandie was baffled by it all. Lust for gold had driven many into a kind of insanity.

"We'll rest for a couple hours, then ride the rest of the night while it's cool," Dunlee told the group. "I'm worried about what will happen when Jib gets his message to his sidekicks hanging around the pass. Endicott may fancy he's got plenty of time, and do nothing right away. Or, his greed may push him fast to get at the gold. As long as they *think* they have you, Mandie, their lust for the gold will spur them to use their leverage."

They made sure Pugley's and Lasko's wrists were tied well. Then they prodded them to the cave, and lashed their legs as well. Dunlee helped Mandie get settled on a bed of blankets just inside the cave mouth.

Luke remained on guard.

Dunlee joined Tom, who had found a burial place, a deep trough on a shelf halfway up the canyon wall. Having toted the bodies there, Tom had scooped out sand and gathered rocks. Now he was wrapping the two bodies in their bedrolls.

"It's a shame, Tom. I've heard a lot about Trowling and the breed he ran with. All bad. Not one Christian thing I can say over these two."

"Dat's right. Jest like Mistah Pugley. He pokes fun at dem dat believes in God. Says dey's weak. But da ones ah knows dat go by da Good Book an' believe da pure way what da Lord done showed, dem's da ones will stand tall when da last word is said."

"That's what Ma taught us," Dunlee replied. "She was dyin' of fever when I promised I'd follow the Lord, too. She died happy when I told her I'd meet her over yonder. One winter I was snowed in. Someone had left an old Bible. When I got through that winter's reading, I was on good speaking terms with the Lord.

"Trowling could follow a man's trail even across the rocks. But he didn't give a hoot about following the trail his Maker left. Gorse never made a place for that either. But I know folk in cultured places who can quote the Book, even some Sunday meetin' people, who live as far from the Lord's trail as Trowling. Still, the trail is there, and it leads to a reward for those who follow it."

"Yessuh!"

The two men bowed their heads, standing in silence for a moment. Then they caved sand down on the bodies and heaped rocks over them.

The day had been harsh. They were glad for a few hours' sleep before they must ride. Dunlee fell asleep only after his thoughts drifted to Hartman's canyon.

Would Shoat be safe from the ruthless ones who plotted to lay hands on his gold?

20

Dunlee's sudden disappearance during the night un-
nerved Teresa. He had been a constant threat to the
grandiose plans Endicott and she had devised. All
their schemes to do him in had failed, and even Chenault had not cut him down yet. But it was at least a
comfort having him where they could keep an eye on
him.

Now he had slipped away, and she could not find
out for sure where he'd gone. Knowing he was shrewd
and bent on stopping her, she wondered if he had
some trick up his sleeve. Had he really gone to deliver
horses as Hartman said? The baron of the pass had
mentioned nothing about that earlier. And why would
Dunlee take time to go away like that when he was
as firm as flint to wreck their plans?

Endicott listened to her frettings as they strolled
out by the cow pasture. The thought ticked in his
mind that Dunlee might somehow have found out
that Mandie was on her way.

He put the possibility to Bucher, who assured
him of Chenault's remarks just that evening. The old
man at the telegraph office was so paralyzed about his

wife's danger that he would never dare cross them. Dunlee could not have found out.

Then one of Pugley and Trowling's outfit hailed Bucher on the ridge one morning. Bucher rode down with the excuse that he'd forgotten his chewing tobacco from the bunkhouse, and motioned Endicott to drift casually over near the bunkhouse door. When Bucher came out, he paused to say to the Virginian, "Jib jest got back from Pugley. Dunlee showed up over north of the Clifton House. Took the lady an' the men off the stage an' hightailed it. . . ."

"What?" A scowl of concern cut worried lines across Endicott's features. "That'll ruin everything. Can't they cut him off? Or we'll stop him before he gets them here."

"Pugley did cut him off, thanks to Jib. They're holdin' 'em in a canyon southwest of the Clifton House. Everything's under control. Even better than you planned. Now you've even got Dunlee."

Endicott relaxed. Then he shot back. "How did Dunlee find out Mandie was coming? Now Hartman must know . . . suspect. . . ." He chewed his lip for a moment. "Tell Chenault and his men to hang close. We may have to change our plans."

Bucher grunted, swung up on his horse, and lifted him to a lope toward the rimrock.

Teresa, sweeping the porch, sensed that something was up when Endicott strode back. Hartman was in the pasture looking at some of his newly-busted broncs, rifle in hand. So they could talk freely. Endicott briefed her.

"Then if Hartman knows Mandie is to arrive, and that Dunlee was to meet her, he's wondering about the false telegrams and the deceit at the telegraph office. And he's unsure of me. Or else he's on to the whole thing. He's just keeping quiet, biding his time. If Mandie doesn't show up, he'll make terrible trouble. He'll really be on a rampage to find out the truth. He'll be more ferocious than a bear. Oh, Trevor, we had better get out of here—quick."

"Not without the gold," he snapped curtly. "We didn't come this far to back off. We need the gold. Whatever Hartman suspects of you now, we can still force him to uncover his gold."

He snapped his fingers. "I know . . . sure, that'll work." Quickly he sketched a plan to her. She liked it—it was a quick way to get the gold and the comforts of home. Away from this wild, lonely place so far west of anywhere important.

Curly came thundering in on a badly lathered horse early that afternoon. He had been riding the line on the west and wouldn't be coming so early unless something had gone wrong. Hartman raced out of a corral to meet him, and Booger came slapping through the brush from the west.

Coot, who had been riding patrol all night and was sleeping in the bunkhouse, was aroused by the hoofbeats. He emerged from the doorway buckling on his gunbelt, his shirt still unbuttoned.

"Three of 'em hit me just outside Hangin' Tree Canyon," Curly shouted before his strawberry roan pounded to a dusty stop. "I'm lucky I got out in one piece." He tossed his Stetson into Hartman's hands and the rancher gazed down at a bullet hole in the top of the crown.

Curly was holding his right sleeve; it was bloody

from a bullet crease. "They was sprayin' lead all around me," he said as he came off the horse and braced himself against a corral pole. "One of 'em yelled, 'Git 'im 'fore he spots the herd an' rides for help.' Well, they chased me like brush-poppers. They tried to close in, but I broke through an' tore out for home. This horse flew like a bat out o' blazes. I owe 'im my life!"

"Stinkin' rustlers!" Hartman thundered. "Coot, get over to the east range. Bring Huck an' Tosh. Ride for the west range. Booger, go bring Max from the north range. All of you meet at the Hangin' Tree. Trail that bunch. This is where we put a stop to the rustling."

He bent closer to Booger and told him about the outlaw hideout in the canyon Dunlee had described.

"Watch for a trick. Like a ruse to draw you all away from here." Booger nodded.

"We'll get our hands on them," said Hartman. "Curly, come on in. I'll patch up that arm, an' you'll stay here with me."

While the men saddled, Hartman worked fast with Curly.

"Recognize any of 'em?"

"Yeah. One of the cusses I've seen with Chenault in town."

Hartman nodded, then raced out to catch Booger before he left. He spoke in guarded tones, as Booger bent down from his saddle to listen. Then the men, armed to the teeth, burst out of the yard. They meant to get their boss some satisfaction.

Hartman would have preferred to ride with them. But he'd better stick near his gold. Anyhow, he was convinced that the men who rode for the brand could handle a pack of rustlers even if far outnumbered. There wasn't a finer riding, shooting outfit in the southwest.

The drum of the horses' hooves had scarcely faded on the ridge when Hartman mopped sweat from his upper lip and chin. He drew up short as he was about to mount the steps to the ranchhouse porch.

What if it was a ruse? Had he made a mistake stripping the headquarters of all save himself and Curly? He was on to Bucher's game. He could trust him like he could trust a rattler. He had only kept him on temporarily to prevent the schemers from knowing he was wise to them. He wanted it to be a stunning surprise when he made his big move.

He planned that to come as soon as Dunlee rode in with Mandie.

"Well, I'll get more ammunition an' be loaded for bear. Then I'll go tell Curly to be ready for anything."

Endicott met him on the porch and asked what all the racket was about. Teresa was at his elbow. Hartman explained as he filled his gunbelt with cartridges.

Then he stomped out to talk with Curly. Later he walked to the barn. As he stepped inside, a pistol was jabbed roughly at his ribs. A voice barked a harsh command.

"Drop the rifle."

His sweeping eyes found two men, both with .44s trained on him from opposite sides. Slowly he relaxed his grip on the weapon and let it drop into the straw near a stall.

One of the men was Choc Chenault. So Chenault had staged his rustling act as a trick after all. He meant to pry the men miles away. Hartman felt the cold, sickening feeling of falling for a trick, of realizing it could happen but not preparing adequately. Outwardly he kept his composure.

"Now, call your man in from the bunkhouse," Chenault instructed. "Any tricks an' he'll get a belly full of lead."

They lashed Curly to a horse stall. No one was left to help. They had him good.

"All right, big man, let's walk outside," Chenault said coldly. As Hartman was going, feeling a gun prodding him in the back, one of the men flicked his Colt thong loose and jerked the gun from its holster. They got quickly to their business.

"You got gold stashed here. We want it, an' we want it fast."

"You go to blazes."

Endicott and Teresa ventured out into the yard.

"What is it, Pa?" Teresa asked. "Why do these men have guns like this?"

Endicott slipped his hand inside his coat.

"You slide that hand out nice, easy, an' empty," called Chenault, "or I'll help you into a quick grave. Git his gun, Lassit." Lassit emptied Endicott's shoulder holster and poked the pistol inside his belt.

Teresa shuddered as if about to faint dead away.

"The gold," Chenault rasped. "Lead us to it pronto. I've been hangin' around a long time waitin' for it."

"You're fixin' things so you'll be hangin' around permanent," Hartman lashed back. "My men'll see it's a trick an' come back. They'll trail you and catch you. The gold won't do you any good."

"Cut the talk," Chenault said meanly. "I ain't got nothin' to lose. We got your man Dunlee. He'll be dead by tomorrow noon if we don't get the gold."

Lassit reached to a saddlebag and pulled out a crumpled black hat. Hartman instantly recognized it. Dunlee's.

"Now," said Chenault, "I figgered that would grab your attention. Got some others with him, a von Ehrencroft, Luke, an' a Tom."

A frown of agony furrowed Hartman's forehead and twisted the corners of his mouth. He glanced at Teresa. Once he had felt his whole world was wrapped up in this girl. Now he could only feel pity and contempt for her.

"Confound it," he said sternly, his eyes drilling hers. "There's things more important in this world than gold ... things like lovin', bein' trustworthy, showin' compassion. I'll take you to the gold. But you're gonna be disappointed. There ain't as much as you may've figgered."

He led off to the barn. Inside, he grabbed a shovel and went into a horse stall next to the one where Curly lay bound.

The others watched as he pushed straw aside, clearing the ground. Then he dug a rectangle in the loose dirt about two by three feet. Soon the shovel iron struck metal. He carefully cleared dirt from it. They stared down at a metal trunk. He flipped the lid up and grabbed one of several cowhide pouches in the trunk. Loosening the leather thong that secured it, he tapped gold dust into his palm. In the light from the doorway it glittered, and the two outlaws saw it. He emptied it with deliberate care back into its pouch and handed it to Chenault. The gunman took it with his left hand, covering him with the Colt in his right.

"Keep 'em covered," the gunfighter said to his partner. Then he stepped back and tapped some of the dust into his own hand, pushed it about with his thumb and studied it. His eyes gleamed with a growing triumph. "Ahh," he sighed. The end of a long quest. He let the dust spill back into the pouch, drew the thong tight.

"Let's have a look at another."

Hartman shrugged, snatched one up, and handed it to Chenault. The outlaw dumped dust into his palm; he liked its richness. His eyes lit up even more with a wild, strange glint. A smile was revelling along the curve of his cheeks, and his lips were quivering with uncontrollable triumph. He was ever so diligent not to let a single particle be lost as he let the dust tumble back into the leather. He motioned Hartman out of the stall, and knelt to look closely into the trunk. Seven pouches were laid out there. He laughed with a deep, hearty gusto and called for a grain bag hanging on a nail. Hartman tossed it to him. He laid all the pouches into it and looped the loose end into a knot. Then he and Lassit marched the other three outside, leaving Curly lying bound.

Lassit went into the trees southeast of the house and brought two horses. Chenault secured the bag to his saddle horn.

"The lady goes along for a ways," he announced. "That'll be security you won't give us no trouble. If you do, you an' everyone else that cares for her won't ever see her agin."

Hartman didn't think that would be such a great

tragedy. But he kept these thoughts locked within himself.

"A man lives for years," he said instead. "He comes across the greatest discovery of his life. Then he can see his riches take wings in one day." He spoke ruefully, a faraway look in his eyes.

"One day?" Lassit snorted. "These bags'll do me a lot of days. A lot of days, big man, 'fore I see the last of it."

"Why not let me ride along, too?" Endicott suggested. "I came all the way from Virginia to see to the safety of this lady. Once you're clear, you can set her free, and she'll need me to help her find her way back. You've got my gun. I'm no danger to you."

"Naw, we don't want you along," Chenault shot back. "I'll get a horse for her an' we'll be goin'."

"Wait a minute," Endicott persisted. "You don't mean any harm to the lady. It's the gold you want."

"Yeah, well, won't do no harm," Chenault agreed. "Lassit, fetch him a horse, too. But if he gives us any trouble, I'll give him some lead pills. He'll come back draped across his saddle—if he comes back."

Lassit saddled two of Hartman's string, ran the others out, and stampeded them toward the east mouth of the pass. He grabbed up every gun he could find in the house and bunkhouse. They left Hartman tied hand and foot in a stall next to his rider. Then they rode for the ridge, tossed the guns off into the brush, and joined Bucher. All five headed out together.

Scarcely an hour had gone by since Hartman's riders had departed to deal with the rustlers.

Hartman spied a nail on a stall pole; it was exposed where the bottom part of the pole had been chipped away by a kicking horse. Lying on his shoulders and neck, he was able to hoist his legs, work the nail into the rope, and pry at the bonds. The position, though extremely painful, paid off. Once free and on his feet, he sawed his arm rope through on a plow blade lying against a wall, though he cut his wrists doing it. Quickly he freed Curly. The gold thieves had been gone less than half an hour.

Three of the tamer mustangs in the corral string had drifted back and stood hipshot by the pole fence near the barn in the afternoon shade. Hartman threw a saddle on a sorrel, and secured an old rifle from the cellar which Lassit had missed. He also brought out a Smith and Wesson revolver from a box on a high kitchen shelf and handed it to Curly.

"Watch the place an' tend to the chores," he instructed. "I'll mosey on behind 'em." Seeing Curly's worried look, he added, "Don't worry. I've tracked bear, mountain lion, lobos, and rustlers. I know this country better'n any of them. They've got some gold I aim to see again, an' a woman to fetch back. The others . . . may not come back."

He loped away, his rifle cradled in his right arm.

21

Bucher led the other riders down a slope, pushing past thick brush to a log cabin near a spring. A clearing lay before the cabin, carpeted by long, lush grass bending in a gentle breeze.

"We'll rest here an' water the horses," Chenault said. He nodded to a bubble of water in some rocks down an incline some seventy paces or so from the front door of the cabin. "We got some reckonin' to do 'fore we go on. Bucher, you an' Lassit water the horses."

He untied the gold sack and swished through the grass to the cabin. A beaten, overturned table made from split logs lay in the center. He hoisted it to an upright position, then slapped the sack down on it.

"I've been doin' a lot of thinkin'," Chenault said to Endicott and Teresa, who had followed him in. "I've been ridin' them ridges, takin' chances. Bucher, too. I figger the lion's share goes to us an' Lassit. Some of our boys with Pugley got some comin' too. They been stickin' with me a long time.

"You two ain't really done nothin' 'cept figger out them lyin' telegrams. You never found the gold like you said you would."

"What's your point, Chenault?" Endicott cut in with a sharp, agitated tone. "You going back on our deal?"

"You figger things real good," the gunman grinned. His gun was suddenly out and resting on the table, his fingers curled about the butt. "You can jest ride back from here. One good thing about that is, you go alive. Course, I wouldn't mind takin' the lady along all the way." He dragged his tongue across his bottom lip, gazing at her beauty. "But she's too delicate. We're gonna ride too fast an' hard for her to keep up. Too bad. Too bad."

Teresa drew out a flowered handkerchief and began to sniffle.

"We need the gold, too," she said brokenly. "It was . . . such a risk . . . and such . . . hard work . . . to try to be . . . another person."

"Lady," Chenault replied slowly, touched by the softness, the feminine delicateness, "you could do a famous job jest bein' yourself. Why don't you stick to that? You're purty, an' charmin'. . . ."

He was so intoxicated with her that he didn't notice what her spread-out handkerchief hid. A pocket in her dress. A small thing, but Chenault would pay. A small hand slipped the tiny Remington .22 derringer into Endicott's hand.

Chenault did not know what had transpired until the little gun coughed and he felt the impact in his heart. He stared across the table in disbelief. For an instant he started to lift his Colt, but Endicott's free hand shot across to hold down his wrist in a viselike grip. The fingers relaxed, and Chenault buckled, sinking to the floor.

Endicott quickly dragged Chenault's body near the door, and put his own hat on the gunman's head so that it would show in the opening. "Back up in the doorway with your hands raised," he told Teresa. Then he grabbed the Colt and disappeared through a side window.

Bucher, tamping tobacco into paper as the horses drank, jumped and spun about when he heard the flat report of a derringer. Lassit, flat on his stomach to drink, reacted so quickly to the shot that he lost his hand grip on a rock and slipped elbow deep into the water, his face submerging as well. When he came up, neither man could see straight to the cabin door through the brush, but once Bucher stepped around a horse he could view the doorway.

"My Gawd, Choc shot Endicott. Endicott's lyin' in the door, an' the lady's got her hands up."

"I'll go see," Lassit replied. He raced up through the brush. He reached the doorway and peered in. Then Bucher heard two quick revolver shots and saw Lassit slammed sideways against the doorpost. Lassit pitched backwards into the grass and lay motionless.

Bucher whipped out his gun, spat an oath, and abandoned the horses. His face was a black mask of cold fury.

"Choc, you ain't got no right," he gasped. Then he slapped through brush to approach the cabin from a side window he'd noticed as they rode down the hill. While he was cutting through the tangle, a shot blasted nearby, and he felt a stinging sensation in his right wrist, then dropped his gun. He knelt and tried to retrieve the weapon, realizing the bullet had hit his gun, not his wrist. Another bullet twanged through the branches only inches from his face.

To blazes with it! He'd better scramble back to his horse and shuck his rifle from the boot. Chenault was stalking him, and the man was deadly with a .44. Many were the men who had found out, too late, that they were no match for Choc in any kind of gunfight. The gold Bucher could do without—at least for now.

Another bullet almost parted his hair as he scrambled astride his horse. The man was getting closer each time. He wheeled his horse about to throw the other horses between him and the gunman. Then he hit leather, drove spurs to his mount, and swished past trees and brush. Half a mile west, he drew up and gave further thought to the matter. He had hankered after the gold. There might yet be a way. . . .

Chenault and Lassit had told him it was hidden in a trunk buried in a stall. But that raised a few questions. Just a few days ago from the ridge almost directly north of the barn he had spotted Hartman emerging from near the side of the barn. He had just seemed to pop up out of the earth, in a deep gully, and was suddenly there, near a scrub oak by the gully bank. Then he had slipped into the barn. Now why would Hartman . . . ?

One thing he did know about Hartman. As fast as he got free, the man would be on the outlaws' trail . . . and a devil to lose. Already he could be on his way. So Bucher nudged his horse and veered southwest in a semicircle. On a small knoll, he peered through piñons and saw Hartman riding a quarter of a mile away along the edge of a large meadow. The rancher must have guessed by now that the direction of the tracks could very well mean they led to the cabin. Now he was closing in almost directly toward it.

That would leave one man at the ranch. Only Curly. Bucher smirked and pointed his mount toward Hartman's pass.

Hartman approached the cabin with a cougar's wariness, stalking slowly toward the door. Near the spring he had spotted two horses, the mounts Chenault and Lassit had ridden. They stood with loose reins dragging in the grass.

Then he found tracks of other horses, and a splotch of blood on a rock. One of the shots he had heard had struck its mark. He crawled on, rifle thrust before him. Suddenly, in the tall grass, he saw a man's boot, then another, finally the entire body. The man showed no sign of life. And inside the doorway Hartman could see the head and shoulders of a man.

A great stillness seemed to envelope the cabin like a lonely graveyard. A dove moaned, and the song of a locust shrilled from somewhere in the brush.

He inched forward, every fiber in his frame alert for fast action.

Chenault! The man in the doorway was Chenault. And the man sprawled in the grass was Lassit. Only the horses remained.

Endicott, Teresa, and Bucher had fled.

As he had suspected, Chenault was alone. Examining the body, he frowned when he saw where the bullet had struck—dead center. He shook his head with deep interest. A small gun, evidently a derringer, had been the undoing of this fast man. Endicott had been disarmed when they had left the ranch yard.

Teresa?

He returned to his horse and led him in a circle

around the place of death. He found one set of hoof-marks pointing off to the west. Two other sets circled the cabin and cut almost due south. Those, he surmised, were laid down by Endicott's and Teresa's horses. One set was cut deep, as by a big horse carrying a big man and, surely, the sack with the gold. The other prints were more shallow, indicating a smaller horse and lighter rider. That would be Teresa.

He followed, certain that they had returned to the pass.

Scarcely ten minutes before this, Endicott had checked four of the gold pouches. Only two contained gold dust. The others merely held rocks. Hartman had tricked them by showing them only the ones with gold.

His eyes shot to the girl mounted beside him as he stood with the pouches of mere rocks. Then he shook them empty in disgust, and she grasped the idea in an instant.

"That's not gold!" Hot fury consumed her. She slammed a clenched fist against the pommel, struck too violently and felt the pain. Then she cursed as Endicott had seldom heard even a man curse. When she exhausted her vocabulary in the outburst, she grabbed up her reins and opened her mouth in a deep growl. "So the old lion thinks he can trick us, does he? Well, we're going back, and we're going to make him show us the gold."

Endicott's eyes narrowed with a glint of anger as he swung up beside her. He knew that Hartman would want to get Dunlee and Mandie back. He and Teresa could just ride back in, show the two pouches of gold, and demand the rest of the gold immediately as the ransom for Dunlee, Mandie, Luke, and Tom. Hartman would be through with his tricks then. And once they had the whole cache of gold, they could kill Hartman and his cowhand, and get away.

Dunlee and his group had pushed on steadily since early that morning. Mandie was riding like a trooper, never voicing a whimper. Dunlee figured she must be racked with pain and weariness from the hours in the saddle and the draining toll of the blistering sun.

He was glad he didn't have to fear the outlaws' pursuit. Pugley and Lasko rode with fallen, surly faces but were no danger now. Pugley's face looked as if he had tangled head first with a Texas longhorn on the prod. He had been smashed into submission. The puffy black eyes, the cut and swollen lips, the torn tongue, the broken nose, and the deep cuts under his chin were painful reminders that he had met more than his match. He had lost a tooth, and had no desire even to try to speak. His whip had been stuffed into his conqueror's saddle bag. Dunlee vowed it had tortured its last victim.

It was late afternoon and they were an hour away from the ranch. Dunlee waved the riders to a halt.

"You bring them on in," he told Luke. "Keep to the trees out of sight an' come into the pass only when you know for sure it's clear. I'll ride on ahead to make sure."

A few minutes later he heard the shots, and veered northwest to see what was going on. He rode along a ridge to find a way down, then he cut across toward a cabin he remembered. When he reached the place, he found the two dead men, one of them Chenault.

He also recognized the boot prints of Bucher out by the spring, and saw that the man had ridden free of the shooting.

Then he came across a print he was certain belonged to Hartman. Following, he saw where it mingled with the tracks of two horses southwest of the cabin. One of the horses left marks that showed it was smaller and carried a small rider. The other left prints indicating that both horse and man were large.

A bit farther on, he was sure the three ahead had headed for Hartman's canyon. He urged his horse to a full gallop.

22

Bucher got the drop on Curly while he was watching toward the east. The puncher had a pistol at his hip and was alert, but the man with the shifty eyes came in slowly from the west behind brush and trees. He stalked him from beyond the barn, and slipped up catlike.

Leaving Curly strapped in the stall where he had been before, Bucher went around to the scrub oak at the base of the gully's far bank. He realized that Hartman could not have popped up from the gully if there was no hole. So he began to paw around in the dry, loose brush and long grass. Shoving brush aside, he exposed an opening that had been hidden down below the tree's roots. A tunnel large enough for a man to crawl through.

Bringing a lantern and a pick from the barn, he crawled into the aperture. A few feet in, he paused. Where might the gold be cached? The ground was rocky, none too comfortable for his knees. As he moved forward, his fingers pressed down into softer soil. He poked around, using the pick eagerly.

He clawed dirt away, and his fingers felt something soft. Pawing more dirt away, he yanked up a leather pouch. He loosened its thong and his eyes, gleaming in the lantern light, saw gold dust. He shouted in delight, then drew the thong tight and dug frantically farther along the tunnel. Soon he discovered a second pouch. Guessing the distance from the first pouch, he inched forward and turned up still another.

A surge of great elation raced through his frame. In a frenzy of excitement, he worked feverishly and uncovered several other pouches. They were coming up easily, now that he had hit upon the pattern.

A smart man, that Hartman! He had anticipated some trick, such as Chenault's, and planted only select pouches in the trunk. If forced to uncover those, he hoped to divert attention from the existence of others. Chenault and Lassit, crazed for gold, had been carried away with that single find.

But not Bucher! He congratulated himself. He was the man to ride out of this with the big haul.

"Better take 'em out, an' come back for more," he mumbled. "I can be far from this place 'fore Hartman gets back—if he gets back. Chenault may finish him, though."

He reached the tree and dumped the pouches from a bag he had made of his loose shirt. There in a spacious crotch between the deep roots, they would lie hidden for the moment. He mopped his brow, crawled back, and brought out several more.

The sun was sinking low. In a short time it would disappear behind the snowcapped western summits. But, he told himself, his own sun had just risen. It wouldn't go down for a long, long time. He was cackling, his whole body tingling with his fortune.

A slight sound reached his ear, like the soft impression of a boot on grass and sand. He glanced up and gasped. Standing belly deep in the hole, he was staring wide-eyed into the snout of a revolver. The gaping circle was trained on his heart. Behind it, smiling with pleasure, stood a man who had just come back from the dead. Trevor Endicott. Bucher had seen him lying motionless in the cabin doorway. A step behind him was Teresa.

Bucher's face drained into shocked whiteness. Was this a ghost? He fumbled for words, tried to summon a natural voice, but knew he quivered from the very shock.

"I . . . I thought you was dead. You was stretched out in the door, done for. Chenault, he kilt you . . . he tried for me, too."

"No," Endicott corrected. "Chenault died the first shot. Then Lassit. Now you, and it'll be a day."

"No . . . no! I ain't ready . . . I don't wanta die." Bucher fumbled the words, feeling a terrible thickness weighting his tongue, a dryness in his mouth. Panic had seized him. He had never expected things to come to this. His hands were filled with gold, but Curly's gun was in his holster. It seemed as far away as the ridge he'd guarded so long. Never had he wished, as he now wished, that he had no gold in his hands . . . only a gun . . . or was far away . . . or this was simply a bad dream.

Visions raced through his mind—his mother pleading through tears with him not to run away with that bunch of outlaws. How had he turned wrong? How had he stuck to the outlaw trail all these years, outlived every crisis, only to wreck himself stupidly on this?

289

"They's plenty for us all," he pled. "You can have most. . . ."

"No, there's just enough for us." Endicott's eyes were cold, expressionless, merciless. They did not hold the slightest hope of a bargain.

"Shore, shore. Take it all. All of it. Jest put that gun down. I'll climb on my horse . . . jest ride out."

He stepped on a root and climbed out of the hole, extending the two pouches still in his hands toward the man behind the gun.

"It ain't worth dyin' for. I'll go."

"Yes, you'll go," Endicott agreed. And for a second Bucher knew relief, thinking he had talked his way to freedom. He was halfway through a short stride to get to his mount when Endicott shot him in the chest twice. His face contorted with surprise and pain, then he crumpled and fell back across the roots over the other pouches of gold.

The sun had gone down.

Teresa stood still, her hand clamped over her mouth. Endicott yanked the limp body out of the opening and dragged it into some nearby brush. Then he came back with the six-gun Bucher had used, and laid it on the ground by the tree. He looked into the pouches, laid them beside the gun, and went and hitched two horses to the buckboard.

"Go get just what we need out of our suitcases," he told Teresa. "Stuff things in the saddlebags." He grabbed them off their horses. "Be fast about it. Hartman may drift back in a while.

"I'll see if I can find more pouches, then we'll beat it out of here."

Teresa raced to the house.

Endicott, using the lantern, found the places where Bucher had dug in the tunnel. Hartman's caching pattern quickly became apparent. Working furiously for a few minutes, Endicott brought out what he had thought must be the last pouches.

In the house, Teresa stuffed things frantically into the bags. Things were moving fast. Soon they would be clear of this place—away from the crude place with no bathtub, no parlor. . . . These thoughts were a relief.

Her mind leaped to the shootings, especially the stare of utter hopelessness in Bucher's eyes as he clutched his breast. The man had wanted to live. Maybe he had someone he wanted to live to see. Never had she witnessed anything so unnerving.

All along she'd had it figured that if anybody died in their plot Trevor or one of the men he paid would take care of it. She would not have to see it happen. But she felt she could dismiss Bucher's death as something . . . necessary—that was the word Trevor had used. It need not concern her at all.

The important thing was the gold. The gold—yes, that would help her quickly forget.

She pulled Mandie's diary from beneath the bear-skin and poked it down into the bag. Her game of deceit was rushing to an end. Soon she could forget the trivial things in Mandie's diary. Bigger, more important things beckoned.

Only one last detail remained—Hartman had to be disposed of. Trevor would send a man back to kill the rancher. Then this little matter would be tied up neat and proper. No one would ever come after them. Teresa had only one regret. She would not be there to see him sink into the dust. She bitterly despised this man who had humiliated her father into the dust.

She had almost finished packing. Her heart felt light and happy. A movement outside the window caused her to glance up. She rushed to the side of the window and drew her hand to her mouth, startled.

Hartman was back! The rancher had slipped in stealthily, hidden by trees, brush, and rocks. Now he was circling the house, bending low to keep concealed by brush, heading around to the bank and the scrub oak.

He must have spotted Trevor from the ridge. Now he was stalking him, and soon would get the drop on him. If he did, there would be no chance to take the gold . . . unless. . . .

Her hand dropped into her pocket, clutched the derringer, which Trevor had reloaded. Her heart was thumping as fast as her mind was racing.

Depositing the loaded saddlebags on the porch, she studied the brush to the west, spotted Hartman's hat bobbing above the lip of a gully, then darted off quietly into the brush to come in behind him. He would never suspect . . . so intent was he on closing in on the man removing his gold. It would be easier from behind. His great, broad back would make an easy target. She would do it quickly. In five minutes she and Trevor would be out of danger.

Emerging from the hole, Endicott was obsessed with his fortune. Turning the wick of the lantern to kill the flame, he set the lantern on a broad root, then stuck the six-gun into his belt. He opened one of the pouches, pouring some of the dust into a cupped hand. Rich, very rich. The treachery was paying off in big dividends. They would never be sorry. . . .

A low *click* behind him caused him to spin about. He peered up the bank, pouches in one hand, the other hand curled about his revolver inside his waist coat. A man towered there with a Winchester aimed at his heart.

Shoat Hartman!

"Better forget the gun," the rancher drawled. "You'll die in your tracks. This rifle will punch your rotten heart out."

Endicott's swarthy face twisted into a tight sneer of contempt. He pondered his chances. Half-turned, he would need to slide the gun from his holster, spin around, aim it, and press the trigger. Chances were, he could hit his target if he got off the shot before Hartman fired. But suppose Hartman fired first. . . .

All he needed was a second . . . one lousy second.

Rising up from a clump of brush, Teresa lifted the derringer in both hands, anxious not to miss the massive back. Her hands were trembling. It was easy . . . yet difficult. Shooting at a human being was different from shooting at targets in Trevor's gallery at Ridgetop Manor. A person could feel something. Her emotions ran rampant; her mind was playing tricks on her. . . .

Her foot pushed down on a bit of dry, brittle brushwood just as her finger pressed the trigger. At that same instant, Hartman flung himself sideways, having heard the crackle behind him. He felt the sting of the bullet high in the right shoulder.

Endicott, seeing him move, reacted on impulse. He jerked his own gun free, whirled, and scrambled to get behind the buckboard.

Hartman hit the grassy shoulder of the bank, rolled, and came up to catch Teresa in the path of his rifle aim. She stood frozen, gun lifted but not knowing what to do next.

In the same instant, off to the side, another gun barked on the cool air of dusk. Teresa felt a terrific shock in her left arm and was spun to her knees, her empty derringer flying into the dust.

Hartman, down low where Endicott could not see him over the bank to get a shot, had held up momentarily at the prospect of shooting a woman. Now he flung a glance off to the south into the brush.

"Good heavens!" Ten paces away he saw another woman who looked exactly like Teresa! She was standing with Luke, deliberately pointing a six-shooter that emitted a wisp of smoke.

Was that Mandie? Had she shot Teresa?

He gasped, and knew he had a winner. The real Mandie. . . . Hartman heard the crunch of a footstep over the bank and instantly remembered Endicott. He stood up, hauled his rifle about to throw down on Endicott. A bullet whined past his head and sung itself to silence in the depth of the pass behind him. He slammed a bullet of his own into the buckboard seat near the crouching Endicott.

For a left-handed shot, he'd done pretty well.

Dunlee, hurrying into the yard, came up behind Endicott. He was ready to bark out a command to throw up his hands. But Endicott glanced back, as if thinking of getting to a horse to make a getaway, and saw him.

The Virginian spun about on his knees where Hartman could not see him, and jerked up his pistol to take aim at Dunlee.

"They can't seem to kill you," he shrieked. "But I'll stop you!"

Dunlee halted in his tracks. His hand streaked to his gun butt, whipping the Colt up in a blur. A bullet screamed past his face. He triggered the revolver twice, saw the crouching man fall back against a wheel and double up. Then Endicott, holding on gamely, whipped up the gun again. Dunlee's Colt barked a third time, and the big man slumped sideways, toppling into the dust. His gun spilled free of relaxing fingers.

Bending over the crumpled form of the gold-seeker, Dunlee relieved him of the gun stuck in the belt, felt for other guns, then motioned Hartman to come on down.

Peering more carefully, he saw blood soaking Endicott's vest around two bullet holes over the chest. A third perforation, high in the muscle of the gun arm, had cut off Endicott's second, desperate shot.

Luke and Mandie moved through the brush toward Hartman. Luke scooped up Teresa's derringer and closed in on the deceiver, who had fainted dead away into the dust. This game was too much for her. Mandie rushed to her father.

"Pa?" Mandie's eyes were tearful. She looked anxiously into the face of the rancher she had not seen for twelve years. Though eager to greet him, she was concerned about his wound.

"Mandie! My girl!" A great smile triumphed over Hartman's grimace of pain, and he grabbed her with his left arm as he climbed to his knees. "Been waitin' a long time."

"Oh, Pa!" She threw her arms about him and buried her face in his left shoulder, sobbing uncontrollably. Luke, grinning, came over and laid a gentle hand on the left shoulder of his boss and friend.

Just then Booger Towns came riding hard into the yard, his rifle ready in an upraised hand.

"Got back jest in time," he grinned. "We were lured away by a rustlin' scheme. But it was jest a trick. Found the hideout, kilt one. The boys are bringin' in two others. I figgered they was tryin' to pull us away from here, so I burnt the breeze gettin' back."

Not far behind Booger, Frenchy rode in with another man. They both dismounted and took in the scene following the shots. Dunlee recognized Dike Bellis, deputy at Cimarron.

"Come on over," Dunlee yelled. "We've got us some killers. Both tame now."

Frenchy and the deputy came over. Bellis had a star pinned to his cowhide vest.

Dunlee nodded to the lawman.

"Figured on this sooner or later. Well, I don't have anything to hide. I cleared out of Virginia because the deck was stacked. We may as well just clear up the whole thing right now."

"It's not you I'm after," Bellis said. "It's a man named Roe Pugley. Seems several bits of evidence make him a prime suspect of murder. Authorities in Virginia had word he might have come here."

"I'm dying," Endicott groaned. "You win, Dunlee. Seems . . . like . . . you won all the way." The fallen man's eyes showed a deep bitterness. His voice was like a blade that could twist and slash the man who bent over him.

"It helps to play it fair and square," Dunlee replied. "You pay the price for treachery. It's a hard way to go, Endicott. By the way, now that you've got nothing to lose—who killed Mueller and tried to pin it on me?"

"Not . . . me. Pugley . . . was killing mad when you . . . cleaned him out in the . . . the game at the inn. That only added to your whipping him . . . like salt rubbed in an old wound. He . . . hated Mueller for promoting you over him. So . . . he killed Mueller, took his money, and said he'd fix you for good."

Deputy Bellis, bending close, took in these words.

"Where will I find Pugley?" asked the lawman.

Dunlee glanced back and saw Tom riding in with the two prisoners on the road from the canyon's eastern mouth. "He'll be here in a minute, tame as a kitten."

Teresa, finally revived, crawled down from the bank. Her face was buried in her one good hand. Luke was helping her; her right arm was a mess. When she looked up, saw the men, and then realized Endicott was on the ground, her face drained even whiter with shock. Her voice was a weak, tortured whisper.

"Is he . . . is he still alive?"

"Barely." Dunlee looked her straight in the eyes. "He confessed to us who killed Mueller."

"Oh!" she came more alive. "Well, it wasn't me . . . or him. It was Pugley. I . . . I heard Pugley admit it. He wanted to kill you to make sure you never could prove you didn't do it."

"You'll testify to that?" asked Bellis.

"Well, I . . . yes, of course. If it will help me and Trevor."

Endicott's good hand had managed to drag a pouch of gold dust from the pocket of his coat. As he clutched it, the dark scowl of a beaten, hurting man pinched his face. It was obvious even as the light grew dimmer in a deepening dusk.

"Nothing," he said in response to Teresa's words, "can help me now." He cleared his throat, set his teeth hard against the pain that tortured him. "All for nothing . . . nothing. We were fools. It isn't important at all . . . now."

"A pathetic, empty way to go," Luke muttered to Hartman, shaking his head at the shame of it. "A man buys his own ticket. A woman buys hers."

Teresa's eyes looked up, then dropped in shame. She broke into sobs when she looked down at Endicott and the fact hit home. He had just died.

"Back in Virginia he once had everything," Dunlee said huskily. "Land, horses, money, power, a beautiful woman. Then he drew a dark plot to steal what meant everything to another man. In the end, he gets nothing."

"I . . . I thought he would always get what he wanted," Teresa sniffled. "And *you* would never amount to much. It was . . . a fool's choice. What will happen to me now?"

"Frankly," said Dunlee, "I don't know yet. You have a lot to answer for, and you'll have a freight wagon of guilt on your conscience. I wouldn't want to live with the load. But you may come out better if you testify to the truth and clear this whole thing up."

"I will. I will tell everything, this whole awful masquerade, Trevor shooting those two men today, then Bucher, and. . . ." She did not mention her own attempt this day at murder, or another attempt in her room at the St. James Hotel.

298

"Didn't Endicott take a crack at me on that gully bank the other day, too?" Dunlee queried.

"Oh, no. That was Bucher. He slipped around from the ridge."

Mandie came near Teresa.

"Why, Teresa? Why? You even meant to shoot Pa in the back. You . . . you planned to kill Pa."

Teresa blushed, buried her face in her fingers. Then she tried to regain her composure.

"I have been very mixed up, so wrong. I can't face you anymore. I've done wrong to all of you. It's too much to ask for your forgiveness."

"We'll see," said Mandie. "Come, Pa, come Teresa, we've got to see to those wounds."

Bellis turned to Dunlee.

"Well, young man, for your sake, what I've been findin' out looks all right. But I want Pugley."

Dunlee, having heard hoofbeats coming into the yard, glanced over. Tom was bringing in Pugley and Lasko. Dunlee pointed to the newcomers, and stopped at the bullwhip man.

"I'm through with him," he said. "You can have him."

Frenchy followed Hartman into the house, caught him off to the side.

"I almost forgot in the excitement. I told Doc Cunningham I was riding out here, and he asked me to give you this letter."

Hartman walked out behind the house alone and opened the letter.

"Well, Doc, I'm ready," he said aloud. "Mandie's home, and. . . ."

His eyes fell on the words halfway through the paragraph.

. . . my specialist friend went over all your symptoms I described in detail. Having dealt with a large number of cases he says are like yours, he distinguishes them from varieties that have been beyond cure. We must wait and see, of course, and I do not want to hold out false hopes. However, we now have very encouraging reasons to think positively in your case. I know I discouraged you, so I wanted to give you this bright note. And I will hope, with you, that you can yet have many good years.

You will need, of course, to stay clear of such things as that boulder you say a man rolled down at you, bulls that get you down, and bullets. And the good news Henri Lambert tells me of your daughter coming back will surely be a tonic. . . .

"Whoopee!" The rancher exulted. "You bet it is!" Folding the letter, he strode back to join the others.

Booger and Luke helped Dunlee carry the gold into the house until Hartman could decide where to put it. The other men of the outfit had arrived to help. Curly, set free, was also lending a hand. Luke paused with Dunlee at the porch steps.

"We did a lot of talkin' durin' the trip back. I mean Miss Mandie, Tom, an' me," he said. "I figger from what she thinks of you an' the way you look at her we're gonna have us a weddin' 'fore long."

Dunlee looked at him in the light of the lamp shining through the open doorway across the porch. A broad grin crept over his face. That was a plumb good idea, he thought. Wouldn't it be nice if Mandie really did feel that strong about it?

Hartman yelled out to Luke.

"Hey, Luke. Way I figger, you got some time off comin'. Now there's a certain lady named Ellie in town. Frenchy says she's been watchin' every stage-coach from Pueblo hopin' you'll be on it. Me, I'd get all fancied up, an' go fetch her. Drive her out to the range I promised. You an' her decide where we're gonna build the new house . . . part of my weddin' present."

Dunlee whooped it up with Luke. That LS brand was going to look good on the range. Then he went inside, figuring he might find out how Mandie felt. Luke, following, looked at Mandie who was putting a bandage on Hartman's shoulder.

"Now that you've come to the pass," Luke said, "you'll have to meet all the folk out here." He scratched his head and looked wise. "We've even got a parson who rides the circuit, Cimarron to E-Town. Really warms up to weddin's."

She glanced at him, her eyes growing wide, then looked at Dunlee. He swept off his hat and took a swing at Luke. The ramrod went out to the porch again, chuckling.

A few minutes later Mandie went out to the kitchen to rustle up supper for the bunch. Teresa had thrown herself across her bed, daubing her eyes. She was crushed under the weight of guilt and sadness.

"You know," Mandie smiled at Dunlee as she peeled a potato, "I think I'm going to like Luke more and more."

He looked up from slicing off a slab of beef, and caught the look in her eye. It was a look he could not mistake if he knew anything about women.

He swept her into his arms and knew he was right.